THE HOLIDAY KILLER

by
Stephen Zimmerman

This book is a work of fiction. Names, characters, places, and incidents are the product of the authors' imagination or are used fictitiously. Any resemblance to actual events, locales, or persons, living or dead, is coincidental.

Sword and Suspense Books LLC

Printed in the United States of America
Worldwide Distribution

Second trade edition

ISBN 979-8-9903541-4-2

Halloween

Detective Sam Cross lifted up the yellow police tape in front of the store and walked toward the crime scene. As part of his promotion following the takedown of Hive and rescuing the Missing, Sam had been moved to Homicide. This was his first case – a murder at a Walmart five days before Halloween.

The sun was just peeking over the city skyline and the wind blew bitterly causing Sam to pull his overcoat tightly around his neck. A few steps later, the sliding glass doors opened and Sam, relieved to be out of the cold, stepped into the entryway. The store seemed to be in that in-between stage of decorations: the fall décor coming down and the cheer of Christmas going up.

Sam looked down at his phone screen to familiarize himself again with the notes he'd taken that morning before the drive over. The store's redecoration efforts had been interrupted by a gruesome discovery in the Holiday section. A woman had been murdered – and Sam had been warned to prepare himself for this to be a "weird one."

Sam's thoughts were interrupted by a familiar voice calling his name. He looked up, surprised to see Tiffany Gunn walking briskly in his direction.

"Tiffany!" Sam exclaimed with both surprise and concern. "What are you doing…" he began to ask, but then saw her blue employee vest. "You work here." Not as a question, but a statement of observation.

"Yep," replied Tiffany with an awkward smile. "First job in the city. I thought about working at a burger place – but yeah, no. I'm going for a clean break and a fresh start, so I decided to try retail. Plus, they were looking for holiday help, so it was an easy hire without having any retail experience."

"How long have you worked here," Sam asked.

"About six weeks or so, I guess," Tiffany said. "It's sure good to see you. Sorry I haven't been over for dinner yet," she continued. "It's just been a full schedule with school and work and settling into the apartment with Laura."

"Oh, nice," Sam said. "That's cool you're rooming with Laura. And hey, don't worry about not getting over to the house. I understand completely. I'm sure it's been quite the transition."

Tiffany was about to reply when Sam held up a finger. "One sec," he said as his partner, Detective Alisha Palmetto walked up.

"I see you've met the employee who found the victim," said Detective Palmetto. "I took her statement while I was waiting for you to drive over."

Sam blinked with surprise and looked back at Tiffany. "Were you going to mention that you were the one who discovered the victim?" Sam said a tad more harshly than he intended.

Tiffany looked somewhat taken back. "Um, you didn't ask, and we were kinda catching up, and I was about to when you interrupted me."

Sam shook his head. "No, it's ok. Sorry that came out wrong. And it *is* good to see you. Sorry. That must've been a shock. I know you already gave your statement to Detective Palmetto, but if you don't mind, I'd like to hear it straight from you."

"Catching up? Y'all know each other?" interjected Detective Palmetto.

"Sadly yes," Sam began, "Wait, that's not what I meant. It's a complicated story."

Detective Palmetto's eyes got wide and then narrowed, "She looks a bit young to be an ex-girlfriend," she said with an accusatory tone.

At that Sam let out a belly laugh and Tiffany snorted. "No, nothing like that," he said after a second. "You remember the Hamlin case?"

"How could I not?" replied Detective Palmetto. "It's hardly all anyone's talked about since I transferred in from Miami last month. Wait, is *this* the sheriff's daughter?"

Tiffany's eyes dropped. "Yes, ma'am. Sherriff Gunn is...was my father."

"Wow. Wow." was all Detective Palmetto could think to say. Finally, she found her words, "I'm sorry to hear about your father. I hear he's a real hero around here."

"Thanks," said Tiffany with a weak smile.

"Um, so, yeah," muttered Tiffany, turning back to Sam. "Me and my coworker, Esteban, and my manager, Amy, got here at six this morning to open up and begin the reset on the Holiday aisle – that's where we change out a section of the store. The Halloween and Fall stuff are getting moved to clearance, and we were supposed to put out the Christmas stuff. Esteban and Amy headed to the back to pull out the Christmas merchandise and I went to the Holiday aisle with some shopping carts to start clearing the shelves – and that's when I found…her." Tiffany's voice trailed off.

After a few moments of silence and Tiffany not continuing, Sam spoke up. "That's ok. Thanks. That's good enough for now."

"No, no, it's ok," Tiffany continued after a deep breath. "I didn't really stay to look very long. I just started hollering for Amy. She called 911 after taking a look for herself."

"Well," said Sam, turning to his partner, "I guess it's time for me to take a look too. Thanks Tiffany. I'll perhaps talk to you more afterwards."

Tiffany nodded, and Sam and Detective Palmetto turned to walk toward the Holiday aisle of the store. "Just a warning," Detective Palmetto said with a tone of disgust, "Prepare yourself. Trust me, you ain't seen nothing like this before."

At the Holiday aisle, Sam ducked once again under a strip of yellow police tape. As he approached the aisle, he jumped at the sound of a demonic laugh to his left. "Jeez!" he exclaimed. He looked to see one of those motion-activated skeleton yard decorations. It was oddly but purposefully placed – not dropped or thrown, so as to warn anyone who approached the crime scene to beware.

Sam rounded the corner of the aisle and froze, mouth gaped open at the scene before him. He fought dual urges to both cringe away and be sick. The Holiday aisle had been arranged like a scene from a haunted house. A chair had been set in the middle of the aisle and a small side table placed beside it. In the chair "sat" a woman's body. It was headless. And on the table next to her was a carved pumpkin. The woman's hand pointed towards it, or perhaps was intended to look like she was reaching for the jack-o-lantern.

The whole scene had been carefully decorated and arranged. The woman was dressed in a red devil Halloween costume, and other decorations such as artificial cobwebs had been draped and wrapped over and around the chair and side table. Placed on the woman's lap was a large bowl filled with various Halloween candies. Pooled underneath the chair was a sizeable puddle of blood.

Sam finally turned back to Detective Palmetto, and once again started at the laughing skeleton. He resisted the urge to punt it as far as he could.

Sam must've had a strange, shocked look on his face. "I told you so," quipped Detective Palmetto. "Coroner's on the way. Should be here shortly."

"Do we know where her…" Sam paused.

Detective Palmetto finished his thought. "Head? Not yet. But we haven't searched much though. Waiting for CSI and the coroner to get here. Didn't wanna disturb things too much."

"Yeah, we definitely don't want to lose any evidence on this one for sure." Sam said grimly as he glanced over his shoulder again at the grisly scene behind him on the Holiday aisle.

* * *

Four hours earlier…

Professor Harold Barnes pulled into his garage, pushed the button on the visor of his car to close the garage door, and then waited until it was completely shut before opening his car door. He looked at his watch. Professor Barnes figured it would be nearly three more hours until his "decoration," as he called it, was discovered. *Actually*, the Professor thought, *it could be significantly longer, considering the dimwitted, incompetent Holiday help that these stores hire during the Holiday season to peddle their over-priced, cheaply made, merchandise that will be broken or forgotten within days of being purchased.*

The Professor stepped out of his car onto a black tarp that he'd prearranged before driving to the store. There he stripped out of the disposable blue surgical gown he'd worn during his time "decorating" the Holiday aisle of the Walmart as well as the rest of his clothes just out of precaution. He proceeded then to wipe his body down from head to toe with a bucket of water and dishrag he'd also placed there ahead of time.

10

He patted himself dry and then took a large step off of the tarp onto bathmat and lastly slipped into his lounge clothes – a pair of dark green pajama pants with a grey t-shirt, topped with a maroon robe. Once dressed, Professor Barnes gloved up and returned to the edge of the tarp, carefully folding it in on itself, enclosing the contents inside. He then rolled the tarp as small and tightly as he could and placed the folded tarp inside a vacuum bag which he sealed. He planned to vacuum pack it at the car wash when he vacuumed out the inside of his car later that morning. He had already disposed of her head the night before by zipping it inside a bowling ball bag before dropping it in the dumpster at a random apartment complex on the way to the store that night. He placed the vacuum bag inside his trunk and then entered the house.

Professor Barnes lived alone except for a ferret named Houdini. He opened the fridge and poured himself a tall glass of milk. From the cabinet he took a package of ramen noodles. About five minutes later, he was settled into his couch with the bowl of hot ramen and his glass of milk. Houdini ran over next to him but cringed away at the steaming bowl of soup.

The Professor turned on the TV and began watching an infomercial for some kind of high-tech watch while he waited for the local news to begin.

***

Over the next couple hours, Detectives Cross and Palmetto talked to the other employees, gathered store security footage, and took well over one hundred photos. CSI was meticulous in their evidence collection, meaning the poor woman's body wasn't taken away by the coroner until after lunch.

Speaking of lunch, Sam had skipped it, his appetite ruined by the scene on the Holiday aisle. Instead, he and his partner returned to the squad room to begin trying to make sense of the little evidence they'd gathered.

The woman's red devil costume had come right off the Holiday aisle shelf. So had the other decorations. The chair and the small side table had been borrowed from the home décor aisle. It was impossible to tell, but very likely the carved pumpkin "head" was also from the store's grocery section. Speaking of heads, the victim's had not been located anywhere at the store. Sam wasn't yet sure what that meant. But from the amount of blood, his initial assessment was that the woman had been killed where she sat and then dressed up.

"Alisha," Sam said, breaking his own thoughts. "Do you think she was a kidnap victim forced to the store and made to change into that costume before her death? Or do you think they were like, I dunno, on a date and broke into the store and she thought she was just dressing up for a game of some kind?"

"What makes you think her being there was consensual?" asked Alisha.

"Just the lack of a struggle is all. No immediately visible defensive wounds," Sam replied thoughtfully.

"Maybe the killer cleaned up any signs of it afterwards," said Alisha. "He would've had plenty of time. Time clock records show that the last employee was out of the store just before midnight. And the witness, uh…" Alisha scanned her notes, "Tiffany said they didn't arrive until 6:00 a.m. That's a lot of time to stage the scene, murder the girl, and do any cleanup necessary."

She was interrupted by Sam's desk phone ringing. It was CSI, "Cross here. Whatcha got?"

"Just more puzzle pieces for you unfortunately," said the lab tech. "First of all, there's no security footage."

"What? Why?" asked Sam. Alisha looked at him and raised an eyebrow.

The lab tech continued, "It's just not there. Looks like the camera's recording function was turned off at, uh – exactly 10:31 p.m."

"Ten thirty-one?" Sam repeated, taking notes. "The store would've still been open. That's very, very curious."

Alisha reached over and hit the speaker phone button on Sam's phone so she could hear as well.

"That's not all," replied the lab tech, "The coroner's initial findings are that the victim was *not* killed at the store. In fact, she was most likely dead for several hours before being brought there. And get this: the coroner says that her blood was drained and then poured on and around her once she was put in that chair."

"Are we sure it's her blood then?" asked Alisha.

"Same blood type," replied the lab tech.

"Anything else?" asked Sam.

"Not much," the tech said. "There's a serious lack of evidence on this one. We haven't yet found any usable prints. In a busy store like that you'd expect there to be thousands of prints, but the entire Holiday aisle was wiped clean. I'll let you know if we find anything else."

Sam thanked the lab tech and went to hang up. "Oh wait, one more question. Do we have a cause of death?"

"Desanguination," replied the lab tech.

"So, she bled to death?" Sam asked.

"No, technically that would be exsanguination. She didn't bleed to death. She died from having her blood literally pumped out while she was alive," explained the lab tech. "The only other wound on her body was a hole on her neck at the jugular – most likely where her blood was drained. Her head was then removed post-mortem."

"Alright, well that answers some questions me and my partner were just hashing over. Thanks again, and call me the minute you find anything else," Sam replied.

"Will do. Better cross your fingers though. The killer seems unusually methodical." And with that the lab tech hung up.

"Well, there you have it. I didn't know Oklahoma had vampires," Alisha joked. "So, she was killed elsewhere. Brought to the store, and then dressed and staged like that. Is Halloween always this weird in Oklahoma?" she added with a disgusted laugh.

"Sometimes the occasional masked robbery, domestic murder, or gang violence, but nothing like this," Sam said shaking his head. "I haven't been a detective that long, but I promise I'd have heard about any cases like this before now. This is a whole new level.

"You got any insight on this kind of thing from Miami?" Sam continued. "I'm getting a satanic, occultic, voodoo vibe from the whole setup."

"Not really. Wouldn't hurt to investigate that angle though. But could just be a Halloween thing," replied Alisha.

Over the next ten days, Detectives Cross and Palmetto reinterviewed Tiffany and the other two employees who'd been there at the discovery, as well as all the employees from the previous night's shift. Nobody had anything helpful to say. Neither could CSI figure out how the security cameras were disabled. The record function was not turned off from inside the store – it just stopped working for exactly four hours: from 10:31 p.m. to 2:31 a.m. And CSI had said that it had the least amount of evidence they'd seen in a murder case: no foreign hairs or fibers on the body; no DNA not belonging to the victim – everything clean as a whistle. The victim was identified by her fingerprints as a thirty-one year old retail employee with nothing helpful in her past.

And so, much to the annoyance of Sam, Alicia – as well as Captain Durant and the story-hungry media – the case went cold. At least, that is, until…

Thanksgiving

Four days before Thanksgiving, Sam was fast asleep when his cell phone began vibrating on the nightstand beside the bed. His wife Jennifer gave his shoulder a nudge and mumbled, "Honey, your phone." Sam reached over and pulled it towards his face, wincing at the brightness of the screen.

"It's the office," Sam said sleepily. The clock read 4:53 a.m. *That's odd*, Sam thought. It was Sunday and he was supposed to be off this week for church. Sam cleared his throat and answered in a hoarse voice. "Yeah, Cross here."

"Hey it's Alisha. You should try answering your phone," said the voice of Sam's partner.

"I did. I'm talking to you aren't I?" Sam retorted, sitting up in bed.

"Yeah, on the third call. You need to get down here," she said.

"What is it? The Halloween case?" Sam said anxiously as he slid his pants on.

"No, it's a new homicide – but looks like it might be connected to the Halloween one," she said.

"How so? What makes you think they're connected?" Sam asked. By this time, Sam's wife had also sat up in bed and flipped the nightstand light on. She looked at Sam, worry etched on her face.

Sam buttoned up his shirt and then turned to his wife and mimed "tie." She smiled and pointed towards the closet. "Hanging up where it belongs," she said. Sam rolled his eyes but then winked at her as he opened the closet door.

Alisha continued filling Sam in over the phone. "Supposedly it's got all the staging and theatrics of the Halloween case. I've not seen it yet. I just got the call about ten minutes ago."

"Ok, meet you at the office in fifteen," Sam said strapping his holster to his belt.

"Actually, you know the Food Mart at Northwest Expressway and the Lake Parkway?" she asked. "That's the crime scene."

"Yeah, I know it," Sam said as he ran a quick razor over the stubble on his face.

"Ok, just meet me there. And bring me a coffee – payment for not answering your phone on the first call. White chocolate mocha, extra hot, extra stirred." Alisha said and then hung up.

Sam threw on his suit coat and then his winter overcoat and apologized to his wife for missing church again. He gave her a quick kiss and closed the front door. It was another cold, windy morning and felt even more so since the sun hadn't yet begun to rise. Sam blew in his hands to warm them as he gripped the frigid steering wheel and backed hurriedly out of the driveway.

It was about a twenty-five minute drive to the Food Mart and it'd be a five minute detour to get him and Alisha a coffee. Sam made a mental note to give her a hard time about her froofy coffee drink.

Traffic ended up being a mess on the Lake Parkway and it was nearly forty minutes before Sam pulled into the Food Mart parking lot. He immediately recognized Captain Durant's SUV parked near the front door. Not every day the boss showed up at a crime scene, but understandable considering the media frenzy around the Halloween case. Already three separate news crews were setting up outside the store.

Sam instinctively took a deep breath as he ducked underneath the police tape, bracing himself for another gruesome scene. Alisha greeted him immediately inside. "Thank you," she said sarcastically as she took the coffee out of his hand.

"That'll be $6.22," Sam said but his partner acted as if she hadn't heard him and walked towards the crime scene. "You know, if you'd learn to drink real coffee, it'd save you about three bucks," Sam called after her.

"Or just have a partner who doesn't answer his phone the first time, and it'll save you about – what did you say? $6.22?" she replied wryly.

More crime scene tape blocked off what appeared to be the Holiday aisle of the store filled with wall décor containing festive phrases like "Give Thanks," and other such items in preparation of the upcoming Thanksgiving Holiday. There were also displays of canned cranberry sauce, turkey gravy, and other Thanksgiving staples.

And there *it* was: displayed in the center of a stack of boxed stuffing was the crime scene. Both Sam and Alisha froze. Alisha rested her hand on Sam's shoulder as if to steady herself. The victim this time was a man. He was undressed except for his boxers and seated on an office chair. He had been cut open from neck to waist and something appeared to be coming out of the open cavity. At least this victim had his head attached, but a bright red apple was wedged in his mouth.

"What is that coming out of him?" Sam asked horrified, his fist instinctively covering his mouth.

"Dear God, please don't let that be stuffing. Thanksgiving turkey will be ruined for me forever," Alisha said in a disgusted tone.

Sam stepped gingerly forward to get a better look. It was most definitely several pounds of bread stuffing. Sam nodded but said nothing.

Alisha cursed. "Y'all crazy here in Oklahoma. We didn't kill each other like this in Miami."

Sam gulped back bile and shook his head. "This one's going down in the record books for sure."

As they continued to take in the scene Captain Durant walked over. His lip curled at the sight. "The media's gonna have a field day with this one. It's starting to look like we've got a madman of a serial killer on our hands. Cross, Palmetto, you two up to this case?"

Sam could detect some doubt in Captain Durant's voice – likely because the trail had gone cold on the Halloween case. "We got this boss," Sam replied confidently.

"Alright," answered their boss not sounding entirely convinced. "Give any other cases you're working on to another detective and make catching this killer your number one priority. And I want all updates channeled straight through my office. The last thing this Holiday season needs is a crazy slasher running around."

****

Four hours earlier…

Professor Harold Barnes gently pressed the brake pedal of his car and came to a stop in his garage. He reached up to the visor and pushed the button for his garage door to close and then waited it for it to fully descend before exiting his vehicle.

Like before after his Halloween "decoration," Professor Barnes stepped onto a pre-arranged tarp neatly spread on his garage floor. He undressed and went through the careful decontamination process before dressing once again into his dark green pajama pants, grey t-shirt, and maroon robe.

He methodically folded up the tarp and stuffed it into another vacuum bag and placed it in the trunk of his car like before. The Professor had taken the previous vacuum bag to a mortician friend of his to be incinerated in the crematorium. The mortician, Walt Emmer, shared some similar "philosophies" but not necessarily the same "dedication" as the Professor. Yet he'd been convinced to let the Professor use his incinerator as needed. Professor Barnes would visit Walt later that day after a trip to the car wash.

Once inside, Harold was greeted by Houdini as the Professor made his way to the fridge where he removed a tray of sushi, poured a tall glass of milk, and then headed for the couch. Houdini ran over to him, sniffing curiously at Harold's meal.

Professor Barnes switched on the TV and turned to the news channel. It was still too early for the news, so he watched the infomercial that was playing. An overly cheerful lady was proclaiming the virtues of a set of over-priced, cheaply made kitchen knives. Since the Christmas Holiday was just a month away, the infomercial studio was decorated in festive lights, white and green Christmas trees, complete with tinsel and garland. Harold could feel his rage growing the longer he watched. Every product had an agenda. Every Holiday was exploited to the max to sell as much merchandise as possible – merchandise that America's spoiled, stupid consumers greedily purchased just to stick them in storage to be forgotten or placed on a shelf somewhere to collect dust and never be used.

***

While CSI did their thing, Sam and Alisha interviewed the store employees. A similar story to the Halloween case emerged: the morning crew arrived to open up the store only to discover the murder a short time later. The store had closed at eleven the night before – and of course the previous night's crew reported nothing unusual before they left.

Sam collected the security camera tapes while Alisha began taking photos. By 10 a.m., they wrapped things up and headed back outside. Alisha pitched her untouched coffee in the trash by the door on the way out. "Sorry about your $6.22," she said, "I just couldn't drink it after seeing him like that. Next one's on me."

As they ducked under the police tape, a herd of reporters and camera crews rushed their way clamoring for a statement. Sam pushed his way through the mob while repeating that they couldn't comment on the case and to expect a statement from the department spokesperson.

"Is it the same killer as the Halloween case?" a female reporter shouted after them, but Sam and Alisha ignored her.

At Sam's car, Alisha asked, "Can I ride back with you? I caught a ride over with Captain Durant."

"Sure," he replied. "Do you want to stop and get a bagel or something on the way?"

"You're kidding me, right?" Alisha said with a shudder. "I don't want food – maybe ever again."

***

Captain Durant was livid. Someone had talked to the press. He had been trying to keep a tight lid on the details of the Thanksgiving case, but either a grocery store employee or one of his officers had leaked crucial information to a Channel 6 news reporter. Captain Durant had set up a news conference for noon that day and his briefing had gone perfectly at first. He'd announced that there had been a murder of a white male and that he would share more information as the investigation progressed and as it was appropriate to do so.

He'd then agreed to take some questions. Out of the blue, the Channel 6 reporter – the one who'd tried to get a statement out of Cross and Palmetto, had asked him, "Is it true you think we have a serial killer on the loose."

Captain Durant had tried to deflect by saying, "We're just in the beginning stages of the investigation and I can't comment on that line of questioning."

But the reporter had pressed, "But isn't it true that the details of this murder are almost identical to the Halloween murder last month – theatrically staged using items from the store in the Holiday section?"

Captain Durant had frozen, unable to think of a suitable reply. Sergeant Ellis had thankfully stepped to the microphone and bailed him out. "I don't know where you are getting your information, but none of that is confirmed and we can't comment further."

The reporter pressed still, "Will you be bringing in the FBI to assist on the case to create a profile for the serial killer?"

Captain Durant's response was to curtly thank the reporters for attending the briefing and then to walk away. Back inside the store, Captain Durant turned angrily to Sergeant Ellis and swore. "What was that? Who's talking to the press? And where did that looney reporter get my words to quote back to me?"

"I don't have a clue. My officers were given strict orders not to talk to the press," Sergeant Ellis replied. "I'll make sure they get the memo again."

"We do *not* need the city in panic thinking about serial killers or anything like that," retorted Captain Durant angrily.

"Yes sir," agreed Sergeant Ellis and then hurried away.

***

"Did you see the Captain's briefing?" asked Alisha back at the squad room.

"Yep, what a train wreck," said Sam shaking his head.

"That reporter had a point though," replied Alisha. "Unless we think we have a copycat on our hands, it does appear to be the work of the same killer. It was just too similar with the staging of the crime scene in the Holiday section."

"Yeah, I'm super curious to hear back from CSI," answered Sam as he began to arrange the photos they'd taken on his desk. Sam let out an audible huff of breath. "I'm going to ask Jennifer to do a ham this Thanksgiving instead of a stuffed turkey I think."

"No kidding," replied Alisha. "I'll probably just eat take-out Chinese this year."

"Aw, why don't you join us at the house, Alisha?" offered Sam. "We always have enough food to feed an army anyway, and my wife is a

24

phenomenal cook. There'll be pies and cookies and all the fixin's. Plus, the Cowboy game afterwards."

"Ha! I just might take you up on that – so long as you don't mind me rooting against the Cowgirls," Alisha replied with a wink.

"Oh, it'll be on for sure," laughed Sam. "Dem Boyz gonna have it in the bag by halftime. Lunch is at noon sharp. Don't be late."

Sam and Alisha poured over the crime scene photos, sketches, and employee interviews while waiting for CSI to call. On her desk, they spread out the contents of the case file from the Halloween case for comparison.

Indeed, everything pointed to the two cases being connected – of course not yet hearing back from CSI made that just speculation. But both murders took place in a store's Holiday aisle. They both were theatrically staged. Both bodies had been mutilated. And Sam wasn't sure whether this was a part of the killer's pattern or not, but both victims had been white – though one was female and the other was male.

About three in the afternoon, Alisha pushed back her chair and announced she was going out for coffee. "Want anything? It's on me," she said to Sam.

"Just regular – black. I don't need to cover up the delicious taste of a cup of joe," Sam said with a grin.

"Whatever," was all Alisha said, as she grabbed her coat and exited the squad room.

Sam headed to the breakroom to grab a snack from the vending machine. He had just made his selection for some peanuts when he heard his desk phone ring. His peanuts didn't fall out like they were supposed to. He started to holler for Alisha to get the phone but then remembered she'd just gone out for coffee. The phone rang again. Sam hit the machine and then dashed back out of the breakroom towards his desk. He arrived breathless just as the phone rang the fourth time.

"Cross," he panted.

"Uh, CSI here. You ok?" the lab tech asked through the phone.

"Yeah, I was just away from my desk. What do you got?" Sam replied. "Actually, hang on, let me grab a pen. Ok go."

"Well first things first, your victim is named Brandon West," began the CSI tech. "Do you want the details about him?"

"No, that's fine. I'll look him up," replied Sam. "Just tell me your part."

"Sweet," replied the CSI. "Ok so…you're not gonna like this, but there's no security camera footage again. Looks like it was cut off same as before."

"Same stop and start time as the Halloween case?" asked Sam writing.

"No, this time it was at 11:26 p.m.," answered the CSI. "It was off for exactly three hours through 2:26 a.m."

"And I guess now the weird part," continued the CSI. "Your victim was most likely killed by drowning – hard to say for sure with no lungs to test. And then he was cut down the chest all the way to his waist, and all of his internal organs were removed."

"So, he could be stuffed, right?" asked Sam.

"Yes," replied the CSI, "but before that – get this: he was brined first…like a turkey. Our initial analysis indicates that the killer used standard ingredients for brining: salt, cider, herbs, orange juice, and juniper berries. As far as time of death, that's gonna be hard to pin down for sure because of the brine's preservation of the tissue, but if I had to pick a time, I'd say day before yesterday, November 21."

"Are you getting all of this?" asked the CSI.

"Yep, just writing," Sam replied. "Never thought I'd write 'man was brined'."

"Right? Ok, so last thing," continued the CSI. "Looks like the killer used nine pounds of stuffing."

"The boxed kind or homemade?" asked Sam.

"I mean, I didn't check for that specifically," replied the CSI, "but I'd just guess the boxed kind because the onions and other herbs looked rehydrated rather than fresh – and the bread cubes looked too precise. Oh, and no prints again. Everything was meticulously wiped down."

"Alright, thanks," answered Sam and hung up the phone. Sam sat there deep in thought, going over all the notes he'd just written down. *What in the world? How is any of this real?* Sam wondered.

He turned to his computer and did a records search on Brandon West, the latest victim. Twenty-six years old. Worked as a marketing consultant for a local company that advised retail chains. No criminal history. And like their last victim, for all practical purposes: a boring individual.

Just as Sam was finishing up his search on their victim, Alisha returned from her coffee run. She'd also brought Sam half a Reuben sandwich. Sam thanked her and then proceeded to open the sandwich and scrape the sauerkraut into the trash can.

"Picky, picky," Alisha joked.

"Nah," answered Sam. "I'm just a plain dude – nothing fancy: black coffee and a basic roast beef sandwich works for me. But I appreciate it. My peanuts got stuck in the vending machine."

"You mean these peanuts?" asked Officer Travis from across the squad room, holding up a bag of half-eaten peanuts.

"Yeah. You're welcome," Sam hollered back.

As Sam took a bite of his sandwich, Alisha pointed at his computer screen. "Who's that?" she asked. "Our perp or our vic?"

"The victim," replied Sam through a mouthful of food. "Brandon West: twenty-six year old marketing consultant. No priors. Nothing interesting about him."

"Any relation to the last victim?" Alisha asked.

"Not sure," replied Sam swallowing another mouthful. "I hadn't got that far yet."

Alisha looked at the notepad on Sam's desk. "I see you've talked to CSI. Wait…does that say he was…brined?" she asked with a horrified tone.

Sam nodded. "Yep. Definitely skipping the turkey this Thanksgiving."

Alisha made a face. "Yeah, and maybe every Thanksgiving after this."

"What's with twenty-six though?" Alisha asked.

"Huh," asked Sam as he washed down the last bite of his sandwich with a swig of coffee.

"The number twenty-six," she repeated. "11:26 p.m., 2:26 a.m., twenty-six years old. That's a lot of twenty-sixes."

"Nice catch," Sam replied. "That *is* a lot of twenty-sixes. I wonder if it means anything or if it's a coincidence? Hey, get out the Halloween case file. I wonder if there were any repeating numbers from that case."

After a couple minutes of laying the case file out on Alisha's desk, Sam tapped his index finger on several spots in their notes. "There," exclaimed Sam. "10:31 p.m., 2:31 a.m., the victim thirty-one years old – the number thirty-one."

"Ok, that definitely can't be a coincidence," Alisha urged. "But what do thirty-one and twenty-six mean? Is it some kind of code?"

"You mean like a numerical substitution?" pondered Sam. "Three is the letter C, one is the letter A – so CA? And twenty-six then would be BF? Do CA and BF mean anything to you?"

"CA as in California? And BF maybe the initials of the killer?" Alisha thought out loud. "Is our killer telling us he's from California and his name is BF?"

"Well, if he is," replied Sam, "it's not much of a clue to go on. There's gotta be thousands of people in California with those initials? I feel like maybe it's more about the numbers themselves – like thirty-one and twenty-six stand for something else."

"Let's make a list of any other similarities," Alisha suggested. "We've got different causes of death, but still both bodies mutilated. Both bodies arranged in the Holiday aisle of the stores. What kind of work again did they do?"

"Uh, the Halloween victim worked retail at a clothing store in the mall, and our latest victim worked in market consulting. I dunno if there's a connection there," Sam mused.

"We need to track down their contacts and see if they knew each other or had ever met," added Alisha. "Their home addresses are pretty far apart, so it's not like they were neighbors. Maybe they knew each other from church or the bar or something."

Sam looked at his watch. It was nearly 5:30 p.m. "Phew, I'm beat. Let's call it a day and hit it again early tomorrow."

"Sounds good to me," Alisha answered, "though I may hang out here a bit and see if anything else jumps out at me." When Sam hesitated, she added, "For real, you go ahead. I won't stay long. See you in the morning."

"Alright then," Sam said grabbing his coat. Sam walked quickly towards his car. If he hurried, he could still make Sunday night church with his family.

***

Professor Harold Barnes pulled away from the car wash and drove towards Walt Emmer's funeral home. It had been a good day. The seven a.m. news had launched with the story of the professor's "decoration" at the Food Mart. Coverage had been nearly wall to wall on all the local stations throughout the morning news hour and then picked it back up at noon as well.

Professor Barnes hated to miss the evening news, but he'd lost track of time, and he had to get to Walt's to dispose of his vacuum bag. In addition to the vacuum back, Professor Barnes also had a five-gallon bucket containing the organs he'd removed from his Thanksgiving "decoration." He decided that disposing of them in a random dumpster like he'd done with the head from his previous "decoration" was too risky and after some persuasion, Walt had agreed to incinerate them along with the vacuum bag.

Ten minutes later, Professor Barnes pulled into the back of the mortuary. The door had been propped open with a wooden doorstop, so he headed inside carrying the vacuum bag and the five-gallon bucket. Walt greeted him nervously and mumbled for the professor to follow him.

"It's just tissue, right? No bones?" asked Walt. "Bones don't always incinerate."

"That's right Walt. We don't want any evidence left behind of your work," Professor

Barnes assured with a wicked smile. "If you don't mind, I'll wait this time while you incinerate it – just to be sure things are done thoroughly."

"I was thorough last time," Walt said with a wounded tone in his voice. "I do this for a living."

"Of course, you do," the Professor said with the same reassuring tone. "But I'd like to watch, if it's all the same to you."

Walt responded with a nod and a thin smile. A half hour later, Professor Barnes was back in his car, driving home. Along the way, he pulled into a McDonald's parking lot, and when he was sure it was clear, he tossed the five-gallon bucket into their dumpster.

***

Over the next three days until Thanksgiving, Sam and Alisha worked tirelessly tracking down the families, friends, acquaintances, and coworkers, both present and past of each victim – trying to establish a link between the two. Yet despite talking to easily sixty different people, they had to concede that, as best as they could tell, the victims had never crossed paths and didn't have any acquaintances that had either. Credit card receipts from the Thanksgiving victim showed that he had never even shopped at the mall where their Halloween victim worked. There was zero connection.

Captain Durant constantly reminded Sam and Alisha that he needed results, which just added to the pressure to solve the crimes before the killer struck again –if that was indeed his plan. Late Wednesday evening, Sam sat at his desk, head in his hands – exhausted. Alisha rested a hand on his arm. Without looking up, Sam said, "I just hate to admit it, but we're in the same boat with this one as the last one. We're no closer to solving either case. Durant's gonna be on my back even worse than before if we don't come up with something."

"Hey, the case'll break," Alisha said reassuringly. "We must just not be looking at it right. But we're both tired and tomorrow's Thanksgiving. It'll wait until after the Holiday. Let's get outta here. Tomorrow's the big day."

"Big day? What do you mean?" Sam asked.

"When yo Cowgirls gonna get whooped," Alisha said playfully.

"Ha! Tomorrow you'll see," Sam said with a laugh. "It's gonna be Cowboys all the way. Ok. Let's go. I'm sure Jennifer could use the help getting ready for tomorrow's meal. Lunch at twelve sharp. See you then."

"No turkey, right?" Alisha asked.

"Not a turkey in sight," Sam replied, making a gesture over his chest of crossing his heart.

"Alright. See you then," she said. "Oh, can I bring anything? Rolls maybe?"

"How about some vanilla ice cream for the apple pie?" Sam suggested.

Alisha gave a thumbs up and headed out of the squad room. Sam sat there a minute longer, but then forced himself to get up and go home.

***

Professor Harold Barnes pulled back the covers on his bed and lay down. Houdini curled up at his feet. Professor Barnes smiled as he closed his eyes and began scheming of what his Christmas "decoration" would look like. He was determined to make his next decoration worthy of the year's biggest Holiday.

The Pattern

Thanksgiving morning was bustling around the Cross house. Jennifer Cross was whipping together last minute dishes; Sam put the ham in the roaster; and about 10 a.m. Tiffany arrived. Her roommate and best friend Laura had opted to return home to Hamlin to be with family, but Tiffany accepted the Cross' invitation to join them for the day. Jennifer was grateful for an extra, experienced pair of hands in the kitchen – and Tiffany set about making the sweet tea and the cranberry sauce.

Tiffany tried a couple times to probe Sam about the cases, but Sam remained tight-lipped. "Maybe after the noon meal," he conceded, "but let's not ruin dinner." Instead, they chatted about Tiffany's classes. She hadn't yet decided on a major but was doing well in her first-year college basics.

"How're things at work," Sam asked. "Have things returned to normal – after what happened there?"

"Ugh, not in the least bit," Tiffany said. "The weirdness of the story has brought out the crazies. Almost every day we have these gawkers with some kind of a murder fetish show up and just stand around the Holiday aisle – as if another dead body is going to materialize. Honestly, it's annoying and more than a little creepy."

"That's actually a helpful bit of information," Sam said thoughtfully. "We may put an officer on that and see if there's someone who shows up every time. Sometimes killers, especially of this type, return to the scene of their crimes – to sort of relive the moment."

Tiffany's eyes got wide. "Aaaand I'm calling into work tomorrow."

Sam's wife cut in. "If you don't mind me interrupting, I need someone to set the table. Your new partner Alisha is still coming, right?" she asked Sam.

"That's what she said last night," Sam replied.

"Alright, so that's" —Mrs. Cross paused to count— "six places we need set. Can you get the boys to help you?"

Sam called for his boys and let them get the silverware while he carried the plates to the table. He glanced at the clock: 11:52 a.m. Alisha should be there shortly. As if on cue, Sam heard a knock at the door. He set the plates down to let her in.

"Hey, sorry. Am I late?" asked Alisha as she handed Sam a grocery sack with two gallons of vanilla ice cream inside it.

"Nope, we'll sit down and eat in just about five minutes," Sam replied.

It was slightly odd for Sam to see Alisha in "street clothes." He'd only ever seen her at the office, where she always wore slacks with a button up white or blue dress shirt and her hair pulled back in a smart-looking ponytail. However, for the present occasion, she was in jean shorts, flip flops…and a New York Giants jersey – the opposing team playing the Cowboys that afternoon.

As Sam closed the door behind Alisha, he called out to his wife, "Babe, I dunno if we can let Alisha stay. She's in a Giants jersey."

"Ew!" the two Cross boys yelled in unison and Jennifer Cross said, "I think I have an extra Cowboys t-shirt she can wear."

"I see I've walked into the home of a cult," Alisha said.

"What's a cult?" asked the youngest Cross boy.

"Never mind," Jennifer said with a laugh. "Now finish getting butter and salt and pepper on the table."

A couple minutes later, they were all seated around the table, and Sam led them in a prayer of Thanksgiving – he also prayed that God would help them solve their case.

As soon as Sam said "Amen," Alisha, quipped, "Ah, doesn't that ham look good this year," followed by a nervous laugh.

"Yup," was all Sam said despite the quizzical look on Tiffany's face.

Before long, everyone's plates were heaped high with food and they were chowing down. By one o'clock, the meal was over, and Jennifer and Tiffany began rinsing the dishes while Sam carried the roaster pan outside to dump the drippings on some weeds. Alisha followed him.

"So, I know I said I wasn't going to stay long at the office, but I was actually there until nearly nine last night going over our case notes and comparing both files," Alisha said.

"Yeah?" asked Sam as he turned the water hose on to rinse the pan. "Did you learn anything for your trouble?"

"I think I found more of the interesting numbers." Alisha replied. "Among the evidence CSI collected was the empty packaging for the costume the Halloween victim was dressed up in. It cost $26.99."

"Well, that doesn't make sense," replied Sam as he turned off the hose. "The number twenty-six goes with the Thanksgiving case."

"I thought that too," continued Alisha, "But I checked the price of the pumpkin that the killer used for the head, and that week they were on sale for $3.99. So, if you round up, twenty-seven and four which equals thirty-one."

"Ok, I'm intrigued. Did you find anything like that with the Thanksgiving case?" Sam asked.

"Well, that's where it got a bit muddier," she replied. "The CSI tech said the killer used nine pounds of stuffing. I looked up how much is in one of those stovetop boxes of stuffing, and each box makes about a third of a pound. Nine times three is twenty-seven boxes though, not twenty-six. But maybe the killer only used twenty-six boxes, and the nine pounds wasn't exact. It's just a working theory."

"Ok," replied Sam, "Even if that's another number set of our numbers, I don't know how that helps us get any closer to catching our perp."

"Well, here's my thought," Alisha continued, "twenty-six boxes of stuffing is a *lot* of stuffing – not a usual amount that someone would buy. So, I thought if we canvassed grocery stores, we could perhaps have them look up any single transaction of twenty-six boxes of stuffing. And even if the killer used cash, maybe an employee would remember selling such an unusually large number of stuffing boxes to one person."

"That's really good, Alisha," Sam praised. "We just might get both a credit card receipt as well as security camera footage."

"They teach us how to do real detective work in Miami," Alisha smirked.

Sam laughed. "Well, they don't teach you how to pick football teams," he said, pointing at her shirt.

"This shirt?" asked Alisha. "I don't even like the Giants. I borrowed it from Officer Treyer just to get under your skin."

Sam checked his watch before heading back inside. It was about quarter past one. A few minutes later, the kitchen was cleaned up, and Jennifer got the desserts out and arranged them on the kitchen counter. Both of the Cross boys opted for two cookies each. Sam went for cheesecake and a cookie. Jennifer heated a slice of apple pie in the microwave and then topped it with the vanilla ice cream. Tiffany got both cheesecake and apple pie, minus the ice cream. And Alisha shot Sam a "don't judge me" look as she got one of each dessert.

"I haven't had a home-cooked meal since moving here, and so I'm gonna take advantage while I can," she explained. "Any beer for the game," she asked as she took a bite of cookie.

"Sorry, no." Sam answered, "Neither me nor Jennifer drink."

"No worries," Alisha replied. "Though you might start after the Cowgirls get pummeled," she added with a wink.

By two, dessert was finished and cleaned up, and with about an hour until the Cowboys game, Sam and Alisha gravitated back outdoors to talk shop. Tiffany followed them out.

"You don't mind me listening in, do you?" she asked.

Sam looked at Alisha, and she shrugged, "I guess it's ok," she conceded.

"Any solid leads?" Tiffany asked.

"Not on a specific suspect," Sam began, "But the killer seems to have a thing with numbers. In the Halloween case, we found several instances of the number thirty-one, and with the Thanksgiving case, it appears that he used the number twenty-six several times – though we're not sure what the numbers stand for, if anything. Maybe he just is an OCD person and likes things with patterns."

Sam was about to reveal more of what they'd found, when Tiffany held up a hand to silence him while she looked intently at something on her phone. After half a minute, Tiffany announced matter-of-factly: "I know what the numbers mean."

There was a few-second long pause, and finally Alisha asked, "Is this a gameshow where we have to guess, or are you going to tell us?"

"No, sorry," answered Tiffany, "I'm just surprised you didn't see it. They're dates of Holidays. What's today's date," she asked.

"The twenty-sixth," Sam said eyes widening. "And today's Thanksgiving."

"And the thirty-first of October was Halloween," interjected Alisha. "Hey, I like this girl."

"I can't believe we didn't think of that," Sam said annoyed at himself. "It seems so obvious now that you say it, Tiffany. Both of us poured over the evidence for days and you come up with the answer in less than a minute."

Tiffany beamed. "So do you think that he only kills before Holidays?"

"Sure seems that way," answered Alisha. "Which means, we should be able to predict at least around when he'll kill next. I wish I had one of those pocket planners that lists all the Holidays. I mean, is it Christmas that's next? Or is there something in between?"

"I think Jennifer has one from church," Sam said as he ducked back inside. A couple minutes later, Sam returned with his wife's planner.

"It looks like the killer perhaps only goes for major holidays – because between Halloween and Thanksgiving, you had, like Veteran's Day, and he didn't kill then."

"So is there anything between now and Christmas," Alisha asked, looking over Sam's shoulder.

"Uh, Pearl Harbor Day," Sam muttered, scanning the calendar.

"That strikes me as too minor of a holiday," Alisha opined.

"Hanukkah," declared Sam. "It starts December twelfth and runs through the eighteenth."

"Is Hanukkah a big enough Holiday to catch the killer's attention though?" Alisha asked.

"Don't ask me," Sam replied. "I'm not Jewish. But I think it's a big deal, right?"

Both Alisha and Tiffany shrugged. Their discussion was interrupted by the Cross boys barreling outside to announce that the kickoff was moments away, so they agreed to table the discussion until maybe halftime. Tiffany was excited to watch the game. Growing up in Hamlin, she'd never seen a live football game. This would be her first.

The halftime show turned out to be a decent classic rock band, so they all opted to stay inside and watch it rather than continue their discussion outside. After about three hours of football, the game finally came to an end. For the Cowboys, it certainly wasn't one of their best, but to Sam's delight, the Giants played an even worse game. And so, in the end, the Cowboys squeaked by with a one-touchdown win.

Alisha, of course, complained about bad refs and the Giants' roster being plagued with injuries, but Sam gloated, "A win is a win." After a bit more friendly banter, both Tiffany and Alisha said they were going to call it a night. Sam offered to drive Tiffany back to campus, but she declined and called an Uber.

An hour later, the Cross boys were in bed, and Sam and Jennifer settled in for a quiet evening. As they lay in bed reading, Jennifer broke the silence. "Your new partner Alisha is pretty," she stated.

"I guess so," replied Sam, not looking up from his book.

"The Miami sun has given her a nice tan," Jennifer continued.

"Do you have a crush on my partner," Sam joked.

Jennifer swatted his shoulder. "No, I'm just saying."

"Ok, then let me just say it. No, I'm not attracted to my partner, Babe," Sam said putting down his book.

"I didn't say you were," Jennifer replied. After a pause she continued. "It's just that she's single and pretty and tan and fit…and y'all seem to get along really well."

"Ok, well first of all," Sam interjected, "I don't even know if she's single. Maybe she's seeing someone."

"But she was free for Thanksgiving," Jennifer answered, "so probably means she's not."

"Who knows? Maybe she has a guy back in Miami. Babe, you don't need to worry about me and Alisha," Sam said, pulling his wife close so she could rest her head on his chest. "You're the only girl for me – unless Marilyn Monroe asks me out, so I think you're safe" he added with a laugh.

Jennifer pinched him and laughed. She rolled over and clicked the lamp off and then returned to the safety of Sam's chest.

***

The next day, Detectives Cross and Palmetto shared their findings with Captain Durant. Sam expressed that they believed their perp was killing within a few days of major U.S. Holidays. And they suggest that perhaps Hanukkah was the killer's next target.

"We're not sure though," Alisha interjected. "We don't know whether Hanukkah is a big enough Holiday for the killer to target."

Captain Durant pondered in silence for a minute. "I'd rather be safe than sorry," he finally answered. "So, what then are we looking for as potential targets? Someone who is Jewish?"

"We didn't so far see any connection between the two Holidays and the actual victims," Sam replied. "I mean, it's not like the Halloween victim was a Satanist and the Thanksgiving victim a Quaker or something. We think the killer is choosing holidays and locations, rather than targeting specific victims."

"So, if the killer does end up targeting Hanukkah, then we should be looking at locations with significance to the Holiday," Alisha added.

"Alright," Captain Durant replied, "We've got a couple weeks until Hanukkah begins. Make a list of potential target locations and report back to me. We can assign officers to the locations around the clock and maybe catch, or at least prevent the killer's next attack."

"Oh, one more thing," Sam said. "We might have a lead on our perp. He bought something like twenty-six boxes of stuffing for the last murder. We're going to try and track down where they were purchased and by whom."

"Good work," Captain Durant replied," Again, just let me know what you find."

Sam and Alisha nodded in affirmation and then left the Captain's office. Back in the squad room, Alisha agreed to make a list of potential Jewish target locations while Sam began hitting up grocery stores to see if he could discover where the stuffing boxes had been purchased. He decided to start with the Food Mart where they'd discovered the victim. However, after a couple hours of going over inventory reports, credit card receipts, and store security footage for the last month, it turned out that nobody had purchased anywhere close to twenty-six boxes.

Sam returned to his car with a defeated sigh. "That would've been too easy," Sam grumbled to himself. That now meant that he had to start canvassing other grocery stores across the city. Sam groaned. There had to be dozens if not hundreds of grocery stores around the OKC metro. The first crime scene had been near the state college on the south side of the metro, but the second crime scene was up on the northwest side. So that meant that the stuffing could've been purchased anywhere in the city.

Sam decided just to return to the office. He needed more manpower. He would enlist the help of other officers to make a list of grocery stores, broken down by quadrants of the city. It was almost lunch, so Sam texted Alisha to see if she wanted him to pick up something for her. She replied back, "Coffee – you know how I like it, and a burger with the works."

By 12:30, Sam was back at the station. He sat at his desk with a mushroom Swiss burger – his favorite – and black coffee, while Alisha ate her loaded hamburger and sipped her white chocolate mocha.

"How'd your search go?" Alisha asked in between bites.

"Struck out," Sam replied. "I was hoping it'd be as simple as checking the Food Mart where the victim was found, but there's no evidence anyone bought twenty-six boxes of stuffing there. So that means, we're going to have to canvass the rest of the city and hope to get lucky."

Alisha made an "ew" face as she chewed a bite of hamburger. "Any idea how many stores we're looking at?" she asked.

"Not a clue. That's why I came back here," Sam replied dejectedly. "I'm gonna get anyone who isn't working actively on a case to help me make a list."

"You should check out the Walmart next, where your friend Tiffany works. Might get lucky," Alisha suggested.

Sam gave an "Mmhmm" through a mouth full of food and made a note to check there next. He swallowed his last bite and asked, "How'd your search go? What'd you come up with for Hanukkah locations?"

"Just five synagogues and Jewish centers across the metro actually," Alisha said, sipping her coffee. "So, if he targets Hanukkah, it should be pretty easy to cover each location. I was thinking, if we could pinpoint the one that would be the most likely target, you and I could take it as a stakeout."

Sam nodded. "Hanukkah starts on 12-12 and ends 12-18, so if he follows the pattern of shutting off the security cameras at the time that corresponds with the date of the Holiday, then we should be able to pinpoint the killer's arrival."

"I wonder if there's any significance to the number of days before the Holiday that he does the murder," asked Alisha. "The first murder was five days before Halloween, but the second was just four days before Thanksgiving."

"Maybe he's counting down to something," suggested Sam. "Like: five, four, three, two, one."

"Then boom?" asked Alisha.

"I sure hope nothing goes boom," Sam said seriously, "but this killer seems to like patterns and numbers and consistency, so I think there's a chance we could be looking at three days before the next Holiday for the next murder."

"Just to cover our bases, we could start a week ahead and do every night through the eighteenth – I know that's nearly two weeks of stakeouts, but the Captain is after us to catch this guy – assuming it's a guy," Alisha responded.

Sam didn't answer. After the conversation he'd had with his wife last night, he knew that Jennifer would not be a fan of him being alone in a car for two weeks straight with Alisha. But it also needed to be done.

Sam broke from his thoughts. "What do you think? Is our killer a guy or a girl?"

Alisha shrugged. "I've kinda been assuming that it's a guy. I mean, aren't most serial killers male to begin with? And I just have a hard time picturing a woman beheading and gutting someone. Plus, while I could see maybe a woman lugging around the first female victim, no way a woman moved our second vic by herself. Didn't his profile say he was over two hundred fifty pounds? Yeah, I'm going with a guy killer."

"Unless it's a team of killers," Sam suggested. "There have been a handful of serial killer teams."

"True, but I'm still sticking with my original idea of a single male killer," Alisha replied.

"No, you're probably right," Sam said. "I was just thinking through all the possibilities."

"Anyway," Sam continued, "I need to get making this list of grocery stores to check for the stuffing purchase." He then spoke loudly to the whole squad room. "I need every available detective and officer who's not working an active case to give me a hand – Captain Durant's orders."

Captain Durant hadn't exactly said that Sam could enlist whoever he wanted, but he *had* said that he wanted progress. Sam divided the city into twenty-nine different communities. Five officers joined him at his desk, and so he gave four communities to each officer and then divided up the remaining nine between himself and Alisha. "Don't forget to include supercenters with grocery departments as well, not just regular grocery stores," Sam instructed.

By the end of the day, Sam had his answer: a depressing ninety-two chain grocery stores and superstores in the OKC metro. And God help him if the killer had purchased the stuffing at a mom and pop grocery store – though Sam felt it wasn't likely a smaller grocery store would have twenty-six boxes of stuffing on hand.

"We've got a couple weeks before Hanukkah to go through this list," Alisha said. "If we spend three hours max per store, and run twelve hour shifts, that's eight stores per day minimum: if they're closer together, maybe more. So, we should be through the list in hopefully ten days or less. And maybe luck will smile on us, and we'll hit the jackpot before we get too deep in the list."

"Or we'll go through the whole list and the killer will have purchased them online," Sam said.

"Well, aren't you just the optimist?" Alisha shot back.

"I'm headed home. My brain is fried. I'll see you bright and early tomorrow," Sam said.

At home, Sam opted not to tell his wife yet about the stakeout he and Alisha had planned. He'd tell her closer to the start date so that she had time to hopefully forget about her insecurities from the night before.

***

The next morning Sam rolled out of bed a full hour before his alarm was to go off. He'd tossed and turned the whole night with weird dreams. He hoped his flopping around hadn't kept his wife awake. He couldn't help but feel an uneasiness over him – that the killer would strike again before they could stop him. Sam decided to head into the office early. He kissed his wife goodbye and headed out the door. Twenty minutes later he walked into the squad room – to see Alisha already at her desk.

"Do you ever go home and sleep?" asked Sam.

"Sometimes," answered Alisha through a stifled yawn. "This case – it's just got me feeling different."

"Yeah, same," replied Sam. "I slept terrible last night. We need to get out there and catch this monster so I can get a decent night's sleep."

"And to stop him from killing again, right?" Alisha said.

"You know what I mean," Sam said with a laugh.

He looked at his watch: quarter after five. "For the list, do you want to take different quadrants of the city or work the same quadrant and move through them like that?"

"I say different, that way we're not potentially focusing all of our attention on the wrong part of town," Alisha said. "It's too early to head out though. Most of the list probably doesn't open for another hour at least. Wanna grab a real breakfast for a change? My treat for the good Thanksgiving meal."

"Sure," said Sam, slipping back into his overcoat he'd just taken off. "Some biscuits and gravy and sausage would help my mood immensely."

Alisha made a face. "Or a cheesy omelet topped with salsa. You need to expand your food horizons."

"My horizons are just fine," feigning defensiveness. "It's worked perfect for me for my entire life. If it ain't broke…"

"You gotta go to Miami some time. You'll get some real food there," Alisha urged.

"Hey now, biscuits and gravy is real food," Sam replied.

Sam and Alisha drove in separate cars so that after breakfast they could split up to begin looking for the person behind the twenty-six boxes of stuffing. They decided on a family diner chain not far from the station. Sam went for the biscuits and gravy with a slice of cold apple pie on the side. Alisha decided a southwest burrito. A half our later, they headed their separate ways: Sam towards the Walmart on the south side where Tiffany worked, and Alisha to the west side of the OKC metro.

Forty minutes later, Sam pulled into the parking lot and headed inside. Much to Sam's annoyance, it took a good ten minutes before a manager finally led him back towards the office – Sam tried to lessen his frustration by reminding himself that it was right in the middle of the busy Holiday season. While the manager checked order and purchase histories, Sam scanned at five-times speed through hours of security footage from before the Thanksgiving murder. He went back for six weeks, but to his dismay, neither the security camera from the stuffing aisle or from any of the registers showed anyone buy large bulk quantities of stuffing. The manager's receipt and order search turned up the same – nothing.

Sam dutifully thanked the manager and then politely refused to answer why he was so interested in the purchase of bulk quantities of stuffing. He then dismissed himself from the office and decided to see if Tiffany was working. As he walked past the Holiday aisle, he noticed the "murder groupies" Tiffany mentioned milling around. Tiffany had described the group as being larger in number than what he observed at the present – leading him to believe that interest was dying off. He made a note to check with the Food Mart to see if a similar phenomenon was taking place at the scene of the second murder.

Tiffany, as it turns out, was working a cash register, but due to the long lines of Holiday customers, she had time for little more than a quick "Hi." Sam told her "No problem" and that he understood – and that he had to run anyway. Back in his car, while the engine warmed up, Sam crossed the first of two dozen stores off his list for his quadrant of town. Bleh. This would be a long day if it kept up like this.

By lunch Sam had checked off three more stores – and struck out on all three. Lunch consisted of a quick chicken sandwich and a lemonade from a fast food drive through, and then he headed for the fifth store on the list, hoping to get lucky.

He didn't – and though he was able to clear nine stores off his list by the end of the day, none of them turned up any results. Palmetto texted him about 6:00 p.m. to say that she'd struck out also with the eight stores she's canvassed. Sam texted back a brief "Alright, better luck tomorrow," and then drove home.

Sam was more frustrated than normal. He'd tried not to let it show, but his words and tone towards Jennifer and their kids indicated that the case was getting to him.

"Did you see the news?" Jennifer asked.

"I caught some here and there – what specifically are you referring to," answered Sam.

"You remember the reporter who ambushed Captain Durant at his press conference a few days ago," she asked.

"Yeah, what about her?" Sam asked.

"She went on a national news interview." Jennifer replied. "And she's given the killer a nickname: the Holiday Killer."

"Great. Just great," Sam muttered.

Sam's phone buzzed. It was a text from Alisha: "Our perp has a name now apparently."

Sam quickly texted back, "Yeah, my wife just told me."

His phone buzzed again with Alisha's reply, "It's kinda catchy actually."

Sam texted back an eye roll emoji.

"Who's that?" Jennifer interrupted.

"Just my partner," Sam replied.

"Oh, what does she want?" his wife asked. Sam detected a slight bit of jealousy in her tone.

"She was just texting me the same thing you just told me about the reporter giving the killer a nickname," Sam said reassuringly. "She said she likes the name. I guess we'll know soon enough whether the name fits."

"How's that," she asked.

"If he kills this next Holiday," Sam said grimly, squeezing her hand.

The Judge

After two more grueling days of visiting dozens of grocery stores and supermarkets, watching hours of security footage, and combing through thousands of receipts – they finally caught a break.

Detective Alisha Palmetto sat in the store office of a midtown grocery store, eyes glazing over as she watched several days' worth of security camera footage on super speed. Suddenly she reached over with lightning reflex and smashed the spacebar on the computer keyboard to pause the video. Carefully using the arrow keys, she walked the video backwards and then stopped. She switched the playback speed to real-time and began to watch.

What appeared to be a middle aged man with thinning dark hair, stood in the middle of the baking aisle with an empty shopping cart. He then looked up and down the aisle in a nervous fashion and began putting boxes of something in his cart one at a time, as if counting. At eighteen boxes, the shelf was empty.

The man dropped to one knee to look at the back of the shelf as if looking for boxes. He then began scooting other boxes to the side in a frantic search for more. Alisha watched as he finally stood, the section of shelving in front of him in disarray.

The man lingered there for a moment and then pounded his fist on the handle of the shopping cart.

After a moment's pause, he began walking rapidly to the end of the aisle, looking left and right. He returned and collected the cart with the eighteen boxes in it and pushed it quickly towards the front of the store, almost barreling into a woman who was turning down the aisle.

As the man turned left and out of sight, Alisha paused the feed to find him on another camera. A couple minutes later she spotted the man by the doors leading to the back of the store, in what appeared to be an argument with a store employee.

Alisha pointed at the screen and said to the grocery manager, "I need to know who that employee is and I need to speak to him ASAP."

"Uh," replied the manger, taking a closer look. "Pretty sure that's Thom."

"Does Thom have a last name? Is he here right now?" Palmetto asked impatiently.

"It's Arnold, Thom Arnold, and his shift doesn't start until four," the manager replied.

"Get him on the phone," Alisha demanded, and then continued watching the video.

After a moment of conversation, Thom, on the security camera video, turned and walked into the back of the store. The customer stood there, hands on his hips, waiting impatiently. About a minute and a half later, Thom returned with a box in his hands. A few more words were exchanged before Thom opened the box. Alisha watched as Thom handed the customer boxes two at a time.

Alisha counted out loud without realizing it: "Two, four, six, eight…"

Thom tried to hand the customer two more boxed, but he held up his hand signaling that the eight additional boxes were enough, before turning and walking quickly to the front of the store. *Eighteen boxes from the shelf. Eight boxes from Thom. Twenty-six in total*, Alisha thought.

"Gotcha!" Alisha exclaimed. She paused the video to find the feed now from the cash registers. A moment later she again picked up the mystery customer unloading the twenty-six boxes onto the conveyor belt at the register.

The cashier said something to him, and he reached into his pocket and pulled out his keychain. She scanned something on it. Alisha paused the video.

"What's that?" she asked. "What's she doing?"

"That's his store loyalty card," the manager replied. "He earns points for discounted gas by scanning it with his purchase."

"What an idiot," said Alisha with gleeful surprise.

"I'm going to need the receipt from that timestamp: 19:41 on 11-20," she said to the manager. "Also, what's the cashier's name? I'll need to speak to her as well."

"Ok, that's Brianna Holt, and she also works evenings," the manager replied. "Also, I called Thom and he didn't answer. I can give you his phone number and address though, and you can follow up."

"Ok, that works. Go ahead and give me Brianna's too," Alisha replied.

Alisha hit the spacebar to continue watching the video. A couple minutes later, all the boxes were rung up. The customer snatched the receipt from her hand and walked quickly towards the store exit, pushing his shopping cart. Alisha paused the video again.

"Do you have security cameras outside?" she asked the manager.

"Not out front. Just in the back where we have the loading dock for deliveries," the manager replied.

Alisha let out an expletive, but then added, "No worries. I think between this footage and the receipt, we should be good."

Alisha scanned the receipt. She cursed again. "He was at least smart enough to pay with cash. I was hoping there'd be a name though from the loyalty card. Can you look up the loyalty number here on the receipt," she asked the manager.

"I can't," he replied, "but here's a new loyalty card. If you call the number on the back, they should be able to tell you."

"Alright, thanks," Alisha said standing up. "You've been a huge help. As soon as I save the security camera footage to this thumb drive, I'll be out of here."

About ten minutes later, Alisha exited the store with the security camera footage, the receipt, and a slip of paper with the contact information for Thom and Brianna written on it. Once she was in her car again and the heater running, she called

Sam. "Grab me a coffee and meet me at the office. I think we got him."

***

Sam drove well above the speed limit back towards the squad room. He whipped into a drive-thru coffee place and quickly ordered Alisha's coffee. Three minutes later, he was back on the road, and soon arrived at the station.

Sam's morning had gone so far just like the last three – store after store without finding anyone whose activity matched what they were looking for. Sam dreaded the thought of several more days of this mind-numbing task, but now that Alisha said she'd found something, a new energy coursed through him. He was so anxious to get inside the squad room, he initially forgot her coffee and had to unlock the car again to grab it.

In the squad room, Alisha already had security camera footage from the store up on the screen and was working to queue up to the relevant parts of the video – most importantly the mystery man's face.

"What'd you find that you couldn't tell me on the phone?" Sam asked hurriedly.

"Did you get my coffee?" Alisha responded, ignoring Sam's question.

Wordlessly, Sam held out the cup of coffee.

"Good, now we can talk," Alisha said. "This is the security camera footage from the Hometown Grocery on Northwest 18th street from the twentieth of November."

"Yeah?" replied Sam anxiously awaiting further details.

Alisha held up a finger signaling Sam to wait a second as she fine-tuned the security camera feed to show a man walking into the store.

"There. This is our guy," she said pointing at a rather ordinary-looking, middle-aged man with thinning black hair. "I'll speed it up, but he goes to the boxed goods aisle and clears the shelf out of stuffing mix, and then forces an employee to give him more from the back until he has exactly twenty-six boxes."

Sam pumped his fist in the air and said, "Dang fine work, Alisha."

"Even better," continued Alisha, "We have the receipt. He did pay in cash, but he used his store rewards number to earn points. The manager gave me an eight hundred number to call – should be a simple phone call to get his name, address where they send coupons, and the rest of his contact info."

"Well, let's do it," said Sam. "I can run the tape down to forensics so we can get an enhanced copy and a good shot of his face while you call."

Down in the lab, he dropped off the tape asking the technician to make a rush on it. Back in the squad room, Sam found an annoyed Alisha impatiently tapping her fingers on the desk.

"They put me on hold," she said rolling her eyes. "The call center worker wouldn't give me our perp's identity, so I told her I wanted to speak to her boss – and now I'm stuck with this elevator music."

"You *would* ask for the manager, Karen" said Sam teasingly.

Alisha just shot him a sarcastic sneer in response.

A few moments later, Sam heard Alisha exclaim, "Yes, I'm still here." Sam couldn't hear the other side of the conversation with the rewards services manager, but he guessed that Alisha was being stonewalled.

"My name is Detective Alisha Palmetto with the Oklahoma City Police Department, badge number 56482…Yes, we have the rewards number for a person of interest in a case we're investigating and it'd be a huge help if you could tell us the name, address, phone number, email – whatever you have on the person it's connected to."

Alisha's voice took on an annoyed tone. "No, I can't give more details than that as it's an active investigation. Just a name and we're done here….C'mon lady, this has the potential to be a major break in a very high profile case. Can you please look up the info? No, I don't have a court order. I didn't know that I'd get the run around here. I thought you'd want to help solve a crime…Fine, I'll get the court order and call back."

With that Alisha slammed down the phone receiver. "Unbelievable. Everyone thinks they're a law expert these days. Where's your warrant? Do you have a court order?" she said in a mocking tone.

Alisha glanced at her watch. 1:00 p.m. "Y'know, it's still early. I'm gonna see if I can get that court order before the courthouse closes at five o'clock." She reached for her jacket and gloves.

"I guess I'll check on the lab and see if they've got a pic for me yet of the perp's face." Sam said dejected at their misfortune with the loyalty card company. "And then I can get with DMV facial recognition and try to get an ID the old fashioned way."

Alisha gave Sam a thumbs up and she was gone. Sam called the lab. The technician on the phone laughed, "Detective Cross, you were down here only fifteen minutes ago. I've barely started."

"I know," Sam said, "but right now I don't need an enhancement of the whole tape. I just need a clear shot of the guy's mug for facial recognition."

"Alright, I'll email it to you as soon as I get it worked up. Give me another fifteen minutes or so," and with that the technician hung up.

Sam opened his email and stared at the screen. The minutes dragged on like hours. With nothing to do until the picture came in, Sam decided to try his luck with the vending machine again. This time his honey roasted peanuts ejected without incident. Sam grabbed a Coke too and then headed back to his desk.

As Sam walked back in the squad room, Officer Travis called from his desk, "Got me peanuts again, Cross?"

"Yep, they're back there in the breakroom in the vending machine," Sam said as he sat at his desk. Still no email. He checked the clock. It'd been *only eight minutes* since he'd hung up with the forensics lab. Sam let out a sigh and closed his eyes.

He must've drifted off to sleep – the case had kept him up nights. But he startled awake as his email made a ding signaling he had a new message. It was from the lab. Sam clicked it immediately. It contained the long-awaited photo. Sam right-clicked to download the photo and then switched to the DMV database program and logged in. A couple minutes later, the photo was uploaded to the system and facial recognition matching had begun its long, slow search of millions of faces. While the database searched the image, Sam began clicking frame by frame through the video to see if he could spot any other clues.

***

Alisha straightened her blouse and put on her blazer she rarely wore. She bent over and checked her lipstick in her car's side mirror and then headed for the courthouse. She needed a favor and it wouldn't hurt to look her best.

Inside the courthouse, Alisha checked in with the court clerk. Lady luck was on her side: there was one timeslot left at 4:00 p.m. with Judge Lawson – *An appropriate name for someone who'd turn out to be a judge*, thought Alisha with a chuckle. Alisha wanted this warrant bad – and she wasn't above turning on the charm if the situation called for it. She'd have to wait two hours however for appearance before the judge. She decided to hang around the courthouse in case things moved faster or an earlier timeslot opened up. She sat in a well-worn chair, pulled out her phone, and clicked on a crossword puzzle game.

She should've known better than to dream of getting before the judge early. In fact, her timeslot came and went without her being called. She checked her watch. It was almost 5:00 p.m. A security guard began locking doors. Alisha rushed to the counter window just as the clerk was about to pull down the metal grate.

"Excuse me. I was scheduled to see Judge Lawson at four, and nobody ever called me," Alisha said hurriedly.

"I'm sorry miss," the clerk said without making eye contact. "You'll have to come back tomorrow."

"Wait," Alisha exclaimed. "This can't wait 'til tomorrow. I've gotta have a warrant today."

"Ma'am," replied the clerk in a robotic, apathetic tone as she packed up her workstation, "everybody says that, and everybody ends up waiting for tomorrow. Our offices open at 8:00 a.m. I suggest you come *earlier* tomorrow," the clerk added with an accusatory tone.

"No!" said Alisha forcefully. "Don't give me that. I sat here for nearly three hours. I didn't come earlier because I just got the evidence I need to break my case wide open. I've *got* to have that warrant – today!"

The clerk wordlessly ignored her and continued to close the window grate. Alisha defiantly put her hand in the way to keep it from closing.

"Ma'am, remove your hand, or I'll have security remove you from the building," the clerk said.

"Let me talk to Judge Lawson – please," said Alisha, her tone softening as she removed her hand. "Please," she pleaded again.

"I'll tell her," the clerk finally replied after a long pause, "but no promises."

"Thank you so much," exuded Alisha. She chewed on her lip while she waited impatiently. The clerk had referred to the judge as a "her" – Alisha had hoped for a male judge in case she needed to flash a pretty smile.

The clerk returned about five minutes later. "Miracles do happen," she said flatly. "Judge Lawson will see you in Courtroom Six.

"Thank you, thank you, thank you!" breathed Alisha as she hurried towards the courtroom. She received no "you're welcome" from the clerk – shocking. Inside, it was just her, the judge, and one bailiff. The judged looked less-than-happy to see her. She stepped quickly to the bench.

"What is it that has you so hot and bothered Detective Palmetto," asked the judge as she peered over her bifocals.

"Yes, Your Honor. Thank you so much for seeing me," began Alisha, but the judge cut her off.

"Skip the pleasantries and get to the point, Detective. I've got a dinner engagement that I'd rather not be late for," Judge Lawson said grumpily.

"Yes. You may have heard about what the news has dubbed the Holiday Killer case," Alisha said quickly as the judge glanced at her watch. "My partner, Detective Sam Cross – you may have heard of him – anyway, we're on the Holiday Killer case. And we've been looking for any evidence to identify a suspect. Well, on the most recent homicide investigation, the victim was…uh…stuffed with boxed stuffing like a Thanksgiving turkey.”

At that, the judge looked up from the notes she had been writing. “That's gross,” Judge Lawson said.

“Yes. I skipped turkey this past Thanksgiving on account of that,” replied Alisha with slight chuckle. “So anyway, we've been scouring every grocery store and supermarket in the city looking for someone who bought a bunch of boxed stuffing – twenty-six boxes to be exact. And this morning, I found security camera footage of a man buying exactly twenty-six boxes of stuffing.”

“Interesting,” interrupted Judge Lawson. “Can you please get to the point of what you need?” she asked looking again at her watch.

“Yes, Your Honor,” replied Alisha. “So, the person of interest – the one who purchased the twenty-six boxes of stuffing, paid with cash, but he used his grocery rewards card to earn his cash-back points. We have the rewards card number from a reprinted receipt from the supermarket – but when I called the rewards company, they refused to give us the suspect's name, address, and phone number without a warrant. But if we can identify this man, we'll likely catch our killer.”

Judge Lawson looked at the notes she'd scratched down and then back up at Alisha. “Detective, your ‘evidence' is kind of thin and circumstantial. Buying twenty-six boxes of stuffing isn't a crime, nor is it terribly suspicious. It's the holidays, and for all you know, this person-of-interest is stocking his pantry, donating to a food bank, or hosting a church dinner."

"But, Your Honor," interjected Alisha, "our forensic lab calculated the exact amount of stuffing found at the crime scene inside our victim and it was exactly twenty-six boxes worth. That can't be a coincidence."

"Detective," Judge Lawson replied, "I'll remind you not to interrupt me again. And coincidences aren't evidence. If the stuffing had been purchased at the store where the murder took place – that might be somewhat more convincing. I'm sorry you've wasted your afternoon and my time here as well. But buying twenty-six boxes of stuffing, however coincidental that may be to your case, just isn't probable cause to force a company to give up the personal information of one of their clients. Good day, Detective. Court is adjourned." Without another word, Judge Lawson rose from her seat.

"Your Honor!" urged Alisha, "We're trying to stop a possible serial killer and we're running out of time and leads. Can you please reconsider?"

"Bring me something more than buying a curiously large number of stuffing boxes and we'll see," Judge Lawson called as she exited the courtroom. The door shut behind her and Alisha was left alone with only the bailiff. Alisha lingered still, petrified by a mixture of anger and frustration.

"Detective," the bailiff said, "if you'll please exit the courtroom."

"I'm going," snapped back Alisha, and spun on her heel.

Back in the foyer area, Alisha pulled out her phone and called her partner.

"Hey!" answered Sam. "Did you get it?"

"If by 'it' you mean a wasted afternoon and the strong urge to slap an old, crusty judge, then yeah," replied Alisha angrily. "But no, I didn't get the warrant. Sorry."

"What!" exclaimed Sam, "How? Our perp literally bought the exact number of stuffing boxes."

"You don't have to tell me," retorted Alisha.

"Who'd you get for a judge?" Sam asked.

"Judge Lawson," replied Alisha coldly.

"Oof," was Sam's reply. "Yeah, she's a tough cookie for sure."

"Cookie isn't the word that I had in mind," said Alisha still angry.

"Well, we'll get an ID soon enough," Sam said trying to cheer her up. "I got an enhanced facial photo from the lab, and it's been running through the DMV database for the last three hours. Hopefully, we'll get a match here shortly."

"Yeah," Alisha said, still annoyed. "Hey," she said, changing the subject, "you wanna grab a beer or a bite to eat or something?"

"I would," Sam replied apologetically, "but I promised my wife I'd be home by six. It's our oldest boy's birthday."

"Ah, ok," Alisha said dejectedly. "No worries then. See you in the morning."

"Yep," said Sam, "and thanks for trying on that warrant. Not your fault."

With that they hung up. Alisha walked towards her car. A light snow was falling outside and she pulled her jacket tighter around her.

***

Sam swung into the grocery store that was about three blocks from the Cross home. Jennifer, his wife, had tasked him with picking out ice cream for the birthday party that evening. He grabbed a half-gallon of both chocolate and cookie dough and headed for the register. Just as Sam was about to step to the register, a man carrying a half-gallon of milk, twelve-pack of ramen noodles, and a tray of sushi nearly bumped into him and slipped into line, rudely cutting him off.

"Excuse me," the man muttered and then placed his items on the conveyor belt to be rung up. Sam thought about saying something about the man's lack of manners, but it'd be a frustrating afternoon and he didn't trust himself not to say something un-Christian. Sam gave a fake smile instead and said, "No problem."

The young lady ringing up groceries was the chipper, friendly type and she struck up a conversation with the man in line in front of Sam. "Just coming home from work?" the cashier asked.

"Yep," was all the man replied.

"Oh cool," the cashier continued unfazed by the man's curt answer. "You're all dressed up. What kind of work do you do? Banker?"

"No," the man replied. Sam could detect a meanness in the man's voice and hoped he wouldn't speak unkindly to the cashier. "College professor," the man finally added.

"That'll be $14.86," the cashier said as she rung up the last item. "And that's so cool. I'm gonna start classes this fall over at the community college. What course do you teach?"

"Consumer Economics," was the man's terse reply as he inserted his bank card in the machine and typed his PIN.

"Oh wow!" the cashier said, "Maybe I'll take your course one day. Sounds super interesting. Here's your receipt. Enjoy the rest of your evening Professor. Happy Holidays!"

The man just nodded and grabbed his groceries. The cashier turned to Sam and greeted him in her same cheerful demeanor. Sam amusedly thought to himself that he should hire her as an investigator for the police force – by the time he'd paid for his groceries, Sam had told her that he was detective, that the ice cream was for his son's sixth birthday, and that he still needed to do all of the family's Christmas shopping.

Sam thanked her, and wished her a Happy Holidays as well, and less than five minutes later, he pulled in his driveway. It was a fun family party, and three hours later, with dinner over, the kitchen cleaned up, and the boys in bed, Jennifer Cross confronted Sam. "I wish you'd leave work at work – especially with tonight being Drew's birthday. I could tell your mind was out there in crime stuff the whole time we were opening presents and eating cake."

Sam sighed. "I'm sorry. I didn't mean to. I'm sure the boys didn't notice."

"But it's like this every night here lately," Jennifer pressed. "We try to sit down and watch something and you don't even know what's happening in the show because your mind is wrapped up in evidence and investigations."

"Well, I *am* trying to catch a deranged killer who's preparing to strike again soon, so forgive me please," Sam replied with a roll of his eyes.

"You know I know that," Jennifer replied with an eye roll of her own. "It's just – it's not like you're going to find the killer and solve the case during family dinner."

"You never know," Sam said sarcastically.

"I just want your attention during the few short hours you're here each evening," Jennifer sighed.

Sam smiled playfully and pulled his wife in for a hug and a kiss. "Then come here and I'll give you some," he said with a flirtatious wink.

Jennifer laughed, "How about another scoop of ice cream now that the boys are in bed, and then we'll see about you giving me a back rub."

"That sounds like a lot of work, but I'm down," Sam said as he applied more kisses.

Jennifer giggled and squirmed away. "More ice cream first…then you may continue."

A few minutes later as Sam followed his wife to the bedroom, he remembered that he'd meant to tell her tonight about the upcoming stakeout – but decided to hold off another night for fear of ruining the mood.

****

Professor Harold Barnes reached down and scooped his ferret Houdini up with one hand and walked towards his study. "Guess what?" he said softly to Houdini. "I do believe it's time for the world to hear from the Holiday Killer. Not the name I would've chosen, but of course nobody asked us, did they?" The furry face just stared back, nose twitching.

Inside his study, the professor seated himself at his old-fashioned roll-top desk and placed his pet on his lap. He slipped on a pair of surgical gloves and then took out a piece of light cream stationary and a cheap click-pen he'd taken from the dentist office a few weeks ago and began to write. He finished the letter, and then taking another piece of paper, copied it word-for-word.

Professor Barnes had decided to send one copy to the police station and another to the news reporter who'd coined the name "Holiday Killer." He folded each letter into thirds and then stuffed them into envelopes – the kind with the peel off sticky strip to prevent leaving DNA evidence behind by licking the envelopes. Once they were addressed and stamped, he placed the letters by the garage door underneath his wallet to drop off on his way to class the next morning, and then tossed his gloves in the kitchen garbage.

"8:00 p.m. Time for the news," Professor
Barnes said to Houdini, and walked to the couch.

The Mortician

The next morning, Sam was early to the office, beating Alisha for a change. Sam didn't even bother to remove his jacket as he hurriedly logged into his computer. To Sam's disappointment, the facial recognition software was still running through its database of faces looking for a match to their mystery stuffing shopper. Sam rubbed his face in frustration. Sometimes facial recognition software brought back a match – and sometimes it didn't. A lot of different factors such as lighting, angle of the photo, and so forth could drastically reduce the software's accuracy and probability of finding a match. The lab tech had done a decent job of providing a usable facial image of the suspect, but it was still a security camera grab at an indirect angle – and the security camera hadn't been top-of-the-line.

After the excitement of finding a suspect, they'd now hit a bit of a brick wall. The rewards card company had stonewalled them and then the judge had rejected their warrant request. Now facial recognition wasn't bringing anything back so far.

Sam opened the image, clicked the print button, and told it to print five copies. Sam would post one in the squad room and then use the others to canvas business and neighborhoods around where the suspect was seen shopping. Sam could only hope that the man in the video had purchased the stuffing boxes from a store either near his home, his work, or in some area he frequently shopped where someone might recognize his face and put a name to it.

While he waited for the painfully slow, outdated printer to spit out the images, Sam texted his partner to request breakfast: "Already at the office. Coffee and a sausage biscuit would be heavenly."

A moment later, Alisha texted back a "thumbs up" emoji. As he put his phone back in his pocket, the final image finished printing and Sam grabbed the stack and returned to his desk. Still no match. It'd only been about four minutes since he'd last checked, yet Sam was still somehow disappointed again that there was nothing.

Sam leaned back in his chair and stared at the ceiling. What a crazy year it'd been – almost made him miss being nothing more than a beat cop: take a statement, make an arrest, write a report, and let the detectives handle the rest. The pay bump had been nice though. And more than ever, Sam felt like he was making a difference.

His daydream was interrupted by the sound of footsteps. Sam straightened up in his chair to see Alisha headed his way with a cup of coffee and a brown sack that hopefully contained his breakfast.

"What're you doing beating me to work? I got a reputation to uphold," Alisha said playfully.

"I couldn't sleep and I was really hoping for a match on that photo – but no luck," Sam replied. He held up the printout of the photo and shot a sarcastic grin of excitement. "Which means more canvassing!"

"Ugh, I think I feel the flu coming on," Alisha replied with a fake "cough, cough."

Sam took a sip of his coffee and inhaled sharply as he burned his tongue. As he unwrapped his sausage biscuit, Sam continued, "I figured we'd hit businesses and possibly residences around the supermarket where our perp bought the stuffing and see if anyone can put a name to his face."

Alisha continued her charade of feigned illness for a moment and then replied with a disgusted tone, "I guess it's better than the last week of watching hours of security camera footage – and it sure beats the two weeks of stakeouts we got coming up."

Sam made a face as he remembered he still needed to tell his wife about the upcoming stakeouts. Alisha shot him a quizzical look, but Sam gave a dismissive wave. Sam chewed and swallowed the last bite of his biscuit and took another swig of his now much cooler coffee. He grabbed the stack of photo pages and said, "Ready, partner?"

Alisha held up a finger as she chewed the last bite of her burrito and then grabbed her coat and followed Sam towards the door. As they rounded the corner to the entryway, Sam almost ran into Captain Durant.

"Ah, perfect timing," began Captain Durant. Sam felt otherwise. "Where are we at on the case?" Captain Durant continued. "Got that suspect ID'd yet? Stakeout all set up?"

"Uh," replied Sam hesitantly, desperately trying to think of something clever to respond. All he came up with was "No…and no."

Alisha saved his bacon. "We would, except for old Judge Lawson," she interjected. "Wouldn't give us our warrant. Rambled on about how it was perfectly normal for a man to buy twenty-six boxes of stuffing," she said with an exaggerated eyeroll. "And we're coordinating with other detectives for the stakeout. Should be all hammered out in a day or two. Anything else before we get to work?" she added with an impatient tone.

"Remember – just keep me in the loop," Captain Durant replied gruffly.

"Will do, Boss," Sam replied and then he and Alisha ducked out the door before the Captain could say anything else.

A few flakes of snow were swirling in the November wind as they stepped outside. Sam looked at the grey sky and felt a foreboding in the weather as he opened the driver's side door of his car and slid inside.

***

Professor Harold Barnes bent over and gave Houdini's head a quick scratch and then grabbed his keys and wallet. He slipped on another pair of surgical gloves before picking up the two letters he'd written the night before. Professor Barnes was leaving earlier than usual. He didn't want to drop the letters near his house or near the university in case their pickup location could somehow be used to trace back to him. He gave himself an extra hour's time so that he could drive clear over to Del City to mail them and still make it to his 9:00 a.m. class.

It wasn't too bad of a drive. Holiday traffic hadn't really picked up yet, and about twenty-five minutes later, the professor chose a postal drop box in a random neighborhood to deposit his letters. Forty minutes later, and with a good ten minutes to spare, Professor Barnes pulled into his faculty parking spot and walked briskly towards his classroom.

***

Detectives Cross and Palmetto pulled into the supermarket parking lot where the stuffing had been purchased and Sam pulled out his phone. He launched the maps app and looked at the businesses nearby.

"There's a little shopping strip about a tenth of a mile that way," Sam said pointing at the screen. "A mobile phone store, hardware store, pawn shop, and an…" Sam paused before saying the final storefront. "And an adult store."

Alisha laughed, "I bet you've never been in one in your life. I can't wait to see the look on your face."

Sam cleared his throat uncomfortably. "Maybe we should split up."

"Sure," Alisha replied quickly. "I'll take the mobile phone and hardware stores."

"Really?" Sam asked annoyed.

"But I'm a lady," Alisha said with a laugh as Sam put the car in gear and headed towards the strip mall.

Sam couldn't think of a comeback, so he just drove in silence.

"Oh, alright. I'll take the adult store," Alisha said as she punched him in the arm. "You're still taking the pawn shop though. Pawn shop owners are sleazy."

Sam put his blinker on and turned into the shopping strip. He parked in the middle of the lot and he and Alisha split up. Sam headed far left to the mobile phone store and Alisha entered the hardware store, the door dinging to signal her entry.

Sam pulled the handle of the mobile phone store, but it was locked. He could see employees inside so he checked his watch. Three minutes until nine. Sam pounded on the door. An employee walked slowly over, distracted by something he was looking at on his phone. Through the door, the employee pointed at the store hours and mouthed sorry.

Sam pulled his badge out and smacked it against the glass with a loud clank. The employee's eyes got wide and he called over his shoulder to his manager. A couple seconds later, the employee unlocked the door and held it open for Sam.

"Sorry about that, Officer," the employee said sheepishly.

"It's Detective, and no worries," Sam replied. "And hopefully I'll only be a minute." He pulled out the photo of their suspect from the folder inside his jacket and held it up. "Just need to know if anyone recognizes this man. He shops locally to this neighborhood, so I'm hoping he might've come in here."

Sam showed it to each of the three employees, but they all shook their heads. "What's he wanted for?" one of them asked.

"Just need to ask him some questions," Sam replied evasively. "Take another look. Are you sure he doesn't look familiar?"

All three employees again indicated no, so Sam tucked the photo back inside the folder, thanked them, and headed back outside.

Sam walked briskly towards the pawn shop. As he passed the hardware store, he could see Alisha still talking to an employee inside. Sam considered going in to see if she'd found out anything but decided to just stick with the plan and check out the pawn shop next.

As Sam entered the pawn shop, the door gave an electronic ding. From the back room came a man – that, like Alisha had predicted, could definitely be described as "sleazy."

The pawn shop owner froze briefly at the sight of Sam. "I don't fence in no stolen items here. Everything's on the up and up," the owner said nervously.

Sam smiled, "How'd you peg me for a cop?" Sam asked.

"Easy," the owner began, but then adjusted, "I mean, I just got an eye for things. So again, I'd get that feeling, ya know if anything brought in was stolen."

"Don't hold it against me if I don't take your word for it," Sam said ominously. Sam could care less at this point if the pawn shop was dirty. But he'd use the man's nervousness to pry out whatever information the man might have.

"Uh, was there anything specific you were looking for?" the owner said uneasily.

"Just a face for now," Sam replied as he pulled the photo out of his jacket again. "Seen this man in here? I just need a name."

"Ahh…nope," was the owner's quick reply.

Sam knew immediately that the owner was lying by the way he looked away. Sam pressed. "I got an eye for things too – and I know you're lying. I just need a name."

The owner rubbed his face with his hands in frustration. "Ok yeah, he comes in here every now and then. But not to move anything. Just buys the occasional odd tool or whatever."

"A name!" Sam replied firmly.

The owner cursed. "I don't know it," he shot back, but Sam fired him a menacing glare.

"Will or Warren or Walker or something like that," blurted out the owner. "I told you; I don't know his name. He's a shifty fella and I've not really struck it up with him. He's not the type for that."

"Ok what else can you tell me about Will or Warren or Walker?" asked Sam, pretending anger. "What kinda car does he drive? Where does he work? What's his last name? C'mon. Give me something or I'll have the Crimes Against Property Unit down here knee deep in your paperwork."

"Bro…I mean Detective. I swear I don't know nothing about the guy," the pawn shop owner said backing up.

"Why you backing up?" Sam asked. "You gonna rabbit on me? Just calm down and give me something I can work with – something besides three different names that are all probably wrong."

"He drives a white car – an older model Buick or something like that," the owner replied with an exasperated tone. "For real man. I don't know any more about him. He's just a regular guy – a bit strange. I've never really paid him any attention. I swear that's it!"

"Fine. But here's my card. And when you think of his name or if he comes in here again, you call me," Sam said sternly. "Got it?"

"Yeah, I got it," was the owner's gruff reply. "So, you're not sending your boys down here, right?"

"Do I need to?" Sam asked.

"Nope. And I'll call you if I see him," the owner replied quickly.

Sam nodded and headed back outside. He didn't see his partner. Perhaps she was still inside one of the stores. Sam was about to go back and check the hardware store when Alisha stuck her head out the door of the adult store and hollered for him to come over.

As Sam walked quickly across the parking lot, he mused to himself: "So we know he shops around here, which means he probably lives in this area too. And his name maybe starts with a W."

About ten feet from the adult store Alisha beckoned for him to come inside.

"I'm good," replied Sam. "Just come on out when you're done. I think I got a lead."

"Would ya quit being a prude," his partner replied. "I've got more than maybe a lead."

Sam sighed and headed inside. He definitely wouldn't be telling his wife that he was inside an adult store with his partner. The interior was just about as Sam had imaged it would be – dress up costumes, magazines, and other unmentionables.

"What's this lead you got?" asked Sam, trying not to look around too much.

"Yasmine here," said Alisha motioning towards the shop clerk, "says she knows our man in the photo. He comes in here at least once a week."

Sam waited for Alisha to continue and then finally asked, "Well are you going to tell me or do I have to guess his name?"

"No, no," replied Alisha, "I was just savoring this moment since you stuck me with canvassing the adult shop," she said with a wink. "Turns out his name is Walt."

"Walt is good," replied Sam. "The pawn shop owner said his name started with a W but he couldn't remember the exact name."

"There's more," continued Alisha. "She said he always pays cash – like at the supermarket, but she's pretty sure he mentioned during one of his visits that he works at a funeral home or something."

"Nice," replied Sam, with a fist pump. "Sounds about like the kind of place he'd work.

And that shouldn't be too hard to track down – it's not like Walt is a super common name. Don't suppose she happens to know Walt's last name."

"Sorry, honey," spoke up the shop keeper. "The name Walt is all I got. People usually want to keep things kinda private in a place like this, if you know what I mean. I can enlighten you to his, ah, preferences, though if you like, Detective."

Sam didn't really want to hear, but on the off chance that it might be relevant to the case, Sam nodded and took out his notepad and pen. Sam cringed at the movie genres and magazine titles he wrote down. Pretty sure he'd need to say a few extra prayers at church that coming Sunday after what he'd just heard. Thankfully, Sam didn't see how any of Walt's "preferences" were in any way relevant to their case.

Just then Yasmine announced, "It's finished," and unplugged a thumb drive from her store computer and handed it to Alisha. "We got a lot better cameras in here than that picture you brought with you. Should be able to get a real good look at your guy. What did you say he did again?"

"We didn't say," replied Alisha with a smile. "But we're very grateful for all your help. If anyone ever asks me for a recommendation for anything up your alley, I'll send them here."

As Sam and Alisha turned to exit the store, Yasmine spoke up one final time. "Now, don't go advertising about my security cameras and me giving the footage to the police. Like I said, my customers like their privacy."

Sam promised to keep it in house to their investigation, and waved goodbye. Outside, Alisha beamed at Sam. "What?" asked Sam. "Were you waiting for a congratulations or a pat on the back?"

"Oh fine. Just coffee then," replied Alisha with a roll of her eyes. Then she giggled. "I can't wait to see you write up the report on our investigation with the things you wrote in your notepad."

Now it was Sam's turn to roll his eyes as he turned and headed for the car. "Did you find out anything else at the hardware store? You were in there for a while."

"Nothing additional," called Alisha from behind Sam as they walked. "One of the guys had seen him but didn't have anything to add, and they said their security cameras hadn't worked in months. What about you? Sounds like you got something from the pawn shop."

"That pawn shop guy is shady as all get out – but nothing likely connected to our case," Sam answered. "Pretty sure he's probably moved some stolen merch, but again, I didn't lean on him too much since that's not what we're after.

"Oh," continued Sam, "he did say that he was pretty sure our guy drives some kind of older white sedan – maybe a Buick or an Oldsmobile. Not a lot to go on, but at least it's something to connect to this Walt guy when we find him. While I drive us to get some coffee, get on your phone and see if you can find a funeral home or mortuary with a guy named Walt who works there."

A few minutes later, Alisha was still scrolling through her phone as Sam pulled into the coffee shop. "You want your usual?" Sam asked.

"Yeah," Alisha replied, "If you wanna grab it, I'll just stay here and keep searching for our Walt guy."

Sam nodded and headed inside.

***

Today's lecture in Consumer Economics was on *Objections to Capitalism*. Tiffany found the discussion quite interesting.

"Now some might get the idea that I'm an anti-capitalist," Professor Harold Barnes said, "but they'd be wrong. The data and history show that capitalism is the fairest and most successful economic system."

"Yes, Mr. Dixon?" said Professor Barnes in acknowledgement to a student's raised hand.

"Professor," replied the student, "How is capitalism more fair than socialism? Socialism aims to give everyone an equal start and an equal finish so that no one is left behind by societal injustices, privileges, and disadvantages."

"You've perfectly described socialism's fatal flaw, Mr. Dixon," replied the professor. "For an equal start does not guarantee an equal finish – unless you unfairly elevate those who have underachieved and unjustly hold back those who would overachieve.

"Yet as I was saying, capitalism isn't without its flaws, for it allows the crooked and those who would take advantage of the system to exploit for profit things that shouldn't be monetized or commercialized. Fact of the matter is that capitalism allows for the sale of almost anything for whatever ridiculous price as long as the seller can find an unsuspecting or foolish consumer to purchase it. All a seller has to do is provide a product for which there is a demand and capitalism allows someone to profit on it."

Tiffany raised her hand. "Can you give us a negative example, Professor Barnes?"

"Sure," he replied. "Take the various Holiday seasons for instance. Tell me, Miss Gunn, what is the purpose of the Mother's Day Holiday?"

"To let our mothers know that we appreciate them," Tiffany replied.

"Correct," replied Professor Barnes. "And, if you look into the beginnings of the Mother's Day Holiday, that's how it began. Anna Jarvis founded the first International Mother's Day to honor her mother and all mothers. But then capitalism got a hold of the holiday – and mind you, I'm a proponent of capitalism – but when capitalism got a hold of Mother's Day, it got completely commercialized. To the tune of, just this year, 26.7 billion dollars. And in fact, Anna Jarvis, the founder of Mother's Day, spent the latter years of her life fighting to have the Holiday *she created* abolished because she was so sickened by its commercialization.

"And capitalism has done the same with every other sacred day in our nation," the professor continued. "Memorial Day? Few, if anyone, actually honor what the holiday stands for. Instead, consumers will spend twelve billion dollars on weekend getaways and bar-b-ques. Same is true of Thanksgiving – it's all about turkey and football. And then the abomination called Black Friday the very next day. Christmas? It's almost entirely about trees and lights and Santa – and the origins of the Holiday are all but forgotten.

"Now this is all well and good for our capitalistic society and the businesses that profit from their commercialization, but at what cost? And I mean more than dollars and cents. I mean the cost of the sacred meaning of our Holidays and the economic enslavement of the consumer. Sometimes it even cost real people their lives."

"So, what do you propose then?" interjected another student. "The abolition of holidays like Anna Jarvis tried to do with Mother's Day?"

"The problem isn't the holidays," replied Professor Barnes. "And again, capitalism isn't a flaw. But if you think about the word 'holiday' it comes from two root words that mean 'holy day' – not necessarily in a religious sense though, but instead meaning 'sacred.' There's a reason that holidays were established: to commemorate some sacred event, or person, or group of people. And the sacredness of the day must not get lost in its commemoration or celebration. Yet that's what has happened to all of our most sacred days as a nation."

Professor Barnes was interrupted by the bell signaling the end of his class period. "Well, you're 'saved by the bell.' I have a whole theory on how to solve our Holiday commercialization problem, but it'll have to wait until next week's lecture. Don't forget your project is due in two weeks…"

* * *

The line was longer than Sam really wanted to wait in, but coffee was a "necessity." Ten minutes later, Sam was back outside. He knocked on his partner's passenger side window to hand her coffee to her. "I think I got something," she said as she took the coffee from him. Sam nodded and headed around to the driver's side.

"There's a Passing Memories Mortuary three miles from here," Alisha said, holding up her phone for Sam to see. "And the website says that the proprietor is one Walter Emmer – could be our guy. So, what's our play?"

"I think we gotta be careful with our approach here," Sam replied thoughtfully. "If we just show up and he has security cameras or if he's not there but two cops are seen poking around – we risk tipping him off."

"I could call and pretend my grandma died and ask if I could come by to discuss cremation," Alisha suggested.

Sam laughed. "That just might work. How's your acting skills?"

"I've been known to put on a convincing act a time or two…so just call now?" Alisha replied.

"Sure," said Sam with a shrug.

Alisha hit the link to dial the number. Four rings later, and the voicemail picked up. A man's voice said, "Hi, you've reached Passing Memories Mortuary and Cremation Services. If you've reached this recording during normal business hours, then I'm either with a family or otherwise occupied with the care of a family's loved one. Please leave a detailed message and I'll call you back as soon as possible. Thank you for considering Passing Memories for your family's needs."

Alisha hesitated, considering just hanging up and calling back later, but then decided to leave a message. "Hello," she said and then sniffed. "Um, my grandmother just passed away yesterday and I'd like to have just a small family ceremony. We're looking for affordable cremation. Could you please call me back? My cell is 786-555-5055. My name is Alisha. Thank you. Bye."

"I guess now we wait," Alisha said with a shrug.

"We could do a drive-by and see if anyone's even there," Sam suggested. "It'd be nice if we could confirm the tip on the car."

"Yeah let's do that," Alisha said, as Sam put the car in drive. "Better than just sitting here doing nothing."

Alisha hit "Go" on the directions on her phone and Sam obediently followed the female voice's navigation. Five minutes later, Sam spotted the sign for Passing Memories Mortuary. He rolled to a stop at the intersection to survey the parking lot and buildings. It was a non-descript tan, cinder-block building that looked like it had been built in the Sixties – maybe even the Fifties, though the paint looked newer. The front entrance was covered by a maroon cloth awning that extended over a pull-through drive. Gold-colored handrails ascended the three steps to the front door. The lawn was meticulously manicured. Sam did not see any vehicles.

Sam slowly turned right to drive around the side and get a view of the rear of the building. Behind the building was a shed with the pull-down door raised and inside were coffin-sized cardboard boxes. And there it was: parked to the left of the shed, mostly hidden, but still visible was the rear quarter panel of a white, older full-sized sedan. From the taillights, Sam guessed it was a Buick, just like the pawn shop owner had suggested.

"There's our car," Alisha exclaimed pointing. "He's gotta be here. What now?"

Just then Alisha's phone rang. Both Sam and Alisha jumped in their seats and Alisha almost dropped her phone. The caller ID read "Walter Emmer." Alisha took a deep breath and answered.

"Hello?"

"Hi, this is Walt Emmer with Passing Memories Mortuary and Cremation Services," the voice over the phone said. "Is this Miss Alisha?"

"Yes, it is she," replied Alisha.

"I'm very sorry about missing your call," Walt said. "I just received your voicemail. I'm very sorry about the passing of your grandmother. You have my sincerest condolences. If I can still be of service to you at this time, you're welcome to come by today and we can talk about the best way for your family to honor her memory."

"Yes, I'd like that very much," Alisha replied. "Do I just come by? Or do I need an appointment?"

"Are you free at 1:00 p.m.," Walt asked.

"Yes, if that's the earliest you have, that'll be fine," Alisha answered.

"Ok ma'am, I'll see you then. Just come to the front door and ring the bell," Walt said.

"Thank you. Goodbye – oh wait!" Alisha added, hoping that Walt hadn't yet hung up. "Are you still there?"

"Yes ma'am, I'm here. What is it?" Walt asked.

"Can I bring my boyfriend with me so I don't have to come alone?" Alisha asked looking coyly at Sam.

"That'll be just fine. Whatever makes you comfortable," Walt replied. "I'll see you then. Thank you."

Alisha hung up the call. "Your boyfriend?" Sam asked with a raised eyebrow.

"You can't send me in there without a partner," Alisha replied. "And plus, I'd like to see if you have any acting skills as well."

"Fine," Sam said with resignation. "It's only 10:30 though. What do you want to do until one?"

"I didn't get any breakfast – just this coffee, so we could grab lunch," Alisha suggested. "And maybe try to do some digging into Walt Emmer before our meeting."

"Sounds good," Sam replied. "Let's go somewhere with Wi-Fi so I can do the search."

A few minutes later, Sam pulled into a fast-food chicken place, and he and Alisha headed inside. Once in the lobby, Sam said, "I'm going to snag that corner table," he said pointing, "before someone else gets it, that way we have some privacy. And looks like it has a plug as well. Just get me a plain chicken sandwich with cheese, some fries, and a lemonade – oh and some bar-b-que sauce."

"I guess I'm buying lunch this time," Alisha said sarcastically.

"Thanks partner," Sam said with a smile and headed for the corner table. It took just a minute to connect to the Wi-Fi and get logged into the records search program on his laptop. Sam looked up and saw Alisha headed his way.

"They said they'd bring it out when it's ready," she said as she pulled a chair over next to Sam and sat down. Sam scooted closer to the wall.

Sam first did a criminal history search. Walt Emmer was squeaky clean – not even a parking ticket. Before Sam could do the next search, an employee in a red shirt and black pants arrived at their table with their order. Alisha had ordered a salad. "One less trip to the gym," she said as she took the carton off the tray.

"Can I get you two anything else?" the smiling employee asked.

Sam looked at Alisha and shook his head. "No, I think we're good," Alisha replied. "Thank you."

"My pleasure," the employee said with a smile and walked away.

Just as Sam was unwrapping his sandwich, he heard a familiar voice call his name. He looked around and then spotted Tiffany walking towards them.

Sam stood up. "Tiffany! Great to see you. What are you doing here?"

Tiffany gave Sam a hug and replied, "Getting lunch of course."

"Oh," Sam said pointing to Alisha, "You remember my partner, Detective Alisha Palmetto."

"Yep," Tiffany said with an awkward, little wave. She then looked past Sam at their table and saw Sam's laptop. "I guess it's a working lunch. I won't bother you. It was good to see you."

"No, no," Sam said quickly. "Uh, why don't you order and join us. I have something I want to ask you anyway."

"Ok," said Tiffany cheerfully, and off she headed towards the ordering counter.

Alisha shot Sam a quizzical look. "I want to show her the picture of Walt and see if she recognizes him," Sam replied as he returned to his chair.

A few minutes later, Tiffany returned to the table and pulled up a chair. "Any progress on the case?" she asked.

"Actually yes – possibly. I got a photo here I'd like you to take a look at," Sam said as he drew Walt's photo out of the folder. "Just tell me if he looks familiar – like maybe you saw him come through where you work."

Tiffany took a long look at the photo and then answered: "I don't think so. I'm pretty good with faces, but this guy – I don't think I've ever seen him. Sorry."

"That's ok," Sam reassured. "We've already likely got a positive ID anyway. I just wanted to see if you'd recognize him as a shopper."

"Yeah, I don't think he's been through – at least not on my shift," Tiffany replied. "Who is he? Is that the killer?"

Sam motioned for her to keep her voice down. "Probably best not to say that kind of thing too loudly. Wouldn't want to attract any attention or alarm anyone. Normally, I wouldn't discuss the case, but we already kinda broke that rule back on Thanksgiving – so yeah, we think so. Do you remember how you figured out the numbers?"

"Yep," replied Tiffany with a self-congratulatory smile.

"Ok, well we caught this guy on security camera buying twenty-six boxes of stuffing," Sam said as he took a bite of his sandwich.

"Twenty-six," said Tiffany thoughtfully. "That was one of the repeating numbers wasn't it?"

"Yes," Sam replied as he input Walt's name in his computer.

"Well, it's gotta be the k…" Tiffany almost said "killer" again but corrected, "the person of interest."

"You'd think so," Alisha interjected, "but we failed to convince a judge the other day, so we're digging for more evidence."

For the next few minutes, in hushed voices, Tiffany, Sam, and Alisha discussed the various aspects of their investigation over their chicken lunch. Sam suddenly spoke up triumphantly. "Got'm! Address, phone, family contacts –

everything on our guy – everything we need to do surveillance if this afternoon's meeting doesn't turn anything up."

"Wait, you're meeting the ki – person of interest this afternoon?" Tiffany said in a shocked tone.

"Yeah, at one – I'm pulling the old 'my grandma died' routine," Alisha said with a smile. "Been using that since high school and hasn't failed me yet."

"I don't know," Tiffany said through a bite of waffle fry. "This guy is a madman. Who knows what you'll be walking into."

"Well, again," Sam interjected, "he doesn't know we're detectives, so he shouldn't be suspicious of us."

Tiffany looked at her watch. "I've gotta get back to class. Good to see you and thanks for letting me crash y'all's lunch." With a wave, Tiffany headed for the exit.

"What is our play?" Sam asked. "Just see what we see? Or are we looking for an arrest?"

Alisha pondered for a moment and then said, "I think just play it by ear. Keep our eyes open, and like you said, see what we see. As meticulous as our perp has been, I doubt we'll find incriminating evidence just sitting out in plain sight."

"Well, we better get headed that way," Sam said as he closed the screen to his laptop. It was almost half past noon. He took one more bite of a now cold waffle fry and then gathered up his trash and tossed it in the bin. Alisha visited the ladies' room while Sam got a refill on his lemonade, and a few minutes later he was backing his car out of the parking spot.

They would be a few minutes early to the mortuary, but Sam figured that might give them the element of surprise and a chance to poke around if Walt was with another customer. Shortly after 12:45, they arrived at Passing Memories Mortuary. Sam had been thinking the whole time they'd been driving. As he parked the car, he said, "Unless we find strong incriminating evidence to make an immediate arrest, I think our goal here has to be just to find anything that will allow us to go back to that judge and get a warrant to search both the mortuary and Walt's home. I don't know what that might be, so let's just keep our eyes open. You ready to earn that Academy Award for Best Actress?"

"Almost," Alisha replied as she let her long hair fall down out of the bun she'd had it in. "We look too much like a pair of suits rather than grieving relatives."

Sam hadn't thought about that. But there wasn't much he could do about his appearance at this point other than ditch his tie, suit coat, and untuck his dress shirt before donning his overcoat. Alisha reached over to his shirt buttons and unbuttoned one more. "There," she said. "That's a bit more casual."

Sam thought about saying something about being able to dress himself, but let it go and reached for the car handle. He pulled his coat tightly around his exposed neck and walked quickly towards the front door of the mortuary, careful to watch for ice patches.

At the door, Sam pulled the handle, but it didn't open. Alisha caught up and pushed the buzzer to the left of the entrance. A minute or so passed. Alisha was just reaching for the doorbell again, when, from the inside, a figure pushed the crash bar and the door slowly opened. It was the man from the supermarket security camera: Walt Emmer.

Interrogated

"Hello," Walt said cheerfully, but with a tinge of nervousness. "Can I help you? Did you call for an appointment?"

"Yes," replied Alisha, "We spoke earlier. My grandma passed away."

"Oh, yes, yes," Walt said opening the door wider. "Please come in. And please accept my condolences." He looked at his wristwatch as Sam and Alisha stepped inside. "I wasn't expecting you for another ten minutes or so."

"Sorry about that," Alisha replied. "We weren't sure where you were located, so we left early. Turns out it was fairly easy to find."

"That's good," replied Walt. "Ah, I do need to finish a few preparations before our one o'clock appointment. If you don't mind waiting here," he said pointing at some chairs, "I'll just finish up and be with you shortly."

Alisha and Sam nodded and sat down as Walt scurried out of sight. As Sam settled into his chair, he felt Alisha take his hand in hers. Sam shot her a side eye and mouthed, "What are you doing?"

Alisha leaned in close enough for Sam to feel her breath on his ear. She whispered, "You're my boyfriend remember? Gotta keep up that Academy Award performance." She set back in her chair and smiled, still holding his hand.

Sam pulled his hand back and said quietly, "I'm going to see if I can find a restroom – and maybe take a wrong turn while looking for it."

Alisha rolled her eyes and mouthed back "Fine."

Cautiously, Sam looked in the direction Walt had gone. There was a short hallway, with a door on either side, and a third door at the end. Sam opted to go in the opposite direction to buy himself more time. There was just one door to the left of the waiting area and Sam entered it.

The light was off, but it was dimly lit by sunlight streaming through several windows. As his eyes adjusted, he saw that this was the showroom. Several different styles of caskets were arranged throughout the room. On a table to the right of the door were four different types of cremation urns: a golden one, a silver one, a brass one, and one made of perhaps stone or pottery. Sam didn't expect to see anything inside the coffins or urns, but he still peeked in each one just for good measure.

On the opposite side of the room was another door. Sam opened it. It was the mortuary's chapel. Sam guessed that there was a funeral soon because the room had flower arrangements by the front stage area. Sam didn't linger, however. He didn't have much time and none of this would help him with what he was looking for – which Sam wasn't even sure of himself.

Back in the coffin showroom, Sam noticed another doorway he'd overlooked because of the darkness. Sam headed quickly for it. On the other side of the door was a pitch-black hallway. Sam fumbled on the wall for a light switch and found one, wincing at the brightness as he flipped it on. Well, he'd found the restrooms he'd claimed to be looking for: men's on the right and women's at the end of the hall. "Rats," Sam thought to himself as he looked at his watch: four minutes until one. He was almost out of time.

Sam exited the restroom area, flipping the light off as he closed the door, and hurried back towards the waiting area where he'd left Alisha. She was nowhere to be seen. Had she gone to poke around also? Or had Walt come back early to retrieve her? Sam didn't like the idea of his partner alone with a brutal serial killer. The only place she could've gone was in the direction he'd seen Walt exit earlier. For good measure, Sam peeked out the front door in case she'd stepped out or gone back to the car for some reason. No sign of her – just a blast of cold December wind.

Sam crossed the waiting room in four large strides and turned down the hallway. He tried the knob to the door on the right. It was locked. Sam gave it a gentle rap with his knuckle and waited. There was no response. Sam turned and tried the door on the left. It also was locked. Only the door at the end of the hall remained. Sam pulled the handle, but it didn't budge.

A growing concern for his partner rose to near panic level and Sam pounded on the door and shouted, "Hello? Alisha? Anyone?" He waited a couple moments and when nobody came, he pounded even harder. Sam was just about to draw his service weapon and attempt to kick in the door when it opened to a very surprised Walt and a wide-eyed Alisha.

"Excuse me, sir," Walt stammered. "Can you please calm down."

Alisha quickly spoke up. "I'm so sorry. My boyfriend is easily excited and very protective."

"So, I see. No, it's ok," Walt replied as Sam mumbled an apology. "Did you find the men's room ok?"

"Yeah. It was fine," Sam replied.

"I was just telling Alisha here," Walt continued, "about our cremation services." Walt held the door so they could walk back through and into a counseling room to the inside left.

Alisha interrupted. "I was very close to my Grandma Palmer. I don't know if we can afford a traditional burial plot and coffin, but cremation seems so – impersonal and, I don't know…disrespectful."

"That's not at all an uncommon feeling," Walt replied. "But I assure you, we take the utmost care and respect for your loved one's remains."

"Maybe if she could see where the cremation process takes place, it might set her mind at ease," Sam suggested, hoping to get a look around more of the back area of the mortuary.

"Oh, that would be great," Alisha said, feigning excitement.

Walt balked. "I do want to be as accommodating as possible, I just don't think that's possible. The crematorium isn't open to the public. I hope you understand."

Sam couldn't tell whether Walt was being genuine as a mortician or he was hiding something. Walt broke into Sam's thoughts with a question they hadn't been prepared to answer. "Where are your grandmother's remains at this present time?"

"I'm sorry, what?" asked Alisha as if she hadn't heard to buy herself some time to think.

"Yes, what I mean is," Walt restated, "what funeral home currently is your grandmother's remains resting at?"

"They're at…" answered Alisha slowly, trying to think of an answer.

Sam broke in: "They're at the police medical examiner's office. They think she might've been murdered."

Alisha's eyes got wide at Sam's response and Walt stammered more than usual. "Oh my. I'm so sorry to hear that. I assumed she died of natural causes. Do you know when her remains might be released?"

Alisha replied slowly, "They haven't told us exactly."

"Yeah," Sam interrupted. He was on a roll. "They're actually investigating to see if her death might be a part of a string of other murders in the area – like a serial killer something."

"Sam!" exclaimed Alisha with genuine shock in her voice.

Sam continued as if he hadn't heard. As he spoke he kept a very keen eye on Walt's reaction. Walt had already grown even more restless at the mention of a serial killer. "Yeah, honey, what is the news calling that madman? The Holiday Killer or something like that?"

"Yeah," replied Alisha, still in shock that Sam was being so forward. "Something like that."

Suddenly Walt stood up and declared, "I do apologize, I just remembered that I have another consultation appointment soon. Here's my card. And do let me know if I can be of service once you have more information on the status of your grandmother's remains. Passing Memories would love to assist you through this time."

Alisha, still taken back by Sam's brashness, managed to tell Walt that she appreciated everything and that they'd be in touch.

As soon as they stepped outside and the door closed behind them, Alisha hit Sam on the arm. "What the heck was that? I thought we were just supposed to keep our eyes open and see what we see?"

"Oh, come on. We weren't getting anywhere," Sam replied. "My poking around earlier turned up nothing. The guy was tightlipped as a clam's shell. I had to try something – ah, creative."

"Creative – that's a word for it. Not the one I would've chosen," Alisha said sarcastically as they arrived back at Sam's car.

"It worked though. Did you see his face when I said the words 'serial killer'?" Sam asked.

"I did," Alisha conceded. "And especially when you mentioned the Holiday Killer. Can you hurry up and start the car? I'm freezing."

Sam sat motionless, clearly in thought. "Hey, boyfriend," Alisha said impatiently. "I'm turning into a popsicle here."

Sam waited a moment longer and then said, "I think we ought to bring him in."

"On what charges?" Alisha asked.

"Just for questioning," Sam said. "Hold him a few hours and see if he gives anything up."

"I dunno," Alisha said slowly.

"I just doubt we're going to find anything here, even if we got a warrant," Sam countered. Sam unbuckled his seatbelt and reached for the door handle. "C'mon, let's do it."

Alisha let out an exasperated sigh and followed her partner. Back at the door, Sam once again rang the buzzer. A few moments later the familiar, nervous face of Walt once again peeked through the partially open door.

"Yes," he said with a hint of impatience. "What can I help you with? I do apologize. I have to prepare for the next appointment."

Sam spoke up, "I think I left my gloves in the men's room. Can I please go get them."

Walt's face took on a downfallen expression but he opened the door for Sam and Alisha to enter.

Walt closed the door and turned around to see Sam's badge near his face. "Actually, I lied," Sam said, "I'm Detective Sam Cross and this is Detective Alisha Palmetto of the Oklahoma City Police. Would you mind if we asked you a few questions – downtown."

Walt's face was frozen, his mouth open, but no words came out. He took a step to his right and proceeded to sit in one of the waiting room chairs. "W-what's this about, detectives?" Walt finally stammered.

"About a murder," Alisha said. "We'll fill you in down at the station."

"I – I didn't kill your grandmother. I'm very sorry about her passing," Walt replied, terrified.

"Oh honey," Alisha said condescendingly, "My grandma passed a decade ago in South Florida." And then to Sam she asked, "Academy Award performance, or nah?"

Sam laughed. "Let's go, Walt. I'll follow you to get your jacket."

Five minutes and many protests from Walt later, they were all back in Sam's car, Walt handcuffed in the back seat.

"I swear I didn't kill anybody," Walt began, but Alisha interrupted him.

"Before you say anything else," Alisha advised, "I need to inform you of your right to remain silent and your right to an attorney. If you choose to waive those rights, or continue talking, anything you say can and will be used against you in a court of law. Do you understand?"

"Yes, yes," Walt replied quickly, "but I'm telling you, I didn't kill anybody."

"Why don't you sit quietly and we'll see about that when you're nice and cozy in an interview room where we can get it all on the record," Sam interrupted.

***

Back at the station, Sam led Walt to an interrogation room while Alisha updated Captain Durant.

"This is all some big mistake," Walt said. "I've never hurt anybody in my life."

Sam lifted a clipboard off the wall near the door. "Just so we have it on record, this is the Warning and Consent form. It's your Miranda rights."

Sam read the form aloud and then asked, "Mr. Emmer, do you wish to have an attorney present?"

"No. I haven't done nothing. I just want to go back to my work."

"Alright, well that all depends on how our talk goes."

The door behind Sam opened and Alisha walked in. "Captain Durant is trying to find a judge who will get us a search warrant for his shop and his house."

"Please ma'am," Walt pled. "I have bodies to take care of and funerals to prepare for." Sam and Alisha looked at each other at the word "bodies."

"And just how many bodies, are there?" Sam asked.

"Not like that," Walt said. "They're for my work – the loved ones of grieving families."

"Are there any bodies at your house?" Sam asked.

"No! Why on earth would there be bodies at my house?"

"I don't know, you tell me, Walt."

"There's nothing. I spend most of my time at work. I'm a very busy man."

From a file folder, Alisha pulled out three photos and placed them on the table in front of Walt. They were stills from the supermarket security camera.

"Is this you in these photos?" Alisha asked.

Without answering the question, Walt demanded, "What is this all about?"

"We're getting there. I just need you to answer my question." Alisha tapped her finger on the middle picture – a zoomed in shot of Walt's side profile. "This is you, isn't it?"

"I don't know. Maybe? Where is this picture from? Why would you be following me?" Walt asked.

"It's from the security camera at the Hometown Grocery store up on NW 18th. And that's you in these photos isn't it?" Alisha pressed.

"I'm not sure," he said. Walt was a bad liar. He had way too nervous of a disposition. Sam and Alisha could see right through his evasiveness.

Sam leaned over the table and tapped the photo repeatedly. "C'mon, Walt. That's you clear as day."

Walt shifted in his chair and looked away. "Even if it is," he said, "What's the big deal? Shopping isn't a crime. I paid for my groceries."

"So, it is you then?" Alisha said. She pulled out another sheet of paper from her folder – a photocopy of the receipt. "We know you paid. We have the receipt. And we have your rewards number right there on the receipt."

A sweat broke out on Walt's brow.

"What is it, Walt? What's got you nervous?" Alisha asked. "That's you in the photos isn't it?"

Walt sat quietly. He clenched his eyes shut as if thinking.

"Hey," Sam interjected. "Where's this guy's keys? We'll just confirm the rewards number ourselves."

"Hey, that's a good idea. They're with the rest of his stuff back with the desk sergeant," Alisha answered. "I'll go get them."

"Ok, it's me in those pictures," Walt finally said.

"Alright," Sam said. "And what did you buy there?"

"It was a while ago. I don't remember," Walt replied.

"Well, we've got it all right here on the receipt and the security camera footage. You bought twenty-six boxes of stuffing. Ring a bell?"

Walt didn't answer.

"I don't suppose I need your answer," Sam said. "It's right here on the receipt. We've got video of you clearing out every last box of stuffing from the shelf and then making an employee go get you more – but not all they had. Just twenty-six boxes. Exactly twenty-six."

Alisha returned with Walt's keys. On his keyring was a small plastic tag for Hometown Grocery. Alisha held up the tag and the photocopied receipt and announced: "See they match. That's you."

Walt still said nothing.

"What did you need twenty-six boxes of stuffing for?" Alisha asked. "You live alone. That's a lot of stuffing for one man."

"I just like it," Walt finally said.

"You're a big fan of stuffing? Ok so, if we go search your pantry in your house, we're going to find a bunch of boxes of stuffing?" Alisha asked.

Walt returned to his silence.

"It's not there, is it, Walt?" Alisha pressed. "You didn't buy it to eat it, did you? What'd you do with it, Walt?"

Walt shifted in his chair and clenched his eyes shut again. He still didn't answer.

"We're not stupid. We know what you did with it. We just need you to tell us," Alisha said.

Sam pounded his open palm on the table causing Walt to flinch. "What. Did. You. Do. With. The. Stuffing." Sam shouted, emphasizing each word.

A knock interrupted from behind Sam. He cracked open the door to see. It was Captain Durant. Sam motioned with his head for Alisha to follow him.

"What is it, Captain?" Sam asked as he pulled the door closed behind him.

"Crack him yet? Our legal assistant says we can't get a warrant unless you get something from this guy." Captain Durant said.

"Only that it's him from the security camera and that he bought the stuffing," Sam answered.

"He claimed he bought it to eat," Alisha said. "But I bet if we search his house, there won't be a single box of stuffing there. So, we could catch him in a lie there."

"That's not going to be enough," Durant said. "Buying or having or not having stuffing isn't a crime."

"I just feel like if we can get in his house and his morgue, we'll find something," Sam said.

"We need more than this circumstantial garbage we have so far," Durant said, frustrated.

It angered Sam that Captain Durant had called their evidence "garbage." What little they had, was the result of weeks of intensive work. "You wanna take a crack at him?" Sam asked.

Wordlessly, Captain Durant pushed open the door and headed inside the interrogation room. Sam and Alisha followed but hung back by the door. For the next twenty-odd minutes, Captain Durant peppered Walt with questions, making subtle threats and insinuations – but ultimately got no further than Sam and Alisha had gotten.

"We got you, Walt," Captain Durant said with false confidence. "You're going down."

Walt, who had barely said a word during Captain Durant's questioning, smiled and replied: "What am I going down for again? You've not accused me of a crime. You've not pinned one single thing on me."

"You're going down for double murder," Captain Durant said, and then exited the room. Sam and Alisha followed.

Once the door was closed, Captain Durant cursed. "That slimy weasel makes me want to ring his neck. He's right though. We have nothing to hold him on or to get a warrant with."

"So, what do you want us to do, Boss?" Sam asked.

After a moment's pause, Captain Durant said, "Cut him loose. Tail him. See where he goes and what he does next. We'll catch him doing something – and if nothing else, he can't kill again with us watching him 24/7."

Sam nodded. "Copy that." Sam had an idea. "Alisha, go get his phone from the desk sergeant."

Sam went back in the room. Walt sat there still with a smug look on his face. Sam sat down across the desk from him and smiled back. A minute later, Alisha returned with Walt's phone.

"What's your passcode?" Sam asked.

Walt hesitated and then answered. "Two…" he began but then stopped.

"Two what?"

"I don't have to tell you."

Sam waited to see if Walt would say anything and then finally said, "Alright Mr. Emmer, you're free to go. You can stop by the desk sergeant and collect your things. We'll be seeing you around."

"How will I get home?" Walt asked.

"Don't know. Don't care," Sam said. "Call a friend if you have one. Stand up and turn around."

Sam removed the cuffs from Walt's wrists and pointed to the door that Alisha was holding open. As Walt walked past her, she said, "Have a good day."

Sam and Alisha headed for the squad room to grab their things. "We'll follow him and see where he goes. I'm also curious to see who he calls to pick him up. He's not married – and I can't picture the guy having a girlfriend."

"Yeah, I'd hate to see the kind of girl that'd date a guy like that," Alisha said.

***

The detectives huddled in Sam's car until finally a taxi arrived to pick up Walt. Keeping their distance, they followed the cab back to Walt's mortuary. Walt exited the cab and looked around before walking to the side entrance of the funeral home. After fumbling briefly with his keys, he went inside.

Sam pulled his car around to a house across the street where he had a view of both exits to the building and then called the cab company. "Yes, this is Detective Sam Cross with the Oklahoma City Police Department. I need the cell phone number for the cab driver in number two seven one. Yes. Got it. Thank you."

"Call that number and see if Walt said anything," Sam said to Alisha.

A couple minutes later, Alisha hung up her cellphone. "Cabbie just said that Walt sat in the back mumbling to himself – nothing he could make out, but that he wasn't really paying attention."

"Alright. It was worth a shot," Sam said.

"I guess we just sit here and wait?" Alisha asked.

"Yeah, I think so for now," Sam agreed. "Like Durant said, see if we can catch him doing something."

As the sun set, Sam texted his wife that he'd be late.

"Save you dinner?" Jennifer texted back.

"Not sure yet. No need. I can stop and get something if I have to," Sam replied.

Jennifer texted back a kissing emoji.

Sam put his phone down and said to Alisha, "You need to text anyone? Boyfriend? Hot date?"

Alisha snorted a laugh. "As if I had time for that." She then winked at Sam. "Besides, you're my boyfriend, remember?"

Sam rolled his eyes and said, "We're not talking about that."

"Oh c'mon. We were great," she teased.

The evening wore on, and neither of the doors to the mortuary opened. Nobody came or went. Sam looked at the clock on the dash: 8:47 p.m.

"When you were in the back with him, did you see a cot or anything?" Sam asked. "Maybe he spends the night there sometimes."

"I didn't. He's just working late. But that sounds like the kind of thing a creepy killer would do – sleep next to dead bodies or something."

Sam pulled out his phone and played one of those language-learning games. He'd been trying to learn a bit of Spanish – figured it couldn't hurt. Jennifer texted him about ten o'clock. for an update. Sam replied that he was still working the case.

As the night wore on, Sam and Alisha took turns taking catnaps. About three in the morning, Sam radioed for a patrol car to come and take over so he and Alisha could go gas up the car, get some snacks, and visit the restroom. Twenty minutes later, they were back on the stakeout. The patrol cop reported no movement.

"What time does Walt open up for business," Sam asked.

"Let me check on the listing again," Alisha said. "Uh, here it is. 9:30 a.m."

Sam let out a groan. "At 9:30 sharp, I'm banging on that door."

"And asking what?" Alisha asked.

"I'm not sure yet. I have more than five hours to figure that out."

At 5:20 a.m. Sam's phone lit up with a text message from his wife. "You never came home. Are you still working?"

"We have a big break in the case. Had to do a last minute stakeout. Sorry. Love you," Sam texted back.

"Trouble in paradise?" Alisha asked.

"No. No trouble. She just worries a lot after the whole ordeal from back this summer," Sam said.

"Yeah, I bet. Wanna call another patrol officer and get some breakfast and coffee? I'll buy," Alisha offered.

"Sure. There's gotta be something around here to grab a bite to eat at besides a gas station," Sam said.

While Sam radioed for a patrol officer, Alisha located a diner only a half mile away. Soon they were seated at a red vinyl booth looking at the menu. Alisha urged Sam to be adventurous and try something besides his usual biscuits and gravy, but Sam declined and went with what he knew. Alisha ordered a Tex-Mex omelet. Sam ordered a breakfast burrito to-go for the officer who was filling in.

Service was slow, and it was almost seven by the time they paid the check and left the restaurant. "I love all these little hole-in-the-wall places you guys have here in Oklahoma," Alisha said. "If there's one thing you guys get right here in the Midwest, it's hospitality."

Back across the street from Walt's mortuary, Sam thanked the patrol officer and repaid him with the burrito. It would be two more boring hours until they could move in. And Sam still hadn't come up with an excuse for being there.

Loose Ends

By 9:30 that morning, Sam was stiff from sitting in his car. He was also cold and grumpy. He put his car in drive and crossed the street to the parking lot of the mortuary. He pulled his coat tightly about his neck and opened his car door.

"Did you come up with an excuse to be here?" Alisha asked.

"We're cops. We don't need an excuse," Sam replied sharply.

"Sheesh Sam, save the attitude for the creepy mortician," Alisha said.

Sam mumbled an apology and loosened his gun in his holster as he headed for the door. Alisha followed a couple steps behind. "I'll just say we had a few more questions," Sam finally said.

Halfway to the front door, Alisha began walking to the right, away from Sam. "I'm going to keep watch around the side of the building just in case he tries to slip out the back. Text me once you're inside – or if anything goes bad."

Sam nodded and took the final few steps to the front door. He blew in his hands to warm them up before knocking sharply. There was no answer. Sam banged again, this time with the side of his fist and waited a few more seconds. Frustrated Sam pounded hard enough to make the double wooden doors rattle. "Police, open up!" Sam shouted.

Sam pulled out his phone and texted Alisha. "No answer. See anything?"

"Nada," Alisha texted back.

Sam called the phone number on the door. It rang five times and then went to voicemail.

He texted Alisha again. "I called and no one picked up. He's gotta be in there right?"

"Has to be. I'll try the back door," she replied.

Sam backed up from the front door where he'd have a wider view of the building including the direction Alisha had gone and waited. A moment later, his phone rang.

"Hey come back here," Alisha said.

The tone in her voice worried Sam and he broke into a run, drawing his gun with his free hand. "What is it? Alisha, you ok?"

"I'm good, but this back door is open a crack," she said.

Huffing slightly, Sam arrived where Alisha stood, gun drawn. He hung up his phone, shoved it into his pocket, and pulled out his flashlight. Alisha was right. The door was ajar about an inch. Through the crack, it was pitch black.

"I wonder why it's open," Sam said in a hushed voice.

"Do you think he was watching us all night?" Alisha asked.

Sam gave a shrug.

"Do we go in?" Alisha asked. "I don't want to upset Durant by not playing this one by the book."

Sam didn't answer right away, but then nodded. "Just a minute though." He pulled his cell back out and called for another patrol car to their location. "You're not going in there alone with that deranged psychopath," Sam said to Alisha as he hung up, "and I don't want him squirting out the front. But I say let's go in and see what we find."

Sam jogged back around the front of the building to watch the main entrance until the patrol car arrived a minute later. "Watch the door and stop anyone who comes out," Sam ordered the patrol officer and then returned to where Alisha waited around back.

"Ok let's go in. We'll just say we found the door open and thought we heard noises inside of someone in distress or something," Sam said as he slowly pulled the back door further open and shined his flashlight into the darkness. Sam took a couple tentative steps inside and then whispered for Alisha to find the light switch. A moment later, she located it and the room illuminated under florescent lights that flickered ominously from a bad ballast.

Sam surveyed the sizeable storage room they now stood in. It was mostly empty except for two coffins and a shelf lined with various colored liquids. They moved quietly and carefully from room to room, but without any sign of Walt. The crematorium was empty and so was the office and rear restroom. In less than ten minutes, Sam and Alisha had cleared the entire building. Walt was gone.

The front door was still locked, yet nonetheless, Sam unlocked it and walked outside to ask the patrol officer if anyone had come out the front. The patrol officer shook his head no. Sam slapped his palm on his thigh in frustration.

Back inside, Sam shook his head. "Where'd he go?" Sam asked Alisha.

"A hidden, secret exit? A trap door? I dunno. He should be here," she answered.

Sam ran his hand over his exhausted face. "He has to be here. Where else would he go?"

"Well, let's look again," Alisha said. "Maybe he's got some secret hidey hole."

Fifteen minutes later, every room of the building has been thoroughly searched a second time. Alisha had even looked inside the coffins to ensure they were empty. And they found no secret passages.

"Since we're in here now, might as well see if we can find something useful to nail him for good," Alisha said optimistically.

"I just don't understand where he went," Sam complained. "Could he have slipped out the back door overnight and that's why it was open like that?"

"Well, unless we uncover a hidden tunnel, that's the only option left," Alisha said. "Though I don't know how. I watched the building like a hawk during my shifts."

"Same. And his car is here. If he gave us the slip, he must've gone on foot," Sam said.

They spent the next hour searching boxes and files in Walt's office, though nothing stood out – just records and receipts from funerals Walt had conducted.

"How is he this careful?" Sam asked, now grumpier than ever.

"Yeah, you'd think we'd find something," Alisha replied. "But forensics has said at both crime scenes there was nothing to go on. Guy's good, I'll give him that. Though I wouldn't have guessed it looking at him. He seems so shifty and not at all who I figured our killer would be."

"Durant still doesn't know we're in here – or that we lost Walt," Sam said. "And I am not looking forward to that conversation."

"Should we get CSI down here to process anything?" Alisha asked.

"Yeah, I suppose so. Maybe they'll find a victim hair or some blood on that cremation furnace," Sam said.

By one o'clock in the afternoon, the crime scene van pulled away and Sam and Alisha walked back to his car. Alisha yawned. "Lunch and then call it a day?" she asked.

"Nah. I'm just gonna head home. Jennifer's going to be worried sick. I'll run you by your car at the station," Sam said.

They arrived to find Captain Durant waiting for them in the station parking lot.

"Good grief," Alisha moaned.

"It's fine. I got this," Sam said.

As Sam parked his car, Captain Durant began walking towards him. Sam opened his car door and Captain Durant unloaded on him, "I know you're the great and decorated Sam Cross, but seriously, what were you thinking? And where is our suspect?"

"Captain," Sam said taking a deep breath, but his boss cut him off.

"You didn't have a warrant. You had no business being in there!" Captain Durant continued.

"It wasn't like that," Alisha cut in. "The door was open when we checked. And I swear I heard the sounds of a scuffle or something. Legal will be fine."

"I don't think I asked you, Detective Palmetto," Captain Durant snapped.

Alisha was hot at being dismissed. "Well, you should have. I found the open door, not Detective Cross."

Sam and Alisha stood there and listened to Captain Durant rant for the next few minutes. Finally, Sam said, "I don't know where our perp went. We were across the street, lights out, well hidden. He must've made us somehow."

"And to be fair," Alisha added, "that back exit was unlit, and we were expecting him to leave in his car. There was hardly any moonlight last night either. It was just one of those things. We'll find him. We put a bulletin out on him on the way over here. Someone will spot him. Detectives Arnold and Morris are headed to the perp's house right now."

"And so, what are you two doing?" Captain Durant asked.

"We were about to go home," Sam said.

"Not until you find the killer you let walk away from underneath your nose," Captain Durant said.

"Boss, with all due respect," Alisha said, "We've been on the job for over twenty-four hours. Arnold and Morris will find him if he's there. And if he's not, it wouldn't matter if it was us or them who went. You're mad. I get it. We're mad too. Plus, I need a shower."

Captain Durant glared a moment and then said, "Fine. But I've got the media and the FBI breathing down my neck and I want this guy nailed and in a cell before he kills again."

"So do we," Sam said. "But we'll never crack the case without a few hours' sleep in a real bed. I could barely keep the car on the road driving over here. We're tired. We'll hit it running first thing in the morning, ok?"

Captain Durant nodded and walked away without further comment. As soon as he entered the station, Alisha looked at Sam wide eyed. Sam let out a sigh. "That went…well," he said.

"Ignore him," Alisha said as she walked towards her car to head home. "He's just blowing off steam. This case has us all uptight. Enjoy your rest. See you bright and early tomorrow."

With traffic, it was almost forty-five minutes before Sam finally shuffled exhausted through his front door.

***

Ten hours earlier…

"No, no. No apology necessary. Come on in, Walt. What's keeping you up at this hour? Couldn't you sleep?" Professor Barnes asked as he held the door open allowing the shivering mortician inside.

"Harold, I got arrested!" Walt exclaimed. "And it's your fault. Why are they knocking on my door instead of yours? I didn't kill anyone?"

123

"Calm down, man. Who arrested you?" the professor asked.

"It was two cops – one male, one female. Detectives Cross and Palmetto or something like that," Walt said, digging Sam and Alisha's business cards out of his coat pocket. "You've got to do something. I'm not going down for something I didn't do."

"Ah yes, the hero cop and his lady partner," Professor Barnes said, taking the business cards from Walt's gloved fingers. "What did you tell them?"

"Tell them? I said nothing. I said they had nothing on me and I didn't do nothing," Walt replied.

"And what makes you think this is my fault? I've been very careful so far. Did you slip up?" the professor said, his voice growing angry at Walt's accusation.

"No, I did everything exactly like you said. And somehow they still found me. Why me and not you, Harold?" Walt retorted.

"You wish it was me then?" the professor asked as he leaned closer to Walt.

"N-no…" stammered Walt. Then his eyes flash angrily as he continued. "Yes, I do. I'm a respectable man. I work hard. I've done nothing wrong – except it would seem to be friends with a killer."

"Walt, Walt. Calm down. Come in here with me to the kitchen and I'll get you a drink. Just tell me everything," Professor Barnes said, gesturing towards the kitchen.

Walt huffed and walked ahead, the professor following. Professor Barnes took two tumblers from the cabinet. "Scotch or Brandy?" he asked.

Walt sat on a high stool in front of the counter in the kitchen and laid his head in his arms. Without looking up, he waved dismissively and mumbled, "The first one, I guess."

The professor poured their drinks – Scotch for Walt and Brandy for himself, and then asked, "Did the detectives say how they found you?"

Walt straightened up and took his drink. After a sip he answered, "It was the stuffing. Apparently they checked every grocery store in the city and found security footage of me buying it all."

"You bought it all – at one store? I told you to spread out your purchases – different stores, different dates," Professor Barnes said, glaring at Walt.

"You know what? I'm a busy man. I have a business to run. I had a funeral appointment coming up and I just wanted to get it over with. This isn't my fault. The stuffing was your sick idea," Walt said downing the rest of his drink in one long gulp. "You've ruined me," Walt moaned.

"Calm down," began the professor but Walt cut him off.

"Stop telling me that! They *know*!" Walt said through gritted teeth. "They were outside my place all night. I had to sneak out and walk here. I can't even go home."

"Have another drink," Professor Barnes said, reaching for Walt's glass.

They drank in silence for the next few minutes and then Walt stood and picked up his gloves to leave.

Professor Barnes set down his glass. "Where are you headed, Walt? You said you can't go home."

Walt shrugged. "I don't know. Out. Maybe I'll kill myself. My life is basically over."

"Don't worry. I've got it under control. Stay. We're friends. You can have the couch. I'll get you a pillow," Professor Barnes assured.

Walt paused as if considering his options and then said, "Thanks. I don't have any other friends."

"That's right Walt, we're friends," the professor said as he locked the front door and retrieved a spare pillow and blanket from the closet. "Get some sleep. It'll take care of everything. I'll make it all go away."

He handed the bedding to Walt and stepped into the garage. "I just need to check on something before I go back to bed," he said over his shoulder. Inside the garage, Professor Barnes slid on a pair of gloves and retrieved a length of rope. He slipped it into the pocket of his pajama pants. He and Walt had been friends since college. He was going to miss him.

***

Sam made it until just after supper before exhaustion overcame him and he passed out in his recliner. Jennifer sent the boys to their room to play quietly and climbed into the recliner and curled up next to him. Sam had barely been asleep twenty minutes when his phone rang. Groaning half asleep, he mumbled for his wife to hand him the phone.

"Who is it?" Sam asked blinking to coax his eyes to focus.

"It's your boss. Can't they leave you alone for five minutes?" Jennifer complained.

Sam pushed his wife off his lap as he hit the green button to answer the call. "Captain? What's up?"

"You've gotta come in, Cross," Captain Durant ordered. "You screwed up. Walt is dead."

"What?" exclaimed Sam standing up and looking around for his keys.

"Looks like he offed himself. And get your partner. She's not answering her phone," Captain Durant said.

"Roger that. See you as quick as I can get there," Sam said and then hung up the phone.

"What is it? What happened?" Jennifer asked, worried lines etched in her forehead.

"The guy we had pegged for the Holiday Killer apparently killed himself," Sam said as he stood up and did his best to straighten his wrinkled clothes. "I'm sorry. I gotta go."

"Honey, you've had no sleep. It's not fair. There are other detectives," she answered.

"It's the job. You know that. I'll see you as soon as I can." Sam kissed her on the forehead and closed the door.

As he walked to his car, he dialed Alisha's number. It rang four times and then went to voicemail. He hung up and tried again – it went straight back to voicemail. *She must be passed out*, Sam thought. *Lucky her*. He looked up his partner's address in his phone. He'd never been to her place, but he had it stored under her contact. *Not too far out of the way*. He'd be there in a few minutes.

Holiday traffic turned it into nearly thirty minutes. Sam jogged to Alisha's front door, knowing that every minute that passed likely meant a longer lecture from his boss. He scanned for a doorbell, but not seeing one, proceeded to knock loudly. There was no answer.

Maybe she's dating somebody and slept over there, Sam wondered. He pounded on her door a little harder. After a minute, Sam finally heard his partner's voice through the door. "You had better be a cop, pounding on my door like that," she said clearly annoyed. Alisha finally unlocked and opened the door. "Oh, it is a cop," she said upon seeing Sam. "What is it? Actually, just come in," she said before Sam could answer. "You tell me while I'm getting dressed. I'm sure you wouldn't be here unless we were going in."

Sam stepped into the entryway somewhat hesitantly. Alisha walked away still speaking as Sam closed the door behind him. As Sam looked back up, he saw her gun in her hand. *I supposed I'd have my gun ready too if someone pounded on my door like that*, Sam thought.

"Excuse the mess," she said as she picked up a bra and a pair of black slacks from off the couch and walked presumably towards her bedroom.

"No worries. I was single once too," he said.

"You know, I was having a really nice dream before you ruined it," Alisha called from her bedroom.

"Yeah, sorry about that. And same, I was happily asleep too when Durant called me," he answered.

"What was so important that we couldn't even get half a day off," she asked.

"Apparently our perp, Walt, was found dead. Durant said they're thinking suicide," Sam said.

"Good. I'm not going to miss any sleep over him. Plus, this means the killings are over, right? Case solved," Alisha said as she emerged from her bedroom, buttoning the last couple buttons on her white blouse. "Don't judge my wrinkled shirt. I can't be bothered to iron it right now," she added.

Sam shook his head. "Durant's mad. His exact words were, 'You screwed up.' "

"He's always mad. And why does he care how the case wraps up? Perp in jail or dead – doesn't matter to me. He's stopped either way," she replied.

Sam shrugged. "It's Durant. He's probably worried about how it'll play out in the media. If he says the case is closed, there will be questions about how we knew Walt was our guy, and then why he killed himself."

"Ok, and?" Alisha asked.

"I dunno. I'm with you. Case closed. Who cares what the media thinks. Everyone should be happy that a bad guy is off the streets and can't kill anymore," Sam said.

Alisha slipped her shoes on, looked in the mirror, and sighed. "I guess I'm ready. Let's go. But we're stopping for coffee. Durant can wait another five minutes and I'm not dealing with his attitude without coffee."

The Letter

Despite Sam and Alisha's initial worries, Captain Durant did not chew them out at the station. Instead, he simply handed them the case folder and gave them the run-down.

"Your perp, Walt Emmer, was found by some hikers out at Overholser Park as you're headed west towards Yukon,' Captain Durant said. "He was found inside a park restroom, hanging from the door."

Sam opened the case file and began spreading the crime scene photos out on his desk. "Yep, that's Walt alright."

"What a cowardly way to go," Alisha said disgusted.

Captain Durant ignored their comments and continued. "As you can see in the photos, a rope was tied to the outside doorknob and then looped over the top of the restroom door. He then stood on the toilet seat to get the noose around his neck, and just simply stepped off."

Sam nodded. "That's definitely one way to do it."

"So, case closed then, right?" Alisha asked. "I mean, it's not as good as catching our guy and nailing him to the wall, but his suicide is pretty much an admission of guilt."

"Well, we still have to confirm everything by processing all the evidence," Captain Durant said.

"Of course, of course. But that's just a matter of time," she replied.

"I would've liked to hear from Walt what exactly his motive was for the killings. Maybe we'll get lucky and find a journal or manifesto," Sam said.

"Get with the detectives who processed the scene at the park and then head over to his house and see what you find there," Captain Durant ordered. "I need to get with my PR team to prepare a statement."

Sam and Alisha spent a few more minutes looking over the photos and notes from the case file and then put it back in the folder. As Sam picked up the last photo, he noticed a stack of mail on his desk. He picked up the envelopes and began idly thumbing through, tossing a couple items of junk mail in the trash.

One letter caught his attention, however. It was in a plain business envelope with no sender's name and a return address he couldn't place. It was addressed to him – but used his full name: "Samuel Allen Cross." Nobody called him Samuel. Or used his middle name. Sam peeled back a corner of the flap on the envelope and then gently lifted up about a quarter of it. Inside he could see what looked like a single folded piece of stationary paper. Alisha noticed his interest in the letter and raised her eyebrow.

Sam didn't answer and instead continued to cautiously open the letter. Alisha watched, hands on her hips waiting for his explanation. He lifted the letter out of the envelope, touching as little of the paper as possible, unfolded it meticulously, and laid it on the desk. Alisha stood behind him looking over his shoulder. The letter was handwritten. It read:

Detective Cross,

Christmas is almost here. Don't you love the Holiday season? Better get your Christmas shopping done. I bet you can't wait to spend hundreds of dollars of your meager detective's salary on cheap presents for your wife and two boys. Maybe you'll even get something nice for your partner. Palmetto, right?

Bet you didn't know that Americans are projected to spend one trillion dollars on Holidays this year? Crazy, right? Think of all the socioeconomic problems that could be solved by an extra trillion dollars each year if people weren't wasting it on cheap gifts, throw-away cards, and over-priced decorations. It might save a life too.

Americans, on average, have $58,000 in debt and thirty-one percent of consumers will go further into debt by upwards of $1400 just to make sure they have a "nice" Christmas. It's the most wonderful time of the year, am I right?

Speaking of decorations, how am I doing so far? Headless for Halloween and Stuffed for Thanksgiving! Brilliant, right? I can't wait for you to see what I have planned next! Sorry to ruin your Holiday cheer. Actually, not really.

By the way, I adore that name you came up with for me. Or was it the pretty reporter lady?

Until next crime,
The Holiday Killer

They both stood there staring at the letter in petrified silence. Alisha was the first to speak. "Oh, heck no. This dude is crazy. Literal nut job. I haven't had enough sleep or coffee for this nonsense."

"Definitely a screw or two loose," Sam replied. Sam looked back at the envelope. "It's postmarked two days ago. Ok, so we have a letter from our killer, but he's dead now, so the letter's threat is empty, right?"

"Yeah, I guess, but still creepy," Alisha said with a shudder. "Got my name in there and everything."

Sam rummaged in his desk drawer for a second and then closed it. "Do you have an evidence bag big enough? I've just got the four inch ones."

"I should, just a sec," Alisha said. She returned a moment later with a letter-sized bag.

"Alright," Sam said, dropping the letter into the bag, "Let me take a pic of it and then I'll run it down to the lab."

Sam was just about to exit the squad room when he heard a voice call his name. "Hey Cross, you're on TV. You too Palmetto."

"What?" said both Sam and Alisha almost in unison.

"It's that reporter who came up with the name 'The Holiday Killer'," said the officer.

Sam looked around for the remote but instead stood on his tiptoes to reach the volume button on the side of the TV.

"…these are the two detectives mentioned in the letter," said the reporter.

"How the heck does she know about the letter?" Sam exclaimed. "I literally just opened it." He scanned the room suspiciously as if looking for a hidden camera or a spy in the room.

"The city is on edge as the Holiday Killer promises another murder before Christmas," the reporter continued.

"Captain!" called Sam.

Captain Durant rushed out of the PR office. "What? I'm busy."

Sam pointed at the TV. "Your press briefing just got a lot more complicated."

"What's this about a letter? Did you know about this?" Captain Durant asked.

Sam held up the evidence bag. "I literally just opened it here at my desk. I have no clue how it's already on the news."

A livid Captain Durant continued to stare at the television set.

"My guess is that our perp mailed the same letter to us and to the news station," Alisha said.

"Find out!" Captain Durant ordered. "Never mind. I'll do it." He turned to Sergeant Ellis who'd been tailing him and said, "Get that reporter on the phone, now!"

The sergeant spun on her heel and Captain Durant stormed after her. Sam looked at Alisha who threw her hands in the air.

Just then Sam's phone buzzed in his pocket. He pulled it out and saw his wife had texted him. He clicked the message.

"Why is my husband on the TV?!" the message read.

Sam rubbed his face in frustration before answering. "I'm just now trying to figure that out myself."

"I don't like it. It's like they're painting a target on your back," his wife replied.

Before Sam could reassure her everything was fine because Walt was dead, she sent him another text in all caps. "THE HOLIDAY KILLER SENT YOU A LETTER!!!!"

"Everything is fine. He's dead. That's why I had to come in so suddenly. The letter was sent two days ago," Sam texted back.

Sam waited for a reply, but none came. He sent another text, "Sweetie? There's nothing to worry about." A few moments passed, but she didn't respond.

"Ugh," said Sam out loud. Alisha started to speak, but Sam held up his hand and shook his head. He grabbed the letter and walked in the direction of the evidence locker.

When Sam returned to the squad room his partner was nowhere to be seen and her coat was gone. He looked at his desk. So were his keys.

He pulled out his phone and texted Alisha, "Should I put out a bulletin for my stolen car?"

A minute later he got a reply. "You need a sandwich. You looked hangry. Or maybe I need to stress eat. I dunno."

"Sorry," Sam replied. "Remember, just cheese and meat please."

Alisha texted back both an "eye roll" and "thumbs up" emoji.

Sam stepped into an empty office and called his wife.

"Hi," Jennifer answered. Her voice sounded shaky.

"Hey, Sweetie. Are you ok? Have you been crying?" Sam asked.

"No, I'm not. And maybe. I'm just scared – seeing your picture like that," she answered.

"There's nothing to be scared of. My face has been on TV before. And the killer is dead. He hung himself," Sam assured.

"I just…I just hate all of this. I don't want to raise our boys by myself," Jennifer said. Sam heard her voice waver as she fought to keep back tears.

"Sweetie, I'm fine. There's no danger. It's all over. I love you. I should be home in time for bed," Sam said.

"Ok. I love you too," Jennifer replied. "Bring ice cream with you."

Sam laughed. "Yes ma'am."

He hung up the phone and was almost back to his desk when Captain Durant hollered, "Cross. My office."

Sam took a deep breath as he stepped inside Captain Durant's office and closed the door.

"Where's your partner?" Captain Durant asked.

"She stepped out. I'll fill her in," Sam said.

"Fine. I spoke with that TV reporter. She was tight lipped on the phone but said she'd share everything she knew if I agreed to give my planned press briefing as an interview with her directly."

"I do not envy you," Sam said.

"Don't feel too sorry," Captain Durant replied. "She demanded you and your partner be there too. I want you TV ready and back here by 7:30 a.m. We're going on the eight o'clock morning news."

"Boss, I'm not an interview kinda guy…" Sam began.

"Well, tomorrow you will be," Captain Durant ordered. "Make sure you tell your partner. I'll have some talking points for you when you get here. Understood?"

"Yes, Sir."

"Alright go home and get some sleep. Those bags under your eyes will look terrible on TV."

"Thanks," said Sam as he turned and exited the office.

Alisha was just walking in and starting to unbutton her jacket.

"Pause that," Sam said. "We'll eat in the car."

"I thought we could eat before heading to Walt's house, but ok," Alisha said.

"Change of plans. I'll tell you about it while we drive," Sam said.

"Why do I get the distinct feeling I'm going to hate whatever it is you're about to tell me?" she asked.

"Probably because you're a good detective and because you're going to hate it," he said laughing.

In the car, Sam thanked Alisha for his sandwich. "I'll buy next time," he promised.

"So, what is it that I'm going to hate?" Alisha asked through a bite of her muffuletta.

"Durant is putting us both on TV tomorrow," Sam moaned.

Alisha nearly choked on her sandwich. "I'm sorry, what?"

"He called that reporter who put our pictures on the evening news," Sam said.

"And offered to have us go on TV? He must actually be mad," she said.

Sam polished off the last bite of his sandwich and explained. "No, it's more like we're being held hostage by that reporter. She only agreed to share what she knew if Durant granted her an exclusive interview instead of the press conference he had planned – and us being there was part of the negotiations."

"He should work on his negotiating skills. Can't he just threaten her with charges for withholding evidence or obstruction?" Alisha said shaking her head.

"I think he's just trying to play nice; you know. Plus, she'd probably claim 'confidential source' or something," Sam said.

Alisha shot Sam a glare. "I'm not putting on a dress. Durant can…"

Sam interrupted, "He just said look 'TV ready.' I'm going to take that as, clean shaven and hair neat, but not black tie. If he wanted more, he should've elaborated."

"Ok good," Alisha said, as Sam pulled up to her house. "I guess, see you in the morning."

"Yup. Goodnight," Sam said.

"Wanna come in?" Alisha asked.

"Can't. Gotta pick up something on the way home," Sam said.

"Alright. Any time you want, open invitation," Alisha said. She waved and unlocked her front door.

A few minutes later, Sam pulled into the grocery store near his house and jogged to the entrance, his breath creating large puffs of steam around him from the cold. Why his wife wanted ice cream on a frigid night like tonight, he wasn't sure. It had always been her comfort treat though – and she had been pretty upset earlier. He grabbed a pint of her favorite: espresso bean, and then drove the rest of the way home.

Once inside, he grabbed two spoons out of the kitchen drawer and headed down the hallway.

He stopped in his boys' room and kissed both of them on the forehead. His wife greeted him in their room with a tired smile. Sam produced the pint of ice cream and smiled back. She eagerly accepted it and Sam began to change out of his work clothes. He was exhausted and tomorrow would be here way too soon.

The Reporter

The interview turned out not to be the nightmare that Sam and Alisha feared it would be. Captain Durant's revelation that the Holiday Killer had been found dead was such a bombshell that the reporter barely asked the two detectives about their appearance in the killer's letter. And what little they were asked, Sam was mostly able to deflect with the boilerplate answer of the investigation being still in the early stages and ongoing.

They did however confirm that the Holiday Killer had mailed a second copy of the letter to the news station, no doubt to generate publicity and fear. It had worked. The reporter said that last night's eight o'clock broadcast was their most-watched newscast of the year and newsstands had sold out of papers.

The reporter wanted their interview to be broadcasted live, but Captain Durant had thankfully stood his ground and demanded it be pre-taped to allow for department editing should one of them "misspeak" at any point. The taped segment would air today at the top of the lunch hour.

And now that Walt was dead, Captain Durant had suspended the surveillance on Jewish centers across the city. In his statement to the reporter, he made sure to stress that citizens could rest easy and go about their Holiday shopping and festivities without fear. The Holiday Killer was dead and in the city morgue.

Captain Durant was also able to secure possession of the duplicate Holiday Killer letter. It was on its way safely to forensics for examination and comparison to the other letter.

Back in the squad room, Alisha plopped in her chair and moaned. "I dressed up for nothing. We were practically invisible once the boss told her about the killer being dead."

"Yeah. Well, better that than be asked a bunch of questions," Sam replied.

Alisha looked at herself in her compact. "Though I could get used to having someone do my hair and makeup for me every morning while I sipped coffee."

"So, what's on the agenda for today?" she asked. "Case is closed. But I guess we still have to finish up the investigation. You know Durant is going to want a neat, pretty little bow tied on this case to pass off to the hungry media."

Sam pressed his lips together tightly and held up his hand to try and cut her off but it was too late. Captain Durant has just entered the squad room – and heard her comment.

"Darn right, I do," he said. "And it has nothing to do with the media, but with doing our jobs right."

Alisha grimaced. "Yes, sir. Sorry, Captain."

Once Captain Durant was out of sight, Sam answered. "I say we follow up with forensics and the medical examiner to see what they've found out. I know they didn't get much in the Holiday

Killer's crime scenes, but no way he killed himself without leaving some kind of evidence, right?"

"You take the medical examiner and I'll take forensics. The blonde guy down there is kinda cute," Alisha said with a wink.

"Works for me," Sam said.

Sam's trip to the medical examiner's office ended up being a waste of time. Doctor Owens had not yet processed Walt's body. "There was that fire with several causalities over off of 10th Street and they've kept me busy," she explained. "Takes a long time to process a body that badly burned."

"I get that – but can't you put a rush on it? This is the Holiday Killer case," Sam began.

She put her hand on her hip and glared at him. "Detective, I don't care if your body is JFK and you're J. Edgar Hoover. They're all dead at this point. And they get worked in the order they come in."

"Okay, okay. Do you at least have a best guess of when you *think* you'll get started on it?" Sam asked.

"After these burn victims, there's three more in front of yours. Give me 'til next Thursday, and if you don't hear from me by then, you have my permission to call," Doctor Owens said.

Sam opened his mouth to argue, but she raised her eyes and glared at him over the top of her glasses, causing Sam to reconsider that idea. Last thing he needed was the medical examiner to "lose" his number or "forget" to send him an email.

He instead flashed a fake smile, thanked her, and headed back to the squad room. Alisha wasn't back yet. Sam hoped that meant she was having better luck down in forensics. While he waited, he decided to back-trace the two envelopes the Holiday Killer's letters had arrived in.

Sam searched the return address on his letter. It was a bust. It was the TV station's address. And he immediately recognized the return address on the letter sent to the reporter – it was their police precinct. Sam groaned. Nothing was ever easy. He'd have to get with the Post Office to track down where the letters had been mailed from – and with all the holiday mail, he wasn't holding his breath for a fast answer.

Alisha returned from the lab a few minutes later looking less than joyful. "He's barely started. Something about a fire. Killed four people. They think it might be arson."

"I got the same thing from Doctor Owens. She said she won't even start on our case until next week," Sam said. "He gave you nothing?"

"Just his phone number," Alisha said. "We had to exchange numbers," she added when Sam rolled his eyes. "That way he could call me when he has something."

"Right. I also got nowhere with the envelopes. The killer put our address here and over at the TV station for the return addresses," Sam said. "I'll have to get the post office to trace it."

Alisha looked at the case file spread on Sam's desk. "I always hate this part of the job. Finding and stopping bad guys is fun. Chronicling and connecting every dot of evidence, not so much."

***

"Miss Gunn," Professor Barnes interrupted impatiently. "There has to be some kind of restrictions on every system or it becomes a source of oppression."

"Does it though?" Tiffany asked. "Is it truly a 'free' market if it's not left alone to meet the supply and demand, or if sellers are regulated in an attempt to make things more 'fair?' That sounds like manipulation and pulling puppet strings to me, not a 'free' market."

"Miss Gunn, there always have been and must be regulation. Do you support the free-market sale of hard drugs?" her professor asked.

"No, of course not," Tiffany replied.

Professor Barnes nodded. "See. Just because there are willing consumers and a market for generating income doesn't mean that something shouldn't be regulated or even completely prohibited."

Professor Barnes was the kind of person who once they decided they were right, that was the end of the conversation as far as they were concerned. It was annoying, but Tiffany wasn't about to let it go. "Ok, but that's quite the leap isn't it from the commercialization of Holidays all the way to selling drugs at Walmart?" Tiffany said.

"Is it in practice though?" Professor Barnes asked. "The illicit drug market is banned because of the addictive and destructive nature of its product upon the consumer. And its sellers are exploitive and dangerous. Again, I'm a capitalist, but everything can be taken too far. Am I not right that the retailers pushing the next shiny this or that are just as exploitive and dangerous? The American public is addicted to buying the next latest and greatest – even to their own detriment. What if I told you that thirty-one percent of all consumers in America will take on upwards of $1400 in debt just this Christmas season? Is that their fault entirely? Or is much of the blame on the shoulders of exploitive and dangerous selling practices by retailers? I promise you that nothing you get for Christmas this year will be anything you need. So, the new debt is for nothing."

Tiffany tried to reply, but Professor Barnes held up his hand and kept talking. "And if it wasn't for the commercialization of Holidays, Americans would be better off and have a combined one trillion dollars back in their pockets. Trust me, if you really need those fuzzy reindeer slippers, then they would be on the shelves every day of the year, not just shoved in your face during a holiday to make a buck and enslave addicted shoppers. Am I not right that going into debt at Christmas for things you don't need, but have been convinced that you do, is bad?"

Tiffany sighed. "I get what you're saying. And I don't know what the answer is. But I stand by what I said about a free and fair market. If there wasn't a demand, then the product wouldn't sell, right?"

"Miss Gunn, you're missing the point. The demand is falsely manufactured by the product maker through deceptive and exploitive selling practices. Wall to wall commercials, product ads shoved in your face, the promise of holiday cheer. The demand is made by the seller, not the buyer. You only buy their product because you've been exploited into thinking you need it. You were perfectly happy before you knew 'X' product existed. But they just told you that 'X' product exists, and then they tell you that since you don't have it, you should be sad. But you have to get it right now during this Holiday or it will be gone forever and you'll be sad forever."

Professor Barnes droned on. Tiffany didn't agree fully with what her professor said. She just didn't know how to give a rebuttal. Maybe she'd ask Sam when she saw him. She'd been invited over again for Christmas and was looking forward to the occasion. Sam was the closest thing she had to family now. She was hungry and her mind wandered to lunch. She'd had enough Economics for the day.

***

Professor Barnes sat down with his dinner of ramen and a glass of milk and flipped on the TV just in time to catch the evening news. To his delight, the Holiday Killer was the subject of the broadcast.

"This morning we had an exclusive sit-down with the very detectives who have been chasing the Holiday Killer and we received an astounding revelation: the Holiday Killer is dead. I repeat, the Holiday Killer is dead. The police captain was tightlipped about the specifics, but a large police presence at a park east of Yukon suggests that's where the serial killer's body was found. How he died is yet unknown, but the Captain promised to be forthcoming as soon as their investigation was complete."

"What's this Houdini?" Professor Barnes said excitedly, nearly upsetting his dinner. The ferret looked at him and twitched his nose. "They think Walt was the Holiday Killer!"

Professor Barnes had killed his friend to tie up a loose end and hopefully create a dead end to their investigation into him. He hadn't dreamed they would think *Walt* was the killer. This meant his next decoration would be a complete and delightful surprise.

The news broadcast cut to a clip from the morning's interview with the captain and the two detectives. "And you're one hundred percent certain that the Holiday Killer is dead," the reporter asked Detective Cross.

"Yes ma'am. There's no doubt about it. His body is lying on a metal table in the medical examiner's office." Detective Cross looked at Detective Palmetto and added, "My partner and I are very glad to put this case to rest."

Professor Barnes let out a belly laugh as the reporter continued. "Now, you're already a decorated cop from your big case this past summer. Have there been any talks of additional medals or maybe a promotion?"

"No, but it was a department effort," Sam said.

The reporter looked at the camera and said, "Such modesty from one of Oklahoma City's finest."

"Stop talking about that stupid detective and talk about me!" Professor Barnes yelled at the television.

***

The rest of the week passed with little in the way of exciting discoveries. Forensics sent over their report, but it revealed nothing helpful. It seemed that Walt had been as careful in his own death as with his victims before him. Hopefully, the medical examiner's report would be more informative – they would just have to wait.

Next week was Christmas and Sam hadn't begun shopping yet. He couldn't shake the Holiday Killer's words from his head: *I bet you can't wait to spend hundreds of dollars of your meager detective's salary on cheap presents for your wife and two boys.*

"Jennifer," Sam said that evening after the boys went to bed, "I don't know what to get you for Christmas."

"Oh Honey, you always find me some little thing that makes me smile," his wife replied.

"But is there anything specific you've been needing or that you want me to get you?" Sam asked.

"Why all the questions this year? Am I that hard to shop for?" Jennifer answered.

"No. It's nothing. Just overthinking," Sam said. He wasn't about to tell her that the Holiday Killer had gotten into his head.

***

Christmas was on a Friday this year – which meant that the medical examiner's report, if it was on time, wouldn't come until Christmas Eve. Sam's hopes of wrapping up the Holiday Killer case before Christmas were looking thin.

"What do you think his motive was?" Alisha asked Sam, breaking him out of his thoughts.

"Aren't they all basically the same?" Sam asked. "The thrill of the kill, sadistic pleasure, psychopathy, terror – that sort of thing?"

"In a way, I suppose," Alisha said. "I've been doing some reading though and watching some serial killer documentaries in my little bit of spare time – and there have been a few serial killers who had a bigger agenda or philosophy of some kind with their murders. Take the Unabomber for instance – he believed that the overuse of technology in America was not only harmful to the environment, but also a danger to society. So, he targeted those he believed were responsible for advancing modern technology."

"Okay…" said Sam unconvinced.

"Hear me out," Alisha continued. "Then you had the 'Butcher Baker' Robert Hansen, who thought that prostitutes were evil and a menace to society – and that's why most of his victims were of that profession."

"Well, now that you're an expert at criminal profiling," Sam joked, "what motive do you have in mind for the Holiday Killer – besides being a deranged lunatic hell-bent on ruining people's holiday cheer?"

"What if it's not entirely about ruining people's fun around holidays, but instead some bigger philosophical campaign against holidays in general? Like he thinks holidays are evil or something like that?" Alisha said.

"Or he just likes to terrorize people during times they're supposed to be happy," Sam said.

Alisha continued, undeterred. "Remember in his letter how he ranted about all the money people were spending and the debt shoppers would incur this coming Christmas? He really seemed to have it out for holidays."

"I remember," Sam said. "I'm just not sure it was anything more than the ravings of a madman."

"I just feel there's a clue in that letter somewhere," Alisha said.

Sam shrugged. "Maybe. But all I saw was a narcissist getting his jollies telling everyone how smart he was. And unless a manifesto or diary is uncovered somewhere that wasn't found at his house, then I doubt we'll really ever know."

***

"Shhh," said Professor Harold Barnes as he reached for the trunk lid of his car. "I'm going to make you so beautiful for Christmas – maybe famous too." A panicked, muffled scream was cut short as the trunk clicked closed.

Mr. and Mrs. Claus

Sam and Alisha were both early to the office the next morning. Alisha continued to analyze the Holiday killer's letter, intent on discovering a motive, while Sam impatiently awaited the coroner's report. Shortly after 9:00 a.m., an email finally arrived from the medical examiner. Sam sat up and leaned forward in his chair and aggressively clicked to open it.

After a couple moments of intensive reading, Sam flopped back in his chair and let out a loud sigh. Alisha looked over at him.

"Doctor Owens got a late start and is still in the preliminary stages of her examination. All she's confirmed so far is that he died of strangulation last Thursday – so basically what we already knew," Sam said.

Alisha rolled her eyes. "Well, that's a letdown. We've been waiting half a week for someone to tell us that a dude with rope marks on his neck died of strangulation."

"Anything new on your serial killer profile, theory, thing?" Sam asked.

"Nothing new, but I still stand by my previous assumption," Alisha said smugly. "Did Owens say when we'd get the full report?"

"Her exact words were, 'Tomorrow, if nothing unusual shows up,' so fingers crossed," Sam said.

Sam started to say something else, but Alisha cut him off. "Don't jinx it," she said."

"I'm just saying," Sam continued. "This case has been weird from start to finish, so it wouldn't surprise me if 'something unusual' does come up."

"There you went and did it," Alisha said.

Captain Durant interrupted their discussion by asking for an update. "I've got a full press briefing lined up for this afternoon to once again assuring holiday shoppers that there's nothing to fear this Christmas. So, I wanted to make sure there aren't any surprises I don't know about."

"Nope. We're kinda just waiting on the final M.E. report. But she said it'll probably be tomorrow before she's done," Alisha replied.

"Ok, thanks," Captain Durant said. "And good work on this one. Don't stay too late. It's almost Christmas."

"Thanks, and good luck on the press briefing," Sam said.

***

It was nearly one in the morning when Professor Harold Barnes pulled in his garage. It had been a good, but exhausting night. He stepped out onto the blue tarp preplaced next to his car and went through his post-murder clean-up routine.

Once inside his house, he went straight to bed. Classes were out for Christmas break, but Harold intended to wake up early and catch the morning news. Houdini curled up at the foot of the bed and soon they were both asleep.

***

Sam felt himself being shaken awake. He was in one of those deep sleeps that leave you groggy when you're awakened in the middle of them. Somewhere in the fog, a voice was saying his name. Finally, after a moment he was awake enough to focus on his wife's voice.

"Sam, your phone's been vibrating like crazy for the last five minutes," she said annoyed.

He sat up and read on his phone screen, "Four missed calls." He was just about to call back when his phone rang again.

He smashed the answer button. "What is it? Did the M.E. report come in? I told you she was going to find something weird."

"Shut up and listen. He's still alive!" Alisha yelled into the phone.

"What? Who's alive? Walt?" Sam asked as he turned to sit on the edge of the bed.

"It's not Walt. We were wrong about everything. The Holiday Killer is still alive. Get down here to the old Crossroads Mall." Alisha hung up the phone.

"Oh God, oh God, oh God," Sam lamented as he threw on his clothes in record time.

"It's *him* again, isn't it," Jennifer asked, dread filling her voice.

"I don't know anything at this point," Sam said.

"But what else could be so urgent or have you upset like this," Jennifer pressed.

"Maybe," was all Sam replied.

As he hurried to his car, careful not to slip on a fresh dusting of snow that had fallen overnight, he quickly texted Alisha. "Coffee?"

"Skip it. Just get here," she texted back.

Sam rarely used the red and blue LED light he kept in the center console of his car, but this occasion called for it. He mounted it on the dash and floored it. It was a solid twenty-five minute drive to the mall. His car tires slipped a few times on slick spots on the highway and he glanced at his phone to check the temperature outside. Twenty-eight degrees. *Driving ninety miles per hour is probably not smart*, he thought. Last thing he needed was to spin out on the highway. He slowed to match the posted speed limit.

The now-defunct mall sat just off the highway, and Sam could see the flashing red and blue lights from other cop cars before he even exited. Less than a minute later, he pulled up next to a gaggle of emergency vehicles. The Crossroads mall had been closed for three years, and despite attempts to revitalize it, it sat abandoned. Now it was a crime scene.

The snow was falling heavier now. The distortion from the many emergency lights made it hard to make out much from where Sam exited his vehicle. He spotted his partner and hurried over.

As Sam approached the crime scene, he noticed one of those Christmas light projectors dancing across several items arranged in front of a vacant department store. He then saw a body – no wait, actually two bodies – displayed at the center of an elaborate Christmas display like you'd expect from someone trying to win "best decorated house in the neighborhood." A man and a woman, clearly deceased, were "seated" behind a cardboard cutout of a sleigh. They were dressed as Mr. and Mrs. Claus and draped with Christmas lights. The man was wearing a fake Santa beard splattered with blood. Behind, as if pulled by the sleigh, was a stack of Christmas presents. In front were inflatable Christmas characters – Rudolph, Frosty, and a gingerbread man – as if about to be run over by the sleigh. Elvis loudly crooned "Blue Christmas" from somewhere in the midst of the display.

"Hey," Alisha mumbled.

"We don't *know* it's him yet," Sam said.

"Unless you think we've got a copycat, it's gotta be him," she replied.

Sam looked at the sky. "This snow is ruining our chances of collecting evidence – not that the Holiday Killer has left any at the previous scenes, but there's always hope. Or there was."

"It'll be daylight soon," Alisha observed.

"Have you checked out the scene at all?" Sam asked.

"Nope. Was waiting for you. Kinda sorry now that I told you to skip the coffee though." Alisha said.

"Agreed, it's frigid out here," Sam said.

"Wonder what's powering all of this?" Alisha asked nobody in particular.

"Good question. All these lights and blowers for the inflatables have to draw some serious power, and I don't hear a generator." Sam didn't figure an abandoned mall would still have working power outlets.

Sam and Alisha began walking a circle around the Christmas display. Around back they found their answer to Alisha's question: a bank of battery backups. Sam looked at the readout display on each of the battery backups, showing their remaining charge.

"I wonder if we can calculate the power draw of each of these devices and figure out what time our killer set up the display – or turned it on at least," Sam said.

Almost immediately Alisha said, "I bet I already know. 12:25 a.m."

"And how would you know that?" Sam asked.

"Because it fits," Alisha said. "On both the previous cases, the security systems went off at the exact time to match the date of their respective holidays. 10:31 p.m. on the Halloween case. 11:26 p.m. on the Thanksgiving case. So 12:25 a.m. for Christmas. And since there's no security cameras to disable, I'd bet that's when he turned the whole display on."

"Perhaps. I wonder which one of these cords cuts off that dreadful music," Sam said.

"What, you don't like Elvis?" Alisha asked.

"Eh, he's ok. *Blue Christmas*, not so much," Sam said.

"Ok, Mr. Grinch," she said, finally cracking a smile.

The sun was beginning to rise giving them a better look at the display – and the victims.

"Wait, I think I know the female," Alisha said, stepping over strings of Christmas lights, careful not to trip and disturb the scene.

"Is that…" Sam began.

Alisha finished Sam's thought. "The reporter lady who interviewed us."

"What was her name?" Sam paused to think. "Taylor…Ashley Taylor?"

"Allison Taylor," Alisha corrected. "A real shame. She was a bulldog reporter but nobody deserves this. Not at Christmas. Not ever."

"Do you recognize the man?" Sam asked.

"Can't tell much with that fake Santa beard on," Alisha said. "But probably not. I don't know any men that aren't cops."

The snow had finally stopped, leaving a half-inch blanket, though muddied and trampled by hundreds of boot prints. So far they'd been spared the media frenzy present at the previous crime scenes due to the out of the way location of this crime scene. After snapping dozens of pictures from various angles, Sam and Alisha began meticulously disassembling and cataloging each piece of the display.

"Twenty-five," Alisha said aloud.

"Twenty-five what?" Sam asked.

"Boxes for the presents," Alisha replied. She sighed. "I think that pretty well confirms the Holiday Killer is still out there. We never made the numerical code angle public so there's no way a copycat would know that part."

"Well, who the heck then was Walt?" Sam exclaimed.

"I hate to think we completely misread him – but our entire connection to him was the stuffing boxes," Alisha answered.

"I feel so stupid," Sam said. "And everyone, including the judge, was telling us that it was nothing."

"Nah, it's still super weird for anyone to buy twenty-six boxes of stuffing. I'm not going to beat myself up over that," Alisha said.

Sam massaged his tired face with his hands. "Do you think…we drove him to commit suicide by accusing him and staking out his place?"

"What if he was like an accomplice or something?" Alisha asked.

"A mortician does seem like a fitting sidekick for a serial killer, to be fair," Sam said.

Alisha pulled off the last string of lights and then paused and started to count the individual bulbs. When she finished counting the entire string, Sam started to speak, but she held up a finger to silence him. Sam watched with curiosity as she looked back through their evidence pile.

Finally, she turned and said, "I found a second set of the Holiday Killer's code: twelve strings of lights with twenty-five individual bulbs each. Twelve, twenty-five. December twenty-fifth, which is Christmas."

Sam groaned. "Yeah, no way this isn't his work. And good catch."

"The boss is gonna be madder than a hornet over all of this, you know," Alisha said. "He gave that beautiful press briefing yesterday and everything."

Almost as if summoned by Alisha's words, Sam saw Captain Durant's black SUV enter the parking lot.

"You know, I wonder if our dead reporter was at his briefing. That would give us a timeline for her disappearance. I also wonder if her news station has noticed her missing," Sam asked.

Before Alisha could respond, Sam's phone rang. It was the medical examiner.

"Cross, here," Sam answered.

"Hey, I've got an important discovery that I thought you should know about right away," she said. "Walt Emmer was not a suicide victim, but rather a victim of homicide. Strangulation was the cause of death, but it was not self-inflicted, and he did not die by hanging in that bathroom. He was strangled elsewhere and then the body was moved."

"You're sure?" Sam asked.

"One hundred percent. It'll all be in my report that should be in your email inbox within the hour. But yes, this was one hundred percent a homicide. And so, I'm sure the whole hanging was staged."

"Wow. That's huge. Thanks," Sam said, hanging up the phone.

"What was that?" Alisha asked. "What's huge?"

"Walt was murdered. He did not kill himself," Sam said.

"Wow indeed. So, another Holiday Killer victim? Or something else?" Alisha asked.

"I don't even know. We're going to have to go back over all the evidence with fresh eyes," Sam said.

"And dig deeper into Walt's connections. His death is so different from the others. I wonder if he's not still somehow personally connected to the Holiday Killer," Alisha said.

"Maybe he was a loose end," Sam said as Captain Durant walked up.

Alisha had been right. It was obvious that their boss was livid. He said nothing as he stood a few feet away watching them work. Together the detectives lifted the presents from the decoration into the evidence van. They were all light weight and empty. Except the last one – it made a light thumping noise when Sam picked it up like something moved inside.

"I think something's in this one," Sam said, balancing it on his knee to keep it out of the snow. He took out his pocketknife and carefully cut the tape holding together the wrapping paper on the box, removing it in one large piece. He handed it to Alisha who carefully folded it and placed it in an evidence bag.

"What makes you think there's something inside this one? And nothing in the rest?" Alisha asked.

"I don't know about any of the others; we can check them later. But this one sounded like there was something loose inside that moved around when I picked it up," Sam answered.

Sam was just about to cut the tape holding the box closed when Alisha yelled for him to stop. "Sam, we're dealing with a psycho killer here. We should call the bomb squad before you go opening boxes."

Sam looked at the box, knife in hand, ready to cut. The sound of crunching tires in snow made him look up. It was the first media van to arrive on scene. Not that Sam thought there was anything to worry about – but he couldn't get out of his mind the picture of his wife watching him get blown up on live TV. Sam looked at Captain Durant who scowled disapprovingly.

"Fine, we'll call the bomb squad," Sam relinquished.

Two hours, and twenty-five checked boxes later, the bomb squad gave the all clear.

"So, I can finally open this box?" Sam asked.

The bomb technician shot a thumbs up and Sam picked up the box to open it. It was a plain twelve-inch cardboard box like you'd find at any office supply store. He lifted up the flaps – sure enough there was indeed something inside: a card in a white envelope addressed to him and his partner.

Alisha, who had been standing over him watching said sarcastically, "Isn't that thoughtful of him."

Sam held the envelope up to the morning sun. As far as he could see, it contained only a Christmas card. It was not sealed, but rather the top flap was tucked inside the envelope. He slid his finger underneath the flap and then pulled the card out.

It was a simple Christmas card like you might buy at any dollar store. On the front was a festive picture of Mr. and Mrs. Claus – appropriately matching the Holiday Killer's current murder scene. Handwritten on the inside of the card it said, "Oopsie. I'm not dead." It was signed "HK."

Sam resisted the urge to angrily crumple the card. It was unfortunately evidence. "Alright, let's let the coroner in here so our favorite M.E. can add these two victims to her backlog."

Captain Durant walked over and looked at the card in Sam's hand. He finally spoke: "My office as soon as you get back." He then turned and walked away.

Sam was in no hurry to have that conversation, so he would take his time getting back. "How about that coffee and some breakfast finally?" Sam asked Alisha. "I don't think the coroner needs us to watch him do his thing."

"Sure," said Alisha as she slammed the back hatch of the evidence van. To the coroner she said, "I know you will, but let us know ASAP if you find anything."

"Well, I can tell you, at least my first impression, of how they died," he said.

"Ok, I'll take it," Alisha answered.

"The woman has both her wrists slit," the coroner said, "and the man has a gunshot wound to head – likely fired into his open mouth. I'm guessing though that it wasn't a double suicide despite being made to look that way."

Sam leaned in and looked for himself. "Right, probably just made to look like it. Thanks."

Twenty minutes later, Sam and Alisha were seated in a diner sipping coffee, trying to decide what to order.

"The chorizo burrito looks good," Alisha said. "And let me guess, you're getting biscuits and gravy as always?"

"I was actually going to get a Belgian waffle, thank you very much," Sam retorted.

They had the corner of the diner all to themselves, so they began discussing the case. "I was so ready to be done with this," Alisha said.

Sam nodded as he swallowed a sip of coffee. "Me too. Somehow we were wrong about Walt. The news is going to go crazy again. Plus, the hectic schedule – my wife hasn't exactly been a fan."

"I think our link to finding the Holiday Killer is going to be Walt though," Alisha said. "He doesn't fit the killer's pattern. He's not murdered on a holiday. There was no theatrical staging of his murder. It was just supposed to be passed off as a suicide to throw us off the real killer's trail. Though I'm sure the Holiday Killer knew we'd figure it out. But it distracted us long enough to carry out his next murder."

"Exactly. And it feels personal," Sam said. "Like I said earlier, maybe a loose end. Somehow Walt knows the killer or figured out who the killer was."

"We're going to have to really dig into Walt's life," Alisha said. "Though I feel like a guy like him can't have that many friends. Should make it easy to narrow something down."

"Speaking of personal, why kill the reporter? She was practically his biggest fan – gave him the Holiday Killer name and everything," Sam asked.

"Yeah, serial killers are usually pretty big narcissists, so I don't know," Alisha said. "Here's an idea: what if they're all somehow personal? As in, they've all in some way angered our killer or are connected to him somehow?"

"That's an interesting theory. But our previous two victims didn't seem to have any connection to each other, which makes it impossible to connect them back to a killer," Sam said.

They had to put their conversation on pause to give their order to the waitress. She was about to walk away when she asked, "Did you hear on the news this morning that the Holiday Killer isn't really dead? Committed a double murder over by the old mall."

"We heard," Sam simply said, hoping they wouldn't be recognized from their TV interview the other day.

"Scary times," the waitress said, shaking her head as she walked away.

Once their waitress was out of earshot, Sam said, "Before we talk about the case any further, we should come up with a plan for what we're going to say to Durant when we get back."

"What is there to say?" Alisha said flippantly. "Everybody, including him, thought Walt was our perp. It's not like we overlooked a big clue – I mean, that we know of. Walt has to be a legitimate lead. We just have to keep digging."

"Is that what you're going to say to Durant though?" Sam asked.

"Why not? He needs to chill," Alisha said rolling her eyes. "We're doing our best, barely sleeping. Most serial killers rack up a lot more than four victims before they're caught and often it takes years – sometimes with whole task forces and multiple agencies involved and still they can't catch them. I mean, it's only been two months. Don't get me wrong, I wish we could catch him today. I wish these last two victims hadn't died. But it's not because we're bad detectives."

"You're right. I just hope Durant sees it that way," Sam said.

"And if he doesn't?" Alisha asked. "What's he going to do, take us off the case and assign different detectives that would have to start from square one? He just needs to let us do our job. It's not like we're slacking."

A moment later the waitress returned with Alisha's burrito and Sam's waffle. While they ate, Sam looked at the medical examiner's report for Walt on his phone: homicide by ligature strangulation last Wednesday or Thursday. Blood pooling on the lower extremities indicated the body had been moved. Definitely a murder.

They paid for their check and headed for the office to face their boss.

The Postcard

Sam and Alisha took a tongue lashing from Captain Durant, but in the end, he grudgingly agreed with Alisha's logic that she'd laid out to Sam earlier at the diner.

Back at their desks, Sam breathed a sigh of relief. "Well, that went better than I thought it would. Good job in there."

"Yeah, maybe it's the Latina in me. I don't like losing an argument," she said.

"I would've never guessed," Sam said.

Alisha ignored his sarcasm. "Let's start piecing this murder together. I'm tired of being outsmarted."

"Same. Go ahead and get the case file spread out for what we have so far while I see if we have an ID yet on victim number two," Sam said.

A few clicks later, Sam said, "Yep, it's in. The coroner had to ID him off fingerprints due to the facial trauma from the gunshot. Looks like one Mark Vance. Twenty-five years old – kinda expected that, with the number twenty-five this time around. Not married. No criminal record. Not much to go on."

Alisha reviewed the case evidence out loud. "So, we have twenty-five Christmas boxes, twelve strings of twenty-five lights, and a twenty-five year old victim – I think that's enough confirmation of the Holiday Killer," Alisha said, writing down each detail on her notepad. "Plus, the card, of course. I'm not going to waste the time calculating battery consumption to prove I'm right about the lights coming on at twenty-five minutes past midnight."

"Are you sure the Latina in you doesn't need to win that argument too?" Sam joked.

"Nah, because deep down inside you already know I'm right," Alisha said with a smile.

Sam continued scrolling through the search result on their victim. "Ok, so Mark Vance worked in advertising. I'll have the guys down in the lab scrub his social media and contacts to see if he was connected to any of our past victims, to Walt, or to the reporter – but I'm not going to hold my breath."

"Very interesting," Alisha said.

"What's interesting?" Sam asked, looking up.

"That our latest male victim worked in advertising. The one before that was in marketing. And the first victim worked in retail," Alisha said, jotting down more notes. "Remember I told you earlier that it felt like our killer was fighting a war against holidays – like philosophically or something. Show me the picture of the letter he sent you."

Sam unlocked his phone and scrolled to the photo he'd snapped of the Holiday Killer's letter. "Ok, what are you thinking?"

"See how he referenced what he perceived to be ills related to Christmas – debt, pointless purchases – that kind of thing?" Alisha said pointing at Sam's phone screen.

"Ah, I see what you're saying," Sam said. "Advertising, marketing, retail – all of that is a part of what drives consumer sales," Sam said.

"Exactly," Alisha said. "So, what if he doesn't have a problem with the Holidays themselves, but with the consumerism that's been injected into them?"

Before Sam could answer, the squad room TV came on with news about their case.

"Breaking news! The Holiday Killer strikes again. Contrary to the assurances we were given in our exclusive interview with the police captain and detectives involved in the case declaring that the Holiday Killer was dead, this morning a new, gruesome crime scene was discovered at the old Crossroads Mall. It had all the earmarks of the Holiday Killer's signature serial murders. And for the first time, there were two murder victims. It is also with great sadness that we report that our very own journalist who broke the case, Allison Taylor, was one of the two latest victims. We will have more details as they unfold, and tonight during the five o'clock hour, we will have a special tribute segment remembering Allison's life and work."

Sam shook his head. "What a mess."

"Anyway, back to the previous conversation," Sam said. "Assuming his motive is a hatred of consumerism during the various holidays, how do we leverage that to both predict his next crime and catch him before he kills again?" Sam asked.

Alisha shook her head. "I don't know that we can. And what Holiday is next? Do we assume he'll strike on New Year's Eve?"

"I don't know, but we can't tell everyone who's thirty-one years old and works in a sales-related industry to watch their back," Sam said. "I still feel like the way to catch him is to follow the evidence rather than trying to predict and prevent the next murder."

Alisha lowered her voice to just above a whisper. "I hate to say it, but it may just be that more people are going to have to die until the killer slips up and leaves us something we can use to identify him or catch him in the act."

Sam nodded. He hated that reality, but it was true – until the Holiday Killer left a fingerprint or DNA or made some other glaring mistake, they didn't have much to go on. "You know, I've been mulling over the way he killed them this time. In the previous two murders, the wounds to the bodies were related to an aspect of the holiday – decapitated woman for Halloween, stuffed man for Thanksgiving – but with these latest murders, we've got slit wrists and a gunshot wound in the mouth. It doesn't seem to fit."

"Yeah, I was thinking about that too," Alisha said. "It does actually sorta fit though. Death by suicide, plus the song *Blue Christmas*. It's probably pointing to the phenomenon of increased depression and spikes in suicides around the Christmas holiday."

"Except that's actually not a real thing," Sam said.

"Uh, yes it is," Alisha insisted.

"Really, it's not. Look it up if you don't believe me. I was just having this conversation with my wife the other day. The Center for Disease Control actually reports December as the month with the lowest suicide rate of the whole year," Sam said.

"Hmm. I stand corrected." Alisha conceded. "So, do we just assume the Holiday Killer got that detail wrong? Or do you think the music and suicide deaths were random or that maybe they meant something else?"

"No, I think you're right as far as why he chose the cause of death and that song. It's a common misconception, and he probably believed it to be true," Sam said.

"Why do you think he killed two people this time? Escalation? Or something more symbolic?" Alisha asked.

"Yeah, I don't know. Maybe to rub it in our faces that he was still out there and we were wrong about Walt," Sam said. "Or maybe he just wanted a Mr. and Mrs. Claus," Sam said shrugging.

***

Professor Barnes was nearly beside himself with child-like giddiness as he watched the news broadcast announcing his return. Every station was wall-to-wall coverage of The Holiday Killer. He closed his eyes, daydreaming about the two detectives, Cross and Palmetto, panicking and trying to figure out where they had gone wrong.

"This is going better than I ever imagined," the professor said to Houdini. "I never dreamed they thought ol' Walt was me. He ended up being more useful than I imagined – though it is a shame we don't have his incinerator to hide evidence anymore. Oh well, back to the old way of ditching in dumpsters."

Professor Barnes continued rambling to his pet ferret while he slipped rubber gloves on and pulled out a greeting card from his shopping bag. "Time for another little note to our esteemed detectives."

It was a Happy New Year card with a picture of a ball dropping on the front. Inside, he wrote:

Tick tock
You watch the clock
At midnight's stroke
Time to croak
A kiss of fear
To ring in the New Year

"Perhaps not my best poetic work," Professor Barnes said to Houdini, "But good enough. We don't have a lot of time before we make our next decoration."

Professor Barnes used a damp kitchen sponge to moisten the seal of the envelope. He had read of a hapless criminal who had left DNA on the flap of an envelope by licking it and was determined not to make the same stupid mistake.

"Time for a drive. I'll be back soon," Professor Barnes said as he opened his garage door.

Twenty minutes later, Professor Barnes spotted a blue mailbox at the edge of a curb and pulled alongside it to mail the card.

*****

Sam and Alisha spent the next couple days finding and piecing together parts of the case. But mostly running into dead ends. As best as they could tell, neither the reporter nor the male victim had any connection to Walt or to their past two victims from Thanksgiving and Halloween, or to each other.

Tomorrow was Christmas, but the return of the Holiday Killer had sucked the festive spirit right out of him. His wife Jennifer was also upset that Sam was working on Christmas Eve and would miss their church's candlelight service. And he hadn't even finished Christmas shopping.

It was just seven days until New Year's Eve and the likelihood of yet another murder that they didn't know how to prevent, made him both angry and depressed. "I just hate this hopeless feeling. Someone else is going to die a week from today and we don't know how to stop it."

"I'm a pretty darn good detective you know," Alisha said with a smile. "I just might have our guy in cuffs before then." Her smile faded. "No, I get what you mean. I've not been sleeping well the last couple nights. Weighs pretty heavy."

"I was giving some thought to who he might attack next," Sam said. "Following your theory of him targeting people associated with the consumer

side of each holiday – the next one is New Year's –
maybe he goes for a liquor store owner?"

"Lots of alcohol sold on New Year's for
sure," Alisha said. "No way though we can stake
out every liquor store. So, let's focus on things we
can control."

"I know. Just having random thoughts,"
Sam said.

"Have you heard back from the crime lab
about whether they were able to get into Walt's
phone yet?" Alisha asked.

"Nope. And I thought the crime lab was
your domain – on account of the hot lab tech and
all," Sam joked.

"Funny. I'll go check though. He *is* pretty,"
Alisha said.

"You could just call," Sam said.

Alisha winked as she walked away. "But
then I can't ogle him."

Sam's cellphone rang. It was Jennifer. "Yes,
sweetie? What is it? I'm working." There was
silence except for rapid breathing on the other end
of the line. "Jennifer? Are you ok?"

"He knows our address," Jennifer blurted
out.

"What? Who does?" Sam asked.

"The Holiday Killer. He sent us a card!"
Jennifer gasped.

Sam grabbed his jacket and keys and jogged
towards the exit. "Don't touch anything. I'm on my
way," he ordered his wife.

"I already opened it," she replied.

"It's ok. Just don't do anything else. Don't toss the envelope or anything," Sam said and then hung up.

Sam drove almost recklessly towards his house, using his lights and siren to pass through intersections. Glancing back and forth between his phone and the road, he shot off a quick text to his partner: "HK mailed something to my house. Headed there now."

The bottom of Sam's car scraped loudly as he whipped into his driveway. Inside he called, "Jennifer?" There was no answer. He spotted the card his wife had spoken about on the kitchen table. Next to it was a sheet from a notepad. It was a note from his wife.

I'm picking the boys up from preschool. If you want to spend Christmas with us, you can join us at my parents' house.

Sam pounded the counter in frustration. He tossed the note from his wife and then took some pictures with his cell phone of the Holiday Killer's card. Just a plain white envelope, ripped open at the top by his wife, and a New Year's card. Sam walked back out to his car and retrieved a pair of gloves and an evidence bag from his trunk. Back inside, he gloved up and opened the card. It contained a handwritten amateurish poem about fearing the coming New Year. They didn't have to guess anymore. The Holiday Killer would strike again in seven days.

Sam took a couple more picture of the inside of the card and then dropped both it and the envelope into the evidence bag. He texted the pictures to Alisha.

"Your wife ok," she texted back.

"She left and took the boys, so I'm going to go with no," Sam replied.

"Sorry. You coming back to the office or…" Alisha asked.

"Yeah. See you in a few," Sam replied.

Back at the squad room, Captain Durant was waiting by his desk. "You should go home, Cross," Captain Durant said.

"I just came from there," Sam said.

"It sounds like your wife needs you," Captain Durant replied.

Sam shot a glare at Alisha and then said, "It'll be fine. I've got to get this card into evidence."

"Ok, but then I want you gone. And take Christmas off too. That's an order," Captain Durant said. "After everything last year, I've got a soft spot for your wife and boys."

"Only if my partner gets the day off too," Sam said.

Captain Durant hesitated and then said, "Palmetto, take the day."

Alisha threw up her hands as Captain Durant walked away. "Thanks for that. I've got the case files all spread out here. Plus, I've got no one to celebrate with so I was just going to work."

"You started it by telling Durant my family business," Sam grumbled.

"He needed to know. You need to be with your family," Alisha said.

Sam didn't reply and headed for the evidence locker. Just then he remembered Tiffany. He pulled out his phone and called her number.

Two rings later, she answered. "Hey, Sam. How're you?"

"Good," Sam said. "Hey, I just wanted to check and see if you were still coming for Christmas tomorrow. If so, change of venue. We're going to have it at my in-laws. You're still welcome. They're good folks. I can text you the address."

"Um, is it ok if I say no? Sorry, I'm sure your in-laws are wonderful people, and I know it's last minute. Something else has come up," Tiffany said.

"Yeah, sure. That's fine. Is everything ok though?" Sam asked.

"Oh yeah, everything is fine – great actually," Tiffany said. "I, um…I met a guy and we've been talking for a couple weeks. He invited me to spend Christmas with him. I told him I already had plans. But since you asked, if you don't mind, I'm sure his invitation is still good."

"Oh nice. Yeah, go for it," Sam said. "You'll have to tell me about him though – I can run a background check if you want. Kidding…but seriously," Sam added with a laugh.

"He seems like a great guy. If I get any weird vibes, I'll let you know. You sure it's ok though? I feel bad changing my mind last minute," Tiffany asked.

"Totally. Have fun. Merry Christmas, Tiffany," Sam said.

"Thanks," Tiffany said. "And you too. Give your boys a squeeze for me. Bye."

Sam hung up and looked at his watch: quarter-to-five. Sam walked back to the squad room. Alisha was packing up the case files. He nodded curtly, still slightly irritated at her. "I guess I'm out. I'm going to grab a couple last minute presents and then maybe make our church's candlelight service. You need anything before I go?"

She shook her head. "Hey, I didn't mean to upset you. Just looking out for my partner."

"I know. Thanks. And Merry Christmas. See you on the twenty-sixth," Sam said.

He drove away in silence. He pulled into the packed Walmart parking lot. Sam wasn't the only last-minute shopper. As he pushed the shopping cart around the store, he couldn't help thinking of the Holiday Killer's words: *I bet you can't wait to spend hundreds of dollars of your meager detective's salary on cheap presents for your wife and two boys.* Sam refused to admit that the Holiday Killer had a point. Even if the gifts were cheaply made and over-priced – nothing beat the joy of Christmas morning and his family's smiles as they opened their presents.

One hour and nearly two hundred dollars later, Sam was back in his car. A couple minutes before 7:00 p.m., he walked quietly into his family's church and slid into the pew next to his wife. She didn't look at him but took his hand and squeezed it. The organist finished the chorus of "O

Come All Ye Faithful," and the pastor stepped towards the pulpit to begin the service.

Christmas

The Christmas Holiday turned out to be exactly what Sam needed. Between food, presents, and family, he barely even thought of the case. Jennifer finally softened her bristly demeanor after opening her gift from Sam: a pair of white gold with emerald earrings. Yet when it came time to pack up and leave, she balked. "I'm just going to stay here a few more days," she said, "just until I know it's safe for me and the boys."

Sam, not wanting to get into an argument on Christmas, nodded and kissed her on the forehead. He hugged his boys, thanked his in-laws, and walked out into the cold. He had driven barely ten minutes when he texted her, "I miss you already. Come home soon."

Jennifer texted back, "Catch him."

He pounded his palm angrily on the steering wheel. The Holiday Killer *had* to be taken down soon. *I'm not going to let him tear my family apart.*

It was nearly nine when Sam arrived home and flopped heavily into his recliner. He sent a "Merry Christmas" text to Tiffany saying he hoped she had a good time with her boyfriend. She replied with two "thumbs ups" and a smile emoji. Sam flipped on the TV and at some point fell asleep in his recliner watching *It's A Wonderful Life*.

***

Sam awoke the next morning with an awful crick in his neck from sleeping in the recliner. *Probably should shower*, he thought as he caught sight of his reflection in the hall mirror on the way to his room. He looked positively hungover despite being a teetotaler. Ten minutes later, he hung his wet towel over the shower curtain rod and pulled on his work clothes. He sent a good morning text to Jennifer and then drummed his fingers impatiently on the counter as he waited for the coffee pot to beep.

Out of habit, he had made a half pot like normal to split with Jennifer, so he texted his partner to see if she wanted him to bring her a cup. "Got my own already," Alisha texted back. Not wanting to waste good coffee, Sam poured the rest into a thermos for later.

At the office, Sam found Alisha already at her desk going over the case file for the Holiday Killer case. Sam nodded and mumbled a good morning.

"Still mad at me?" she asked.

"No. Just a rough night. Honestly, we're good. I did offer you coffee remember?" Sam said.

"True that," Alisha said. "Ok. Well, you want to help me comb back through the evidence to see what we might've missed?"

"What makes you think we missed something?" Sam asked. "We've been over that a dozen or more times."

"Good grief, it's just called being thorough. Unless you have another suggestion. Or did you just want to sit around and do nothing until the next murder on New Year's?" she replied.

"You're right. Sorry. Give me like two minutes to clear my head and I'll help," Sam said.

He walked into the dingy squad room toilet. Someone had been skipping their cleaning duty – for quite a while. Alisha didn't deserve his attitude. Sam splashed cold water on his face and took a couple deep breaths. He glanced at his phone as he dried off. Still no good morning text from Jennifer. Sam silenced it and buried it in his coat pocket. She'd said, "Catch him," and apparently that's what he needed to do to fix things with his wife. Which meant he needed to work, not hide in the bathroom.

Back at Alisha's desk, he said, "Hey, I'm back. Sorry about that. I'm good now."

"No worries. I thought I'd dive into Walt's business records from the mortuary," Alisha said. "There has to be some kind of clue there to point to the real killer."

"Right," Sam said. "I know we misread him, but we can't have been one hundred percent wrong. There has to be a connection there. I guess I'll take the evidence from the staged suicide. Maybe we'll get lucky there. Since the Holiday Killer was trying to pass it off as a suicide, maybe he left some trace DNA on the rope or something."

Sam rang the forensics lab, but no one picked up, so Sam decided to take the walk there. A couple minutes later, he knocked and then entered the lab.

"Oh hey, Cross, what can I do for you," the lab tech asked.

"Just wanted to see if you had run for DNA or any other trace evidence on the Walt Emmer faked suicide scene," Sam asked.

"Oh, wait, that wasn't a suicide? I hadn't got the memo," he replied.

"Yeah, the M.E. ruled it a homicide. She said it was staged to look like a suicide, but the body said otherwise," Sam said. "Since that's what we were supposed to think, I'm curious if the Holiday Killer got sloppy and left us something behind."

"For sure. Yeah, I'll get right on it. Though just be warned, a public bathroom is a forensic nightmare. There's liable to be dozens of different prints and DNA galore," the lab tech said.

"Yeah, I hear you. But at least if we have it all separated and catalogued, then maybe if we get another lead, we can match it to something you found. Thanks. I appreciate it," Sam said.

Looks like someone needs to check their e-mail, Sam thought – it'd been ruled a homicide five days prior.

He was about to leave when the lab tech said, "Oh, I did get into that phone though. You wouldn't believe how many people use their birth year as a passcode. I disabled it, so you don't have to type a passcode each time."

"Awesome," Sam said, taking the phone from the lab tech. "Talk soon."

* * *

"Any luck?" Alisha asked as he returned to his desk.

"Yes and no. He didn't even know they'd ruled it a homicide, so he's just getting started on processing the evidence today," Sam said. "But he got into Walt's phone," he said holding it up.

"Incredible. Because these business records aren't turning up anything," she said. "I was hoping our victims would've been former customers of Walt's, but that doesn't seem to be the case. But let's dig into that phone. Surely there's something helpful there."

"Hope he's not a 'chatty Kathy,' or else running down all his contacts could be a pain," Sam said with a chuckle.

"Why are you always a 'half-empty' person," Alisha moaned.

"Call me jaded, I guess," Sam said. "Rarely is it ever easy. My wife has like five hundred contacts in her phone."

"I think you're still mad at me," Alisha said with a roll of her eyes.

Sam laughed. "Just give me half of the numbers, and we'll knock it out together."

***

After a couple hours, Sam and Alisha were able to narrow down the contacts in Walt's phone to just fourteen potential personal contacts. The rest had been related to his work. They'd check those too if it came to it.

"Who has just fourteen friends or family members they talk to?" Alisha asked.

"Walt didn't exactly strike me as the outgoing social type," Sam replied.

Alisha nodded. "True, true. Good for us though. I sure hope we get a lead here. We're due some good news."

"No kidding," Sam said.

"I can't shake the feeling that we're staring at some major clue and just don't know it," Alisha said as she took a sip of her old coffee and made a face before tossing it in the trash.

"Possibly. But it could be that it's one of those puzzle pieces you can't find a home for until you get more pieces in their proper place – or, the Holiday Killer is that good," Sam said.

"Let me see that card he mailed to your house again," Alisha said pointing at the case folder near Sam on the desk. Alisha read over it in silence for a couple minutes and then conceded, "There's nothing to go on in there. Just a taunt that he's going to kill again – which we already knew."

"Yeah, and the paper came back with no fingerprints, no DNA on the envelope," Sam replied. "And the card could've been purchased at any of a hundred different stores."

"I just had a thought," Alisha interrupted. "What if the killer is a surgeon or in some way connected to the medical field. That could perhaps explain the decapitation of the first victim, and the gutting of the second one. Not anyone can do that. Plus, his easy access to gloves to prevent leaving any evidence. Surgeons are pretty meticulous people – and they have to be somewhat coldblooded and calculated. I read somewhere that surgeons are pretty high on the list of professions that attract psychopaths."

"That's as good a theory as any," Sam said. "Kind of goes with having a mortician friend too. I wonder if any of these contacts are doctors."

Alisha tore the list of fourteen names in half and spun her chair around to her computer as Sam grabbed the other half and rushed to his desk. They worked in silence, the only sound being the click-clack of keyboard keys.

Alisha finished first with a defeated sigh. "A mechanic, an elementary school teacher, a retired Army colonel, a city bus driver, a college professor, and Walt's elderly mom and dad – both in the nursing home. So, we can rule them out for sure – unless we think our killer is a geriatric."

"So far I've got an instructor for a driving school, a lady who works at a pet store, a librarian, a car salesman, and a barista. Just now looking up the last two," Sam said.

"Give me a name of one of them," Alisha said.

A minute later, Sam sat back, his shoulders slumping with resignation. "I struck out too."

"Wait!" Alisha exclaimed. "Victor Guerra, surgeon…ugh – of dentistry."

"I mean, maybe?" Sam said with a laugh. "We still have to track down and possibly interview all of them anyway since they knew Walt, but yeah, dentist is a big leap to serial killer."

"Well, to be fair, any of these professions is a big jump to serial killer," Alisha countered. "For instance, the Son of Sam killer was a postal worker,"

"You're right," Sam said. "Hey, it's lunchtime. Are burgers ok?"

"That's fine. I had Chinese yesterday for Christmas," Alisha said as she grabbed her coat.

As they walked to Sam's car, his phone dinged. It was a picture of Tiffany with a nice looking guy. If Sam had to guess, he was probably twenty-eight to thirty years old though to Tiffany's twenty years. Tiffany was beaming in the picture. *I guess this is the boyfriend*, Sam thought.

He shot off a quick text saying, "Great pic!" and pointed his car in the direction of his favorite burger place a couple blocks away. As they sat in the drive-thru lane, Sam sighed.

"What depressing thing are you about to say now?" Alisha joked.

"Just that it's an atrocious time to be calling people," Sam replied.

"What do you mean?" Alisha asked.

"Well, it's the day after Christmas, and we're going to be calling people about a dead guy they knew. I know I wouldn't want to receive that call in the middle of the Christmas Holiday," Sam said.

"We can't afford to wait though," Alisha said. "We have a murderer to catch and he's going to kill again in less than a week."

***

The rest of the afternoon was spent mostly leaving voice mails – it was the day after Christmas

189

after all. Alisha got two of her half of the list on the phone – the dental surgeon and the retired colonel – and set up interviews for the next day. Sam had slightly more luck, getting interviews set up for three of Walt's contacts: the pet store employee, the barista, and the college professor.

It was nearly six p.m. by this time, so Sam and Alisha called it a day.

"You and your wife all good again?" Alisha asked as she buttoned up her jacket.

"Yep," Sam said.

"I detect a lie in there, but I'll let it go – don't want you mad at me again," Alisha said.

"She's just scared, and I don't blame her. She's one hundred percent supportive of me as a cop – but like every police spouse, the job sometimes gets to her. That stupid New Year's card mailed to our house didn't help things," Sam said.

"She and your boys still at her folks," Alisha probed.

"Yeah. But it's fine. I'm so busy and barely home right now anyway," Sam replied.

"If you're free one night and wanna hang – popcorn and movie or just not be alone – let me know," Alisha offered.

Sam nodded and thanked her for the offer and headed to his car. The wind was brutal causing Sam's eyes to sting and water. Sam ducked his head into his coat collar and jogged to his car, still thinking about Alisha's invitation. Sitting at home in a quiet house all evening didn't sound remotely enjoyable. But he was *positive* his wife would not approve of him hanging out with Alisha after work

– especially alone at her house. Sam lingered a moment longer and then drove home.

191

Guess Who

Sam's first interview of the day was with the college professor listed in Walt's phone contacts. However, he was no-show. *Odd*, Sam thought. *You'd think that a guy who's used to marking people tardy for a living would be the punctual type.* Sam used his freed-up time to give callbacks to those who didn't answer yesterday – an annoying exercise since Sam hated leaving voicemails.

An hour later, they got word that their eleven o'clock interview had arrived – the retired colonel from Alisha's list. Sam grabbed his notepad and headed for the interview room while Alisha went to retrieve the colonel.

Sam sat in a chair towards the back corner of the interview room. Alisha would be taking the lead on this one. Less than a minute later they entered the room. For a retired Army officer, he looked rather unassuming – he was on the shorter side and heavyset. The only indication of his former military status was the black hat he wore emblazoned with the word "Veteran."

"I appreciate you coming in today, Mr. Hatch, on such short notice," Alisha said. "We'll try to make this quick and get you on your way."

"No worries. I'm retired. I got all the time in the world," the colonel said. "So, you said this is about Walt? Sad deal, him taking his life like that."

Alisha looked back briefly at Sam before continuing. "How long did you know Walt?"

"Just a few years," the Colonel said. "My mother passed away and since we live in the neighborhood where Walt has – had rather – his funeral home, he handled her service for us. He did such a good job with Mom that I'd occasionally refer him business. We'd also sometimes run into each other at the grocery store and such. Eventually we became friends and would meet up for lunch. He liked this one diner in the area. Honestly, a real nice guy."

"So, you knew him pretty well then?" Alisha asked.

"I guess. I mean, as well as you know anyone on that kind of casual basis," the colonel said. "Why specifically are you guys investigating his death? I didn't think the police investigated suicides."

Alisha ignored the question and redirected. "What kind of things did you talk about at these lunch get-togethers?"

Colonel Hatch shrugged. "Oh, just normal stuff y'know. He'd talk about his work some – fascinating stuff really. Sometimes football. He was a Sooners fan and I'm a Cornhusker fan. So just some good-natured ribbing depending on who was winning or stinkin' it up that season." The colonel added, "You didn't answer my question. What's the police looking into Walt's death for?"

"Sir, we're sorry to break it to you like this," Alisha said, "but Walt's death was actually ruled a homicide. Somebody killed him and then staged it to look like he committed suicide."

Sam watched the colonel's face intensely to gauge his reaction. The colonel's mouth dropped in genuine shock and confusion. It took him a few seconds to find his words and reply. "That's terrible. I can't for the life of me think of who'd want to hurt a guy like Walt. I'd ask you if you were sure, but I suppose we wouldn't be having this conversation if you weren't. You got any leads?"

"What'd you do in the Army," Alisha asked.

"Nothing terribly glamorous – just a 12A Engineer officer," Colonel Hatch said. "When I wasn't navigating Army politics, I led my troops to perform at a level of excellence. Spent my last six years in battalion command staff headquarters."

"Can you think of anyone that might have wanted to kill Walt? Anyone he mentioned having a beef with or that he was scared of? You said you guys sometimes talked about his job. Did he ever mention a disgruntled customer who might have a reason to kill him? Any falling out with a friend?" Alisha asked.

"Honestly, no. He always bragged about his five-star Google reviews. People loved the guy. Sure, he was quirky and a bit awkward but past all that was a real friend," the colonel said.

"Well, you're the first person we've interviewed about his death. So, as we talk to his other friends, is there anyone you'd recommend we take a closer look at from Walt's circle of friends?" Alisha asked.

"I really didn't know any of his other friends. To be honest, I don't think he had that many. The guy worked probably sixty hours a week," Colonel Hatch replied. "Didn't leave a lot of time for social interactions."

Alisha read out loud the list of names they intended to interview. "Any of those names stand out to you? Do you know any of them?"

"Can't say that I do" the colonel replied. "If anything comes to me, I'll be sure to pass it on. You got a business card I can have?"

Both Sam and Alisha passed their cards to him. They thanked him for his time and help, and Alisha escorted him to the lobby.

A couple minutes later, Alisha joined Sam at his desk. "I think that was a dead end," Sam said.

"Yeah, I don't know that we gained anything helpful there," Alisha agreed. "Who do we have next?"

"Well since my professor was a no-show," Sam said as he scanned his list, "I've got the pet store lady at two and then the barista at three-thirty. When's your dentist coming?"

Alisha curled her lip. "Not 'til seven. He said he had to close up his practice first." Alisha glanced at her watch. "But since we've got over two hours until the next interview, let's eat and then I'm going to do some more callbacks."

***

The rest of the afternoon flew by. They grabbed burgers and Alisha lined up the mechanic and schoolteacher for the next day. The interviews with the pet store employee and the barista turned out to be even less helpful than Colonel Hatch. The pet store employee barely knew Walt – she used to deliver cat food to his house. The barista had looked more promising – she was actually Walt's niece. But they hadn't spoken in over a year.

Sam ran his hand over his face in frustration. "Are we actually expecting one of these names," he said tapping the list with his index finger, "to be our killer and to just walk into the police station and talk to us so we can arrest them?"

"Could be. Why not?" Alisha said. "The Holiday Killer is a real person. And my money is still on him knowing Walt somehow. It's about time we get a lucky break you know."

Before Sam could reply, his phone rang. Sam didn't recognize the number and almost let it go to voicemail, but after a couple rings decided to answer. It was the no-show professor from the morning. The professor apologized for missing the interview and said he'd overslept and could come by tomorrow. Sam lined him up for right after lunch.

***

Professor Harold Barnes grinned with devilish self-satisfaction as he hung up the phone. Tomorrow would be great fun. He'd finally get the opportunity to look Detectives Cross and Palmetto in the eye. He'd have a surprise for them too when he did. Of course, he had lied about oversleeping. Something had come up.

"Today has been a busy day," Professor Barnes said to Houdini as he scratched his pet under the chin. "We hadn't planned on capturing our next guest until tomorrow, but when a perfect opportunity falls into your lap, you don't let it pass by."

The professor had chosen a gym employee for his next "decoration." She'd taken a jog that morning through a secluded portion of the park near her house. And Professor Barnes had been watching and waiting. He attacked as she rounded a line of bushes. He hadn't killed her yet – only knocked her out. It was too early to begin his work so he'd have to keep her alive until then.

"Hopefully she's a fan of ramen and sushi," Professor Barnes said to Houdini. "Or maybe I'll get her a last meal – like they do on death row."

***

"Hey, did Walt have a will? Who did he leave his car, house, and business to?" Alisha asked.

"Not that we know of. They're still going through the mountains of evidence they collected. The guy was a serious hoarder when it comes to paperwork," Sam said. "There were boxes after boxes of records both at his home and office. I don't think they've even catalogued it all yet."

"I was just thinking that maybe Walt and the Holiday Killer were such close friends that he willed everything to him," she said.

"Frankly, that seems like a stretch to me," Sam said.

197

"There you go being pessimistic again – but you're probably right," she conceded. "Maybe we'll get lucky."

"I feel like we keep saying that" Sam laughed ruefully.

"Saying what?" Alisha asked.

"Get lucky," Sam said.

"Well, at this point I'll take anything – good police work, luck, divine intervention," Alisha said.

"Should I call a psychic for you?" Sam asked.

"Stop it. Now you're just being ridiculous," Alisha said. "Come on. It's interview time."

***

The dentist was next – and looking like another dead end. Dr. Nichols and Walt had met at a medical convention years ago and their only ongoing connection was occasionally playing chess online.

Alisha was about to cut him loose when Sam thought of one final question. "Dr. Nichols, I'd like to get your expert opinion as a medical professional."

"Sure, ask away," the dentist replied.

"Do you mind looking at a couple photos of the victims? I know that's not the kind of thing you normally see in your line of work," Sam said.

"Uh sure. I can do that. What did you want to know?" the dentist asked.

"Mainly about the way the Holiday Killer carved up his victims. The first one was decapitated, and the second was cut from the chest down to his waist and had his internal organs removed," Sam explained as he laid out the pictures on the table in front of the dentist.

"My God!" exclaimed the Dr. Nichols as he held up each picture.

"Yeah, I know. My question is: would the killer – in your professional opinion – need medical training to perform that kind of, um, surgery…for the lack of a better word?" Sam asked.

The dentist took a closer look. "I don't know that I can say for certain. I mean if the intent was to perform a medical procedure, then sure, absolutely. But when the intent is to kill or just cut up a body – I would think not."

"And why do you say that?" Alisha asked.

"The incisions don't look precise enough to me," he said. The dentist pointed at the incisions. "The cuts aren't jagged per se, but they also don't strike me as being done by someone who did this all the time. It all looks a bit amateurish to me."

"That's a lot of help doc," Sam said.

"I don't think the killer even used medical tools," the dentist continued. "If I had to guess, just ordinary kitchen knives."

"Appreciate it Dr. Nichols," Alisha said. She looked at Sam. "Do we have any other questions for him?"

"None that I can think of," Sam said. "Here's our cards, and if you think of anything else, please call us any time. Oh, and these photos have of course not been released to the public, so if you would do us the favor of not discussing them with anyone."

"Sure thing. No problem," the dentist said.

***

"Wakey, wakey," Professor Barnes said to his captive. He held a bowl of ramen in one hand and a glass of milk in the other.

She didn't respond so he nudged her leg with his foot. She sat up awkwardly due to her hands and feet being bound. When she saw the professor, she let out a muffled whimper through the gag on her mouth and tried to pull away towards the wall.

"You know, I didn't think this through," he said out loud, more to himself than anyone else. "I've never kept one alive before." This brought further whimpering and a panicked look in her eyes. "I don't know if I trust you if I untie your hands. Guess I'll have to feed you myself."

The professor knelt in front of her and set the milk on the floor. "I'm going to uncover your mouth. Don't torture us all with your pathetic screams. No one will hear you. And it'll just make me mad."

He leaned in with one hand still holding the soup and the other extended to remove the gag. As he did, her legs that had been curled up by her chest suddenly and violently shot out and collided with his midsection. He fell back on his rear, the bowl of soup landing on his lap.

Professor Barnes let out an angry and pained yell intermixed with various curse words. He stood up, noodles and soup dripping from his pants. His large frame towered over her. "I promise you; you'll regret that – painfully." He reached down and grabbed the glass of milk and flung its contents in her face, and then exited the room.

Professor Barnes

Sam slept restlessly that night. He'd fallen asleep in his recliner again while watching a crime show and woken up four hours later to an annoying infomercial. He'd gone to bed, but sleeping alone wasn't his thing, and so when his alarm went off at 7:00 a.m. he'd snoozed it.

Today was slated to be another round of probably boring and mostly unhelpful interviews with Walt's contacts. Sam wasn't expecting the mechanic, the schoolteacher, or the college professor to be their killer. He felt like they were shooting in the dark.

The schoolteacher ended up teaching kindergarten. The thought crossed Sam's mind how creepy it would be to have a kindergarten teacher brutally killing people across the city, but nothing she said was helpful or enlightening. She even denied knowing Walt at all. After doing their best to establish some kind of connection to Walt, they cut the teacher loose.

"Well, that was odd," Alisha said as she returned from escorting the teacher to the building exit.

"Tell me about it," Sam replied as he sat at his computer and scrolled through Walt's phone records they'd received from his cellular company. "Doesn't look like he ever called her either."

"I'm starting to think he fat fingered it or something when he entered it into his phone," Sam said.

"Or the phone number belonged to someone else before her," Alisha added. "In any case, another unhelpful interview."

"I'm going to get some peanuts from the vending machine before the mechanic arrives. Want anything," Sam asked.

"Nah I'm good. Thanks," Alisha said.

***

The mechanic arrived a few minutes early. He was Hispanic and looked to be about twenty-five. Sam immediately noticed that the mechanic looked *extremely* nervous to be in the interrogation room.

"Appreciate you coming in," Alisha said.

The mechanic replied in a hurried manner. "Yeah. No problem. Is this going to take long? I've got work."

"No, shouldn't take too long. Just have a few questions for you," Alisha said.

"You're Latina? Can we talk in Spanish," the mechanic asked. "I don't speak English too good."

"Uh, you're doing just fine, plus my Spanish is iffy. And my partner here, Detective Cross, needs to be able to understand what we're saying," Alisha said.

"Yeah, I'm mucho gringo," Sam said.

Sam's butchered "Spanish" brought a nervous laugh from the mechanic. "So, what's this about? I swear I haven't done nothing."

"We didn't say you did," Alisha replied.

"So, I can go then?" the mechanic asked.

"Look, man. Just calm down," Alisha assured. "We're not here to jam you up. I don't care whether you're here legally or not. We're not Customs and Immigration. We work in Homicide."

"Homicide? Like murders?" the mechanic asked his eyes widening.

"Yeah, murders. First question," she said as she placed Walt's picture on the table. "How do you know this man?"

"I don't. I've never seen that dude in my life," the mechanic said.

"Then why is your number in his phone with your name, Luis Garcia, next to it?" Alisha asked.

The mechanic didn't reply. "Luis, his name is Walt Emmer. How do you know Walt?" Alisha pressed.

"Is the dude dead?" Luis asked.

"Why would you ask that?" Alisha asked.

"Because you said you work in Homicide. I ain't stupid," the mechanic replied.

"No, you're not. Which is why you're going to stop avoiding my question and tell us how you know Walt," Alisha said.

Luis cursed. "Fine. He used to go with my mom back when I was in high school."

Alisha looked back at Sam and nodded. "Walt and your mom dated? What's your mom's name?" Alisha asked.

"You ain't getting me to snitch on nobody," Luis said.

"My partner can go to his computer and in five minutes have your mom's name," Alisha said, "so how about you save him the trouble and just tell us."

"It's Maria Hernandez, but you can't talk to her. She don't know nothing. She don't talk to him no more," the mechanic said.

"When was the last time you or your mom saw or spoke with Walt?" Alisha asked.

"Like eight, ten years ago. For real, lady. I don't know anything about a murder," Luis said.

Alisha could see a hint of a tattoo mostly hidden under his shirt. "Let me see your arms. Do you have any gang affiliations?"

Luis stuck out his arms. He had several tattoos. They looked amateurish, but nothing that she recognized as being associated with street gangs. "Sam," Alisha said, "You see anything you recognize?"

Sam shook his head.

"So, is that it? Can I go?" Luis asked.

"In a minute. As you guessed, Walt is dead. Murdered," Alisha said.

Luis sat up straighter and shook his head. "I didn't have anything to do with that. I never had anything against him. I was like fourteen when he and my mom were together. I swear, miss."

"Alright, Mr. Garcia. You can go," Alisha said. "Do us a favor though. Talk to your mom for us and then call if she says anything you think would be helpful. Got it?"

"Ok. I got it," Luis said as he stood and exited the room.

Back in the squad room, Sam asked, "Ok so what do you think about Luis Garcia?"

"I think he's shady, but zero chance he's the Holiday Killer," Alisha said. "Probably into drugs or some small-time gang stuff. I think I'll pass his name along to Narcotics. He seems soft. I bet they can get him to be an informant or something."

Sam laughed. "I'd take that bet. And if you want lunch, we'd better hurry. The professor who ghosted me yesterday will be here in less than an hour."

***

Sam washed down his burger with a gulp of root beer and picked up his notepad. "Ready for another exciting interview with the most uninteresting people of Oklahoma City?" Sam asked sarcastically.

"Hey, the retired Army colonel was a little bit interesting," Alisha joked.

Alisha headed for the interrogation room while Sam retrieved the professor from the police lobby. As soon as Sam saw the professor, he paused as a brief moment of recollection passed through his mind. *Where have I seen this guy before?* On second thought, the professor could pass for a hundred different generic Caucasian white-collar men in their forties. Still, Sam couldn't shake the thought that there was something familiar about this man.

Sam introduced himself. "Detective Cross. Follow me this way please."

Inside the interrogation room, Sam took the near seat, while Alisha sat in the chair at the back of the room. Sam noticed that the professor didn't look particularly nervous – in fact, he looked almost relaxed.

"Thanks for coming down today. We really appreciate it," Sam said.

"Glad to do it detectives. And my apologies for the mix-up yesterday," Professor Barnes replied.

"It happens," Sam said. "So, we just had a few questions about your relationship with Walt Emmer."

"What about Walt?" the professor asked.

"Well, first of all, how did you know him?" Sam asked.

"We go way back. Friends since college," the professor said.

"Oh yeah? Were you roommates or anything like that?" Sam asked.

"No, just same college. He once considered becoming an educator as well, but decided he didn't have the personality for it," the professor said. "Have you met Walt?"

"We have," was all Sam divulged.

"Then you know what I mean," Professor Barnes said. "An educator needs a certain personality for standing up in front of people and talking for hours. One has to be comfortable having all that attention on you while being able to speak clearly. Walt never could overcome his nervousness."

"So, when did you see him last?" Sam asked.

"It's been a couple weeks. We'd get together for drinks from time to time. Last time I saw him, I had the feeling that something was bothering him," Professor Barnes said. "But he got very quiet that evening."

"And do you remember what night that was?" Sam asked.

"No. I don't keep track of such things," the professor said.

"What do you think was bothering him?" Sam asked.

Professor Barnes straightened up in his chair and his demeanor suddenly became aggressive, his fists clenching. "I think it was actually you two. He said you lied to him and harassed him at his business. Then you arrested him and held him without any reason for hours."

"Whoa, calm down there, Professor," Sam said.

The professor did not calm down. "You accuse people of things they didn't do and drive them to desperation," he continued to rant. "You claim to 'Protect and Serve' but you neither protected nor served Walt by killing him."

"Mr. Barnes, you need to take a breath. We did not kill your friend," Alisha said.

"It might as well have been your hands that put the rope around his neck," Professor Barnes accused.

"So, I take it you know he's dead then," Sam said. "I'm truly sorry for your loss. But it had nothing to do with us."

"He was happy before you made him desperate," Professor Barnes said.

"Professor, you should know that Walt did not kill himself," Sam said.

"Is that your confession?" Professor Barnes asked.

Sam shook his head. This conversation was way off the rails. "Can I get you a bottle of water or something?" Sam asked.

"I'm fine. Let's just get this over with so I can get the stench of this place off of me," Professor Barnes said.

"Ok. So do you have any idea who would want him dead?" Sam asked.

"Besides the cops?" Professor Barnes asked indignantly.

"Yes, let's assume people not in this room," Sam said fighting the urge to roll his eyes.

"No then. Walt was a great guy," Professor Barnes said with a sullen glare.

"We've been told that by everyone who knew him. It'd really help us if you could remember the last time you saw or talked to Walt," Sam said.

"Why so you can shift the blame of his death to me?" the professor asked.

"I don't know – should we?" Sam asked.

"Preposterous," Professor Barnes said.

Alisha chimed in from behind Sam. "We're just trying to trace Walt's steps and contacts before his death. That's all. We're not blaming anyone."

"Are you the 'good cop' supposed to disarm people with siren looks and voice?" Barnes said sarcastically.

"You're not under arrest. This isn't an interrogation. We're just asking you about your friend Walt. We'd like to catch his killer," Sam said.

"Well, as far as I'm concerned, I'm looking at his killers," Professor Barnes said. "That so-called Holiday Killer's not the only one with blood on their hands."

Sam redirected the conversation back to the unanswered question. "Let me ask you again. Do you have any idea at all what day it was that Walt came to your house?"

"I suppose it was about two weeks before Christmas," Professor Barnes finally said.

"Thank you. That's helpful," Sam said. "I think that about answers all our questions for now. If you think of anything else, here's our cards. And we just might be in touch again if we believe you can be of more help."

Professor Barnes stood up and snatched the cards from Sam's outstretched hand.

A minute later back in the squad room, Sam encountered an irritated Alisha. "Let's get coffee," she demanded.

Once seated inside Sam's car, she turned to him and said, "What the heck was that Sam?"

"What do you mean," Sam deflected.

"He got to you and it showed," she said.

"I was fine. It was just a bit of a heated interview," he said.

"You all but accused him of killing Walt," Alisha said.

"And? Didn't you say the other day that one of Walt's contacts could be the Holiday Killer?" Sam asked.

"Yes, but –"

Sam cut her off. "Ok then. I was exploring that possibility. You have to admit that it was a weird interview."

"It was," Alisha agreed. "He went from smug to enraged like the flip of a switch – but that could've been from you."

"I don't get the initial smugness though," Sam said. "A long-time friend of his is dead, so why the initial air of confidence?"

"That's just how intellectuals are. Every professor I had in college was like that," Alisha said.

"I also can't shake the feeling that I've met or at least seen him before," Sam said. "What interviews do we have left for today? I'm ready to be done with them," Sam asked.

"None, unless we can line up some of the ones who never answered or called back," Alisha said.

"Wanna just hit the streets and do it the old-fashioned way – show up at their homes and places of business?" Sam asked.

"Ambush-style. I like it. Sure, I'm sick of the office," she said.

"Same. Let's grab their addresses and go," Sam said.

***

Professor Barnes walked in his front door and exclaimed loudly to his ferret, "Oh, I wish you could've seen it! I put on an Oscar-worthy performance. I had that meathead detective all flustered."

Houdini sniffed his owner's hand as the professor scooped him up. "I wonder how long it'll take those two village idiots to find the surprise I left for them."

Upstairs, Professor Barnes began to remove his dress clothes he'd worn to his interview. "Time to get my next decoration ready, Houdini. We must put it up tonight."

From his closet, he pulled out a brand new pair of blue scrubs. Over that, he donned a disposable hospital gown, including the shoe covers. He caught sight of himself in his mirror. He looked ridiculous, but it was necessary to ensure no trace was left behind.

Back downstairs, he stretched a pair of latex gloves over his hands and then assembled the rest of what he'd need for the night: a Zippo lighter, two bottles of vodka, and a length of rope. He had intended to bring a knife with him too – but after the way his captive had behaved herself, she would not receive his mercy.

***

Sam and Alisha had just three contacts left to track down – the school bus driver, the car salesman, and the driving school instructor. It was early afternoon, so with any luck, they'd be able to wrap up the final interviews before calling it a day. It was winter break from school, so hopefully the school bus driver would be home. They'd find out soon enough. Sam hit "Go" on Google Maps.

Thirty minutes later they parked out front of a trailer – not one of those run-down trailer park ones, but rather a double-wide all alone on half an acre. Alisha was just about to knock on the door, when it burst open and there stood a man with a shotgun. The smell of booze wafted out of the house.

"Whoa, whoa!" shouted Sam, while his partner yelled "Police!"

The bleary-eyed homeowner gripped his shotgun and slurred, "I don't see no police car. Whatcha doin' on my property?"

"We're detectives with the Oklahoma City Police Department. Cross and Palmetto. I need you to put down the gun. We're just here to talk," Sam said, his hand resting on the grip of his pistol.

A brief, tense standoff ensued before the man set his shotgun on the small table by the front door. "I'm still gonna need to see your badges," he said.

Both Sam and Alisha displayed their badges. Not taking his eyes off the shotgun, Sam asked, "Brian Tanner?"

"Yeah, that's me," the man replied.

"What in God's name are you doing answering the door drunk with a shotgun?" Sam asked.

"I just had a couple," the man said.

"I think you had a couple six-packs," Alisha said.

"Yeah, I dunno. No crime in drinking in my own house though," the man said.

"We didn't say there was. We just came to ask you a few questions about a case we're working on," Sam said. "We called you several times, but you never returned our calls."

"Did it ever occur to you that I didn't feel like talking? I'm going through some stuff and want to be left alone," the man said.

"I'm really sorry to hear that, and you can get back to drowning your sorrows after we ask you a few questions," Sam said.

"Fine, what's this about?" the man said, motioning for them to come inside.

As Sam entered the living room, his nostrils were again assaulted with the smell of alcohol. A couple six packs had been an understatement. At least two dozen beer cans along with a mostly empty fifth of whiskey were strewn around the living room. Brian Tanner plopped down in his recliner and popped the tab on another beer. "Ask away," he said.

"Do you know a Walt Emmer?" Sam asked.

"Yup," the man replied.

"Have you been in contact with him recently?" Sam asked.

"Nope. I was kinda hoping I'd never hear his name again, to be honest," Tanner said.

"And why's that exactly," Sam asked.

"Should I be talking to you without a lawyer?" the man asked.

"You're not under arrest. We're just talking in your home," Sam said. "Do you have a beef with Walt?"

"You could say that – used to is more like it though," Tanner said.

"Over what?" Sam asked.

"He cheated me out of a week's pay is what," Tanner said.

"How's that?" Sam asked.

"Poker game," Tanner said.

"I've played a lot of poker," Alisha chimed in. "Why do you say he cheated?"

"Because he wasn't ever any good. He was angry about losing every time. And then he comes back one week and wins big – takes me for two thousand," Tanner said. "Not just me either, but the other guys too. That cheater talked us into playing higher stakes than normal and then walked away with over four thousand that night. And then he wouldn't come back and play anymore. Just collected and ran."

"Ok, so is that what's got you on a bender then?" Sam asked.

"Nah, you can thank my ex for that," Tanner said. "That card game was two years ago and I haven't seen or heard from Walt since then."

"Gotcha. So did you know he was dead?" Sam asked.

"Dead? No, but I'm not going to shed any tears over him," Tanner said, letting out a very juicy burp.

"He was murdered," Alisha said.

"Well, boo-hoo. I'd like to shake his hand. Wish his killer would handle my ex as well," he said.

Sam glanced at Alisha. "Alright, well, we're going to go for now. Two quick questions first though. One, can we get you someone to talk to? That's an awful lot of alcohol you've consumed."

"I can handle my liquor," Tanner said. "Thanks though. What's your second question?"

"Can we take your shotgun with us back to the station? I know you have a right to have it, but we just want you to be safe until you feel better. Deal?"

Tanner sat unresponsive for a minute and then said, "Ok, fine," followed by a loud and foul belch.

"That's a good decision, Brian," Alisha said. "We'll leave you a receipt and our card, and when you sober up, just come on down and pick it up."

Five minutes later Sam and Alisha were backing out of the driveway with Tanner's now unloaded shotgun in Sam's trunk. "Well, that was – I don't even know the word for that," he said.

"I have a word for it: redneck," Alisha said with a laugh.

"I was going to disagree with you at first, but yeah, that was as stereotypical as it gets," Sam said.

"We should probably send a welfare check tomorrow to his house just to be safe," Alisha said. "Gotta make sure your relative is ok," she added with a wink.

"Funny. None of my family is like that. Actually – never mind. There's my cousin Ted…and my brother-in-law Vince," Sam admitted.

"I feel like there's got to be a country song for this," Alisha joked.

Sam rolled his eyes and punched in the next address into Google Maps. The last two interviews with the driving instructor and the car salesman turned out to be dead ends as well, and so Sam headed back to the office to turn in Brian Tanner's shotgun and head home.

Alisha called after Sam as he walked to his car, "You know, if we're right about the Holiday Killer's pattern, he's gonna kill again tonight."

Sam sighed. "I know. I hate it that there's nothing we can do about it."

New Year's Eve

When the call came in, it was nearly 6:00 a.m. It took another half hour for the fire department to finally get the blaze under control. That's when they discovered the badly charred body propped up against the fireworks stand. Still gripped in the victim's bound hands were the remains of a disco ball.

Sam and Alisha ducked under the crime scene tape. The stench of immolation made Sam gag. He covered his mouth and nose with a glove.

"First burned body?" Alisha asked.

"That obvious?" Sam replied. "Do you ever get used to that smell?"

A moment later the Fire Marshal introduced himself. "Inspector Gilliam. I'm going to go out on a limb and guess this to be your serial killer's work."

"Based on?" Sam asked.

"Well, if you take a closer look at the body," the inspector said stepping nearer and pointing, "there's remnants of ropes tying the hands and feet – so not an accident. Plus – and I'm just in the preliminaries – but if I had to guess, the body was the point of origin for the blaze. Also, an accelerant was used."

"Gasoline?" Alisha asked.

"Too early to tell. But I should be able to get you an answer by the end of the day," the Fire

Marshal said. "It also looks like the body was surrounded by fireworks that were set off to begin the fire,"

"That's certainly helpful. Thanks, we'll take the body from here," Sam said.

"Are we going to start with the assumption that this is the Holiday Killer?" Alisha asked Sam.

"It's the right date for his next murder, and there's little doubt from the way the victim was bound that it was homicide. Plus, the staging and that disco ball is definitely the kind of thing the Holiday Killer would do."

"Let's start looking for clues of his pattern then," Alisha said. "Should be something with thirty-one for New Year's Eve, right?"

"Good grief, I don't even know where to start," Sam said, looking at the charred mess and scooting a piece of burned wood aside with his foot. "I doubt there's a note like at the Christmas scene after this fire – not one that survived anyway."

Just then the coroner arrived. "We could use some help," Sam begged.

"I'll see what I can do. Though cause of death is going to have to be determined after toxicology due to obvious reasons," the coroner said.

"A fireworks stand is a strange location," Alisha said to Sam while the coroner began his work.

"Yeah, though I guess it kind of fits," Sam said. "Lots of money is spent every New Year's on fireworks."

The coroner cut in. "I can give you a preliminary identification of the deceased."

"You can? Already?" Alisha asked. "I'm impressed."

The coroner laughed. "It wasn't that hard. She has her ID right here," he said handing Alisha a partially melted, but readable plastic card with a picture on it.

"Plus One Gym. Laticia Williams," Alisha read out aloud.

"A gym employee is an odd choice for a victim," Sam said. "Doesn't fit the sales theme of the first three victims – if you don't count the reporter."

"It's not that far off base though," Alisha said. "Gym memberships are one of the biggest New Year's resolutions. January every year is unbearable at the gym with the influx of people promising themselves to get in shape."

"So, fireworks, a disco ball, and the gym – I guess it fits his pattern," Sam said. "Alright, let's get out of here. I don't think there's much else we can do here until the Fire Marshal and the coroner get us something more to go on."

"Breakfast?" Alisha asked.

Sam shot her a disgusted look. "Just coffee for me. That smell's going to take a while for me to forget."

***

An hour later, they were back in the squad room and Sam began his deep dive into their latest victim's background. Laticia Williams was in fact a

220

gym employee. She was also thirty-one years old –
their first confirmation of the patter and solid clue
that this was a Holiday Killer victim. She had been
reported missing after she failed to show up for
work three days ago.

Sam was interrupted by another officer
calling his name from across the squad room. "Hey,
Cross. You're gonna want to see this." She held up
an evidence bag.

"And what exactly is that?" Sam asked.

"It was found by the cleaning staff in the
interrogation room – looks like your killer left you a
clue in interrogation," she replied.

Sam and Alisha rushed over. Inside the
evidence bag was a small square piece of cardstock
with the initials "HK" written on it. Taped to the
back side was a snippet of rope.

"When was this found?" Sam demanded.

"Last night, I believe," she said.

"What's her cleaning schedule? Is it every
night or…" Sam asked.

"I know it's not every night. Maybe every
other night? She said she would be back tomorrow
if anyone had any questions about it," the officer
said.

"Get her in here ASAP," Sam ordered.
"This can't wait until her next shift."

"Copy that, Detective," the officer said.

"I told you so," Alisha gloated. "You asked
if we expected the Holiday Killer to just waltz in
here – and turns out he did just that."

"Or she. We interviewed both men and
women," Sam said. "Who all came in again? We

can't count the ones we tracked down. They had to have come in."

"Let's see," Alisha said, counting on her fingers. "The retired colonel. Then the dentist. The pet store employee, the schoolteacher, the college professor, the mechanic – I feel like I'm missing one."

Sam mentally counted off their interviews as well. "The barista also," he concluded.

"You're right. But if the cleaning lady only comes every other day, then it could be any of them," Alisha moaned. "We've got to know where she found it."

The officer popped her head back in and said that the cleaning lady would be there in half an hour.

A red banner on the squad room TV caught Sam's attention. He quickly turned up the volume. "Breaking News! Holiday Killer claims fifth victim. Last night around 12:30 a.m. an explosion and fire were reported at a firework's stand at the corner of Broadway and Northwest Tenth Street, just off of the two thirty-five. Fire departments responded and after extinguishing the blaze, a badly burned body was discovered."

"How on earth are they connecting this to the Holiday Killer when we're just now connecting the dots?" Sam asked.

"Probably a lucky guess – if they call it for the Holiday Killer and then they're wrong, they just issue a retraction," Alisha said.

"Well, they did get something wrong," Sam said. "This is the killer's sixth victim because you have to count Walt."

"Oh, while you were digging into our victim, I looked up the 911 call from the fire last night. Call came in at exactly 12:31 a.m. Caller was anonymous. What're the chances it was placed by the Holiday Killer himself?"

"There should be a recording of the call. I'll go get it," Sam said.

"And I'm going to run the card from interrogation down to the lab. Maybe, just maybe, we'll get lucky and they'll find a fingerprint on the tape or get DNA from the rope," Alisha said. "And perhaps if I bat my eyes at the cute lab tech, he'll put a rush on it."

"Female empowerment at its finest," Sam joked.

***

Professor Barnes finished scrubbing the room where he'd held the gym worker hostage and then headed for the shower. *It's not all just fun and games, this killing business*, the professor said to himself. *It's hard work staying one step ahead of the cops.* "But we have to finish our mission," he said aloud to Houdini who was curled up on the end of his bed. "We have to make sure they get the message – even if it costs us everything. We have to do it for *her*."

After his shower, Professor Barnes drove to a secluded wooded area a half hour from his house. There, after making sure no one was around, he doused the tarp and the rest of the rope in the last of the vodka and lit it on fire. He stayed until it was mostly consumed. He then gathered the fragments and drove to a gas station on his way home where he tossed them in the trash. He sure missed Walt's incinerator.

***

"So, of Walt's contacts who came in," Sam said, laying out DMV pictures of those they'd interviewed, "Who are you liking for our killer?"

"I just feel like this is the work of a man," Alisha said. "There have been female serial killers in the past like Wuornos, but she didn't move her victims' bodies, because let's face it, that's a lot for a woman to handle. The Thanksgiving victim was over two hundred fifty pounds. And for the Christmas murders, there were two victims to move. I just don't see a woman doing all that – especially not the ones we interviewed. None of them looked physically capable."

"We'll of course check the women, but basically that leaves us with four male possibilities," Sam said, separating the pictures of the retired colonel, the mechanic, the professor, and the dentist from the rest of the pile.

"Hey, Cross," called the female cop from earlier, "Maria Lopez, the cleaning lady is here."

"Perfect. Thanks!" Sam said.

In the interrogation room sat a very nervous-looking Hispanic lady in her fifties. Alisha took the lead. "Thank you Miss Lopez for coming down on your day off. You're absolutely not in trouble. You

224

did a very good job finding that clue for us. So, you can relax.”

"Ok, thank you ma’am,” she replied in a thick Spanish accent.

"You can just call me Alisha. We just have a few questions and then you can go.”

"Ok, what can I do to help?” Miss Lopez asked.

"Well, tell us first where you found it?” Alisha asked.

"I was wiping down this table like I do every time I clean in here,” Miss Lopez explained. She moved her hand in a circular motion, miming cleaning the table. "When I went to clean under the edge of the table, it just fell down on the floor.”

"So, it was on the side of the table you’re sitting on?” Alisha clarified.

"Yes, Alisha. I think it was more towards the right side,” she said.

"And how often do you clean in here? Every shift?” Alisha asked.

"No, not every shift. I only clean every other day, and I have a checklist for different days in different parts of the building,” she said. "I just clean in here once a week.”

"Oh, ok. And then what did you do when it fell on the floor?” Alisha asked.

"I picked it up and when I saw the letters – I’ve seen about the Holiday Killer on the news, so I thought it might be related to the investigation – I then gave it to one of the officers,” Miss Lopez said.

"You had gloves on then when you picked it up?" Alisha asked.

"Yes ma'am, I always wear them when I'm cleaning," she said.

"Ok that's great. Thank you for being so thorough. You very well may have found a clue to break the case. Thank you for coming in," Alisha said.

After Miss Lopez left, Sam said, "Well, that doesn't get us any closer to narrowing down the timeframe. We'll have to go back and watch the footage from the interviews to see if we can spot someone planting it."

"For sure, but that feels too easy," Alisha said. "

"Now who's the pessimist?" Sam joked. "Sometimes these narcissistic killers can't help themselves and slip up. I mean, that's what we've been waiting for – for him to make a mistake."

"I know. I'm hopeful. It's just that the Holiday Killer has been so careful up to this point," Alisha said.

Sam pointed again at the four pictures of the male suspects. "So, any one of these just jump out at you as more likely? My money's on the dentist or the retired colonel."

"To be honest, none of them struck me as a killer," Alisha said. "The mechanic was shady as all get out, but I think it was drug or gang related, not because he's the killer. The dentist was so nice – but that's also how psychopaths are. They've got that superficial charm. But I dunno. And I'm not feeling the colonel. He seemed legitimately surprised at the news of Walt's murder and offered to help. Which leaves me with the professor."

"Yeah the professor was all kinds of weird," Sam said, "But he seemed to me just to be angry about his friend's death. And you know how a lot of elites in education are – many of them are anarchists and hate cops. So maybe it was just going to be a bad interview no matter what. I was thinking the dentist because he was in good physical shape and would have some knowledge of the medical stuff to carve up the bodies. Or the colonel – even being an engineer, all those years in the military, I'm sure he learned how to kill."

They were interrupted by a phone call. It was the Fire Marshal. "I've got some results for you," he said. "First, the victim's body, as I suspected, was in fact the point of origin for the blaze. The accelerant used was an unusual one. The body was doused in alcohol – vodka if I had to guess."

"That *is* unusual," Sam replied.

"Yeah, that's a new one for me. Not unheard of. But usually, you find it with drunks who passed out while smoking, not in homicides," the Fire Marshal said. "Oh, and the body had fireworks packed around it, and then the whole blaze was started with a Zippo lighter."

"So just to make sure I got everything," Sam said reading from his notepad, "Body doused in vodka, fireworks arranged around her, and then the killer tossed a Zippo and walked away?"

"That does seem to be the story, based upon the evidence," the Fire Marshal confirmed.

"One question," Sam said, "and this might sound strange, but I promise you it's important. We believe the Holiday Killer works in numerical patterns. We're looking for the numbers twelve and thirty-one. We already confirmed our victim was thirty-one years old and the 911 call reporting the fire came in at 12:31 a.m. Did you find anything else that would line up with those two numbers? I don't know – thirty-one fireworks or twelve smoke bombs – something like that?"

"I didn't, but I'll have another look," the Fire Marshal said.

"Thanks, and don't share that numbers thing with anyone," Sam said. "We've not revealed it to the public, so we don't want the killer to know that we've caught on to his pattern."

"Copy that, I'll let you know if I find anything else," said the Fire Marshal and ended the call.

"Now we just need a cause of death," Alisha said. "Hope that coroner gets back to us soon."

"I think we can assume she burned to death right?" Sam asked.

"Not necessarily," Alisha replied. "It could've been a gunshot, stabbing, lethal injection or anything prior to the fire. And even in a fire, most people don't die of their burns, but of smoke inhalation."

"Ok fine," Sam said. "Before we dive into the interrogation tapes, let's eat. I'm starving after skipping breakfast."

"You queue the first one up, and I'll run out for burgers," Alisha offered.

"Sounds good to me. With root beer please," said Sam.

Sam queued up the first video of the retired Army colonel and then called the dispatch where the 911 call for the fire was received and requested the audio be sent over. He had just finished sending an e-mail to the coroner asking for cause of death when Alisha returned.

"Ready for some riveting theater?" Sam asked.

Alisha handed Sam his hamburger and said, "Let's do it."

***

Three hours later, they admitted defeat. Despite multiple pauses, rewinds, and zoom-ins, neither of them could spot any of the four male suspects tape the card with the rope to the underside of the table. They all touched the table at various times, but none of them seemed to be planting anything. And then just to be thorough they watched the interviews from the ladies as well. Still nothing.

Alisha groaned. "Why does our killer have to be so smooth? We just need one slip up – just one mistake to catch him."

"Unfortunately, that's a fact he's no doubt well aware of," Sam said. "He will though. They all eventually get caught."

"Ok, statistically that's not true. But I applaud your positivity for a change, so I'll just agree with you," Alisha said.

Sam's phone rang. It was the coroner finally. "Hey, Detective Cross. This is just preliminary, but toxicology indicates that your victim was alive when the fire was set. Her death was most likely the result of carbon monoxide poisoning with the secondary cause being extreme burns all over her body."

"Thanks," Sam said. "What an awful way to go. I'll keep an eye out for your final report."

Sam hung up the phone. "Well, we have all the pieces to the puzzle it would seem," he said to Alisha. "She was burned to death, posed in front of a fireworks stand, doused in vodka, while holding a disco ball."

"Yeah, I think that pretty much confirms it's the Holiday Killer," Alisha agreed. "Nobody else kills like our killer. And can't be a copycat because our victim is thirty-one."

"I do wonder what other clues the Holiday Killer might have left us that didn't survive the fire," Sam said.

"Yeah, well, unless the Fire Marshal uncovers something, this might be all we got," Alisha said. "But it's very on brand for him – and we can finally say it's a 'him' I think. But we're no closer to catching him than before."

"Unless he slipped up with the card left in the interrogation room," Sam said.

"I guess we'll find out soon enough once the lab calls back," Alisha said. "I'm exhausted from watching the tapes – from everything really. I'm done for today."

"Same. And try to relax tonight. Get to sleep early. Don't let the case consume you," Sam said.

"Same. And try to relax tonight. Get to sleep early. Don't let the case consume you," Sam said.

The Taskforce

"Cross, Palmetto, my office," barked Captain Durant.

Sam glanced at Alisha and mouthed, "What now?"

She shrugged.

"Update. Lay out the full picture. Where you're at. What progress you're making. Leads. Theories. Everything," Durant ordered.

For the next ten minutes Sam and Alisha brought Captain Durant up to speed. "We're waiting on the final report from both the Fire Marshal and the coroner."

"So, what you're really saying you're no closer to catching him than at any point before?" Captain Durant said.

"No, that's not at all what we said," Alisha retorted. "We actually have a suspect pool finally – four men with direct links to Walt Emmer. Plus, he's getting more brazen, leaving that clue in the interrogation room. He's going to slip up soon. We're closing in."

"I've given you time – nearly three months to be exact," Captain Durant said. "We have six murder victims, and the news stations questioning the abilities of our department. And frankly I don't blame them. You *might* have a lead. That's not very promising. You have suspects. Good. But you had one before and he was murdered."

"But, Captain, one of these four men put that card with the rope in the interrogation room. One of them has to be the killer," Sam said.

"Ok, then we tail them. Bring them back in and try to break them," Captain Durant said.

"No offense, but how did that work out for Walt?" Alisha said. "Whichever three of the four suspects aren't the killer could be jeopardized by an increased attention. I'd like to not have that guilt on my conscience."

"And how does your conscience feel about the lady who was burned alive two days ago?" Captain Durant said.

"That's not on us," Sam said. "We're doing our best, and the full responsibility of each death is on the killer, not on us. C'mon, Captain, you know that."

"You're lecturing me now, Detective?" Captain Durant said. "We owe it to the citizens of this city and any future victims of the Holiday Killer to do not just 'our best' but everything we can to bring him down."

"Captain, if we tail our suspects too closely and the killer catches on, he may just go underground – stop killing until the heat is off," Alisha said.

"I'd settle for that at this point," Captain Durant said. "I'd like to go one major holiday without anyone dying in a horrific, headline-inducing death. And that's why I've made up my mind to assemble a multi-agency taskforce."

"So, you've lost confidence in us?" Sam asked.

"You didn't seem to mind interagency cooperation last year when you needed rescuing," Captain Durant said. "The FBI will be sending a team, and so will the U.S. Marshals. You are not off the case. They are not taking over. It remains our department's jurisdiction. But you need help."

Sam didn't know what to say. It was difficult to counter his boss' argument – and he wasn't even sure why he bristled at the idea of a taskforce. Sure, it could be a pain in the neck dealing with different personalities and procedural variations between agencies. But Sam couldn't think of one downside to more help – as long as they didn't spook the killer.

"Roger that, boss." Sam said.

"The state lab will begin by reanalyzing all the evidence so far. Doesn't hurt to have a second set of eyes go over everything with a fine tooth comb. The FBI will look at your suspects and try to determine a profile and the probability of which one is most likely to be the killer. And the Marshal Service will conduct limited surveillance – they're probably the best there is at tracking people. Any questions?"

"Just wondering what we're supposed to be doing since you gave away all our work," Alisha said.

"Watch your tone, Palmetto. And I can put you on leave if you feel you have nothing to contribute to this case," Captain Durant said.

"We're good. Thanks boss," Sam said. He put his hand on Alisha's back and pushed her towards the door before she could say anything else.

"Dang, Alisha," Sam said once they were outside. "Ever hear the phrase, 'don't poke the bear?' Because Durant is the bear. And you were definitely poking."

"And? Maybe I need a Miami vacation," Alisha retorted.

"There's time for that after we catch the Holiday Killer," Sam said. "Trust me, we still have plenty to do. Starting with figuring out when he's most likely to strike again. Last night while I was bored at home, I made a list of the major U.S. holidays."

"That sounds like a relaxing evening. I thought you said, 'don't let the case consume you,' and here you are spending your evening alone working on the case," Alisha chided. "I took a long bath with some wine and went to bed early like you suggested."

"Well, good for you. Anyway, do you want to go over the list or just bicker about who is the most responsible adult?" Sam asked.

"I'd win that argument, but sure let's see what you got," Alisha said.

"Ok, so it seems he focuses only on major national holidays because he skipped Hanukkah," Sam said. "So, we can skip Martin Luther King Day on January 17. Which would make Valentine's Day the next one on February 14," Sam said.

"Bleh," Alisha said. "I don't want to even imagine what he'd do to ruin Valentine's Day."

"And then after that," Sam continued, "if we haven't caught him by then, we can probably skip Presidents Day, and then there's Easter on April 4," Sam said. "And then, if it gets that far, Mother's Day is May 9, and Memorial Day on May 31."

"I would like to hope this doesn't drag out that long," Alisha said. "But at least we know we have some time between now and Valentine's Day – almost a month and a half. Maybe that taskforce will find something helpful between now and then."

***

The next day was a raucous whirlwind of introductions as over a dozen agents from State, the FBI, and the U.S. Marshal Service – all of whose names Sam promptly forgot – descended upon their squad room. The FBI claimed the conference room, while the Marshals took over the break room. The forensic group from State headed for the lab and evidence storage.

Later that afternoon, Captain Durant assembled everyone into the conference room where Sam nervously stumbled through a briefing he'd spent yesterday preparing, complete with crime scene photos, victim profiles, those they'd interviewed, and the ones they'd eliminated, focusing on the four male suspects that they'd narrowed the list down to. Sam also shared details of the Holiday Killer's numerical patterns: thirty-one on Halloween, twenty-six for Thanksgiving, twenty-five for Christmas, and thirty-one again for New Year's Eve.

One of the Marshals raised his hand and introduced himself, "Deputy Lerner. What's the connection with the staged suicide victim?"

"So that's Walt Emmer," Sam replied. "He was seen on the security camera footage buying the twenty-six boxes of stuffing used in the Thanksgiving murder. At first we thought he was the killer. But after he turned up dead, we concluded he was an accomplice or associate, and his murder was to silence him. That's where we got the suspect list – they're all personal contacts of Walt. From there we narrowed it down to the four men we interviewed in our interrogation room based upon one of them leaving a clue taped to the underside of the table."

"Thanks for the clarification," Deputy Lerner said.

Sam continued the briefing. "We've been able to find no connection whatsoever between any of the victims. They appear to have been chosen at random, though intentionally selected for their occupation and age – the occupation related to either the particular holiday or the sales industry in general, and then their age to match the pattern for that particular date."

An FBI agent raised his hand next. "Agent Wilmer. Have you worked up a motive?"

Sam nodded. "I was just getting there. My partner Detective Palmetto and I believe that the Holiday Killer has a vendetta against the over-commercialization of holidays. That he believes holidays are being ruined by all of the sales and shopping that's been injected into them."

"And what do you base that on," the Agent asked.

"Largely on a letter the killer mailed to both me and one of the news stations," Sam said as he clicked to the briefing slide with the letter. He paused a couple minutes before continuing to give everyone a chance to read the letter. "So, we believe that his goal is to expose the ills of holiday commercialization and 'rescue' the holidays from what he sees as predatory sellers."

"Interesting," chimed in another Agent. "I was not expecting this to be ideologically based. Most serial killers murder for personal gratification."

"Reminds me of the Unabomber case," said one of the Marshals, sparking a smug grin from Alicia.

The next half hour was spent with more questions and then the different agency members talking amongst themselves. At noon Captain Durant ordered everyone to break for lunch and reconvene in an hour. Sam could not have been happier. Being the center of attention was not his thing.

"Phew," said Sam as he plopped in the front seat of his car.

"Yeah, I feel you," Alisha said.

"You barely had to talk," Sam said with a chuckle. "I was the one in the hot seat."

"You did great," she said. "A natural."

"You'll never find me in a classroom or at the academy giving lectures," Sam said. "There's a reason I went for detective instead of sergeant. Briefings just aren't my thing."

"If you say so," she said as they pulled into the Mexican place they'd chosen for lunch.

***

It was another late night at work by the time Sam finished answering the multitude of questions from the taskforce. Sam had been working so many back-to-back twelve to fourteen hour days that it suddenly occurred to him he had no clue what day of the week it was. He looked at his phone. It was January second. He ran his hand over his face. It was his wife's birthday. He gunned it out of the parking lot and headed for the Walmart on the way to his in-law's house to grab a gift.

Sam speed-walked through the store looking for something to get for his wife that wouldn't break the bank. A familiar and friendly voice called to him. "Can I help you find something, sir?" Sam turned to see Tiffany's smile. He had forgotten that this was the Walmart she worked at.

"Hey, Tiffany!" Sam said. "It's so good to see you. I was just trying to find a gift for my wife. It's her birthday today."

"Cutting it kinda close, aren't you?" Tiffany teased.

"To be honest, I just remembered. Work has been a nightmare with this case," Sam said.

"I'd love to catch up and hear all I've missed," Tiffany said.

"I'd take any help I could get at this point. And you did discover the pattern," he said in a lower voice, as if some eavesdropping person might hear a sensitive part of the investigation.

"Yeah, I did, didn't I?" Tiffany said. "Classes are about to start up again. Maybe we can get together one day next week?"

Sam glanced at his watch. He really wanted to get to his wife before it got much later. "Sure. I'll call you. I really should find something and get going though. It's late."

"Can I suggest something?" Tiffany asked.

"By all means do," Sam said with a tinge of desperation in his voice.

Tiffany laughed. "Fluffy pajama pants, something that smells nice – lotion, perfume, a bath bomb, and some ice cream."

"You're a life saver. Can you direct me to the right sections so I don't wander around here aimlessly?" Sam asked.

"Absolutely. Follow me," Tiffany said.

Fifteen minutes later, Sam was back in his car and speeding the rest of the way to his in-laws. He hadn't spoken much to Jennifer over the last week since Christmas. She could be terribly stubborn when she was upset or worried for their boys. In this case, it was both.

Sam pulled into the driveway only to find his in-laws' car gone and the house empty. They'd probably gone out for his wife's birthday. Sam let out a defeated sigh and looked upwards. *God, can't I please catch a break*? he prayed wordlessly. He waited a few minutes and then carried the Walmart sacks to the porch and set them neatly on the welcome mat. It was below freezing so at least the ice cream should survive.

He found a blank piece of paper in his glovebox and wrote a quick note on it. *Happy Birthday, my love. Sorry I missed you. Hope you had a great birthday and enjoy the gifts. I love you and miss you. Please come home soon.*

My Professor

Despite having the taskforce combing through every speck of evidence and lead, the next week passed with no real developments in the case. The forensics lab confirmed that the rope snippet on the back of the card left in the interrogation room was cut from the same spool of rope used to tie up the New Year's Eve victim. But as Sam feared, there were no identifying traces left behind.

The FBI team developed a possible criminal profile: educated, detail oriented, and someone with strong beliefs. That basically eliminated the mechanic suspect – but that was no real surprise to Sam or Alisha. They didn't peg him for the killer anyway. That left the dentist, the professor, and the retired army colonel. It would take a more intense deep dive into those three to narrow it down further. Sam's money was still on the dentist, and Alisha leaned towards the professor. Both of them agreed that the army colonel was probably too old at fifty-two to dive into a life of being a serial killer – though him being retired meant he had time on his hands.

That Friday, Sam met with Tiffany for lunch. "You know, I had a hard time convincing Mike that this meeting was ok. He can be very protective," Tiffany said.

"Mike – that's the boyfriend. I think that's the first time you've told me his name," Sam said.

"Yeah, well – I didn't want you digging into his background," she said. "He's really very sweet. But put yourself in his shoes. I'm meeting with a man he's never met, and he's not allowed to come along, and I can't tell him why I'm coming."

"Yeah, I guess that does sound suspicious," Sam agreed. "It is good to catch up with you. And thanks again for the help with my wife's present."

"Of course. Did she like it?" Tiffany asked.

"I think so. She wasn't home when I brought it, so I couldn't judge her reaction," Sam said.

"Oh – haven't you seen her since? Is something the matter?" Tiffany asked.

Sam let out a sigh. "It's just the case. The killer mailed a letter to our house and she freaked out."

"He did what!" exclaimed Tiffany. She looked around and then lowered her voice. "Well, duh, she freaked out. I would too. So, is she in hiding?"

"No, she's just staying at her parents. She said she'd come home when I catch the killer," Sam replied.

"Oh – I'm sorry. I mean, I kinda get it. But still, that's gotta be tough. I know you're doing your best," Tiffany said.

"I'd like to think so. My boss doesn't though. He brought in a team of investigators from other agencies to assist on the case," Sam said.

"That can't hurt right? The more eyes the better. Isn't that why I'm having lunch with you today – so I can add my intuition?" Tiffany asked.

"I suppose so. I just don't warm up to people very well," Sam said.

"So I remember," she said with a wink.

"Let's order and then I'll bring you up to speed," Sam said.

Tiffany ordered a salad. "I've got to keep my figure for Mike," she said. Sam ordered the chicken strips.

"I can't believe it's been so long since we talked," Tiffany said.

"Yeah, it was Thanksgiving I think," Sam said.

"No, remember, it was that one time I ran into you on my lunch break – and you were about to go spy on the 'person of interest.' What ever came of that?" Tiffany asked.

"Well, he was not who we thought he was, and we basically got him killed," Sam said.

"Oh, my goodness!" Tiffany said. "You must've felt awful."

"Yeah, we think he was still somehow connected to the real killer, so it's not like he was completely innocent. But us putting heat on him made him disposable," Sam said. "In the end though, it led us to some really solid suspects. I honestly think we're closer than ever before."

"That's great. So lay it all on me. Let me see if there's anything I can help you figure out," Tiffany said. "Oh, what were the patterns for the other victims?"

"So, Christmas was the numbers twelve and twenty-five," Sam said.

"Makes sense," Tiffany mused.

"And then New Year's was thirty-one again, like Halloween," Sam said.

"Odd that he'd repeat a number, but I guess that's just the way the calendar falls," Tiffany said. "Who do you have for suspects?"

"They are all contacts of the guy we thought was the killer who ended up getting murdered," Sam said. "We had like ten to start out with, but we think we have it narrowed down to just three."

"Hey that's good! Who are the three guys?" Tiffany asked.

"Shoot! I should've brought their pictures to see if you recognized any of them – like maybe one of them came into where you work," Sam said. "Anyway, one's a dentist, one's a retired army officer, and the last one is a college professor."

"That's quite the diverse group there. No offense to all of the wonderful, heroic veterans of our nation," Tiffany said, "but former military sounds the most likely to me."

Sam nodded. "Yeah, I'd agree with you if it wasn't for his size and age. He was not a big guy and he is fifty-two. I just can't picture him lugging around those bodies. Just sounds like a lot for an older guy on the smaller side."

"Well, then I'd go with the dentist – it's in the medical field and the Holiday Killer has carved up quite a few bodies," Tiffany said.

"Exactly. He's the one I'm leaning towards," Sam said. "My partner though is on 'team professor.' But to be fair, the profile that the FBI put together could fit any of them."

"Well, what's the professor like?" Tiffany asked.

"He was what you'd expect from a college professor, really," Sam said. "Self-important, elitist."

Tiffany laughed, "Yeah, sounds like every one of my professors – well except Miss Thatcher. She's super sweet and approachable. But the rest of them – don't you dare question their ideas or try to approach them outside class," she added with an eye roll. "What's the professor teach?"

"Math or something," Sam said.

Something about saying it out loud caused claxon alarms to go off in Sam's head. Numbers. Patterns. Holiday commercialization. *How did I miss it? It was that ridiculous interview. He got under my skin and I never asked the important questions.*

Tiffany broke Sam's internal monologue. "What is it, Sam? You look like you're worlds away?"

"I'm actually blind," Sam said.

"What, Sam! Math?" Tiffany asked.

"It should've been so obvious," Sam said. "Hang on a sec." He pulled out his phone and started scrolling rapidly through his camera roll. "Here," he said, handing his phone to Tiffany. "Read the letter he sent me."

Tiffany's brow furrowed as she read, but then her eyes widened and her face went pale. "Oh. My. God!" she exclaimed, her hand shaking so bad she could barely hold the phone. "This sounds like my economics professor."

"You're not serious," Sam said.

"I think I'm going to be sick," Tiffany said. "That letter sounds plucked straight out of one of Professor Barnes' lectures from a few weeks ago."

"Did you say, 'Barnes' is your professor's name?" Sam asked.

"Yeah, Harold Barnes," Tiffany confirmed. "And it sounds *exactly* like him. I even got into it with him. He was railing against the predatory – oh what did he call it? 'Economic enslavement of the consumer to the detriment of the sacredness of the holiday,' or some garbage."

"Are you sure?" Sam asked.

"Ninety-nine percent sure. In one lecture right before Christmas he even talked about the new consumer debt that would be taken on by Americans this Christmas. And see," she said pointing at one line of the letter, "how he says, 'am I right?' – Professor Barnes says that *all the time*."

Sam sat in stunned silence. This was the break they'd been looking for, but how were they supposed to prove it without a shred of corroborating physical evidence.

"Sam! Say something," Tiffany urged.

"I'm thinking," Sam replied.

"But you've got to arrest him! My professor is the Holiday Killer," Tiffany said.

"I've gotta go," Sam said. "I need to get with my partner and the taskforce."

Sam dropped a couple twenty dollar bills on the table to cover lunch and the tip and started to walk away when he turned back to the Tiffany. "Actually, come with me."

"I don't know if I can. I told Mike I'd be gone only like an hour. He's expecting me at his place in a few minutes," Tiffany said.

"Well, call him and tell him you're going to be late," Sam ordered.

"Ok," Tiffany said as she dialed his number.

Sam listened to the one-sided phone conversation. "Babe, I'm sorry. I can't make it over. No, everything is fine. It's just that the meeting with my friend has turned into something big. No, I can't explain. Mike, don't be like that. I told you he's just an old friend. He just needs me to help him with something. I'm really sorry. I promise. Please don't be mad. No, I don't know how long…"

Sam took the phone from Tiffany mid-sentence. "Sir, this is Detective Sam Cross of the Oklahoma City Police Department. Tiffany Gunn is helping us with an investigation. No, you cannot know what this is about. It's police confidential, and I've instructed her to not discuss details of the case with anyone. She is not in trouble in any way. No, I will not explain. I'm sorry if you don't like that answer. She'll call you when she leaves the police station. Thank you, goodbye." Sam hung up the phone.

Tiffany's mouth hung open. "Sam! You hung up on my boyfriend!"

"We need to go," Sam said. "If your boyfriend is the sweet guy you say he is, then he'll get over it."

It was a twenty minute drive back to the station with Tiffany following. Once inside, Sam quickly assembled the taskforce in the conference room and then escorted in a timid Tiffany.

"Miss Gunn?" Captain Durant asked, confused. "Sam, what is she doing here?"

"I'll explain," Sam said.

For the next several minutes, Sam recounted the contents of the Holiday Killer letter. Tiffany occasionally chimed in with her experiences from being in Professor Barnes' economics class.

When Sam finished speaking, Captain Durant let out a long sigh. "Miss Gunn, you sure do have a way of getting yourself wrapped up in the most incredible series of events."

"And who is this young lady again," asked one of the FBI Agents.

"She's a friend whom I worked with on a case in the past," was all Sam revealed. "She's got good instincts."

The agent looked to Captain Durant for approval and he nodded.

"The problem," said one of the techs from State, "is making this case rock solid. If it's Professor Barnes – and I agree it sounds very much like it could be – he's left zero forensic evidence to verify that fact. We have no DNA or prints from the Holiday Killer."

"We could tail him," said one of the Marshals, "but unless we catch him kidnapping his next victim or in some other way incriminating himself, it's going to be tough making a case before a Grand Jury."

Alisha had said nothing during the entire conversation, but now she spoke up. "We have an insider now though," she said pointing at Tiffany.

"Excuse me?" asked Tiffany. "I am not taking his class again. No way."

"It's perfect though," Alisha urged. "He doesn't suspect you. So, you can continue to surveil him for us as a student in his class."

"Sam?" Tiffany pleaded turning towards him.

"You obviously don't have to," he said. "But you shouldn't be in any danger."

"It's creepy though. I don't want to sit in a room with a guy who kills people in his spare time," Tiffany moaned.

"Just consider it," Sam said. "If you do, great. If not, that's understandable."

The meeting ended a few minutes later and Sam walked Tiffany out to her car. "Sam, I don't want to take his class. I just can't – not after everything last year. I need a normal, stress-free life."

"I get it," Sam said. "It's your decision."

Tiffany looked at her watch. "Ugh, what am I going to tell Mike?"

"Tell him nothing. I already handled it," Sam said.

"He's just going to be annoyed," Tiffany said. "Oh, I know. I'll take a selfie here at the police station so he knows I was really here." She held up her phone, trying a couple different angles before snapping a picture.

"It's your first relationship, so I get that you're worried. But trust me. If he's 'the one' he'll understand and get over it," Sam said. "Plus, when this is all over, you can tell him everything."

Sam waved bye. Alisha was waiting for him back inside. "Is she going to do it?"

"I don't know. She's been through a lot and she's finally found normalcy for the first time in her life," Sam said. "I'm not going to pressure her. But she's tough as nails. She might just come around."

"While you were outside, the taskforce put together a preliminary plan. Since the Holiday Killer has a history of sending taunting letters, they're going to get a warrant to intercept all his outgoing mail," Alisha said.

"Ha! Hope they don't draw Judge Lawson again," Sam said.

"You don't think she'd cave to the feds?" Alisha asked.

"Judge Lawson, from my experience, doesn't give a hoot who you are. If she doesn't want to play ball, you're not getting a warrant from her," Sam said.

"I still can't believe we finally know who the killer is," Alisha said. "We've just got to nail him now before he kills again on Valentine's Day."

The Raid

The taskforce managed to get the warrant for Professor Barnes' mail despite going before Judge Lawson again. They also, to Sam's surprise, got a warrant to raid his house. Sam had tried to talk them out of it, but Captain Durant had overruled him. The raid would take place in two days.

"This is a bad idea," Sam complained. "He's too meticulous. It's not like there's just going to be body parts lying around his house."

"I mean – maybe. Just look at Dahmer," Alisha countered.

"But Dahmer was insane. And a cannibal. I don't think our professor is either," Sam said.

"Maybe he keeps souvenirs. That's a common feature of many serial killers," Alisha said.

"You mean like trophies from his victims?" Sam asked.

"Yeah, some serial killers keep their victims' ID's, or take photographs of them, or take a piece of jewelry. I think the Dating Game Killer did all three, if I remember correctly," she said.

"You weren't kidding when you said you did a deep dive on serial killers a while back. I still don't know though," Sam said. "None of that seems to fit the Holiday Killer's profile. I don't get the sense that he gets any pleasure from killing his victims or that he relives the experience in the same way that a sadistic serial killer does. It's all about his deranged ideological message he's trying to send."

"Well either way, we've got the best of the best going in. Surely they'll find a clue – a hair, some DNA. He can't be *that* good can he?" Alisha asked.

Sam shot her a sideways glance as if to express his doubts.

***

"We've got a lot of work to do, Houdini," Professor Barnes said. "These last couple weeks were busy, busy, busy. I've barely had time to prepare for my class."

Houdini's nose twitched as the microwave beeped indicating that the professor's ramen was done. Professor Barnes set a bowl of food on the floor next to him for his pet as he settled in at his desk to eat and look over course material for the upcoming semester.

"I would've never thought running a one-man campaign against the entire corporate world would be so time consuming. But nothing of value and lasting change happens without dedication and hard work. Thankfully, we have time before we have to start preparing for our next decoration. I want to pick someone special this time. But for now, we have to focus on our day-job."

His house still had a lingering smell of disinfectant from the company that had come yesterday to deep-clean the house and steam the carpet. Tomorrow he'd take his car to be detailed – necessary expenses for carrying out his work.

***

Professor Barnes was not home when the taskforce conducted their raid two days later. The warrant they had secured was the "no-knock" type, so the professor would need a new front door after they left.

The taskforce searched the house for nearly three hours dusting for prints, swabbing surfaces, and snapping hundreds of pictures. Sam and Alisha seized various items – kitchen knives, stationary, ink pens, and sections of rope from the garage, hoping to find something to connect the professor to one or more of the murders. Under the couch hid a ferret, but despite Sam's best efforts, he could not coax the creature out.

A member of the forensic team from State walked over to Sam. "This place has been cleaned. And I don't mean your typical housecleaning or even a homeowner doing a thorough cleanup. The carpets have been steam cleaned within the last couple days and a professional cleaning company has been over this house like you might get done before putting your house up for sale."

"That honestly doesn't surprise me one bit," Sam said with a sigh. "Every crime scene we've investigated has been just like that – zero prints, zero DNA. Not a thing to go on."

"I wasn't trying to sound pessimistic," the tech said. "If there's something here, we'll find it. I was just letting you know."

"Yeah, thanks," Sam said.

"Hey, look," called Alisha. Sam turned to see her holding the ferret. "Isn't he a cutie? Kinda creepy to think of a serial killer having such a cute pet."

Finally, the taskforce called it quits. Professor Barnes had no basement or attic, so the search for evidence was pretty straightforward. Sam and Alisha carried their evidence bags out to the police van.

"Wonder where our esteemed professor is?" Sam asked as he walked to his car.

Alisha joined him at the passenger side. "There's no way he had a heads-up was there? Though it is kind of a coincidence that he cleans his house right before we come and then he's not here."

"Yeah, I don't like it. But you're right. There's no way we've got a leak. It was literally just us on the taskforce that knew we were hitting today," Sam said. "He just got a lucky break."

Sam took one last look back at Professor Barnes' house. A half dozen boards had been crudely nailed over his broken front door and yellow police tape was zigzagged across it. Sam took a small pleasure in imagining the professor's annoyance at coming home to find his door looking like that.

Sam looked over at Alisha in the passenger seat. The nose of Professor Barnes' ferret poked out of her jacket. "What is that?" Sam asked.

"It's a ferret, Sam," she replied.

"Right, but why do *you* have it?" Sam asked.

"Because I couldn't leave the poor thing there. The front door is busted and what if it escaped and got eaten by hawk or froze to death out here?" Alisha said. "I left him a note saying he could retrieve his pet by coming to the police station."

"You love to poke the bear, don't you?" Sam said.

"Yup. Maybe we'll see Professor Barnes today after all," she replied.

***

Professor Barnes arrived home shortly after noon. He entered through his garage as usual, so he did not see his wrecked front door. But what he did immediately notice was that his usually meticulous garage was not in the same condition he'd left it.

He quickly exited his vehicle and looked around. Someone had rummaged through his garage, and the empty pegs on the tool bench indicated that items had been taken. Professor Barnes reached back under the seat of his car and pulled out a handgun. Cautiously he pushed open his garage door leading into the kitchen. On the table was a stack of paperwork. Professor Barnes glanced around and then looked at the papers. He let out a curse.

"Houdini!" he called. "Who's been here? Where are you?"

Nearly every surface of his kitchen and dining room were covered with black and pink fingerprint powder. Professor Barnes set his gun on the counter and began walking through the house looking for his pet. *Probably terrified and in hiding*, he thought.

He then noticed his broken front door. *They better not have let him escape or someone will die!* "Houdini!" he called again. "It's ok. It's just me. The bad men are gone." After a thorough searching of the house, under the couch, the bed, the closet – all of Houdini's favorite hiding places, Professor Barnes returned to the kitchen. In the stack of paperwork, he found a note.

Mr. Barnes, due to the possibility of your ferret slipping through your drafty front door, I have taken him with me for his own safety. You may retrieve your pet at your convenience at the Oklahoma City Police Department, Station 7. Request either Detective Palmetto or Cross.

Professor Barnes cursed again. "My drafty front door," he spat. "The door you destroyed!" *Better keep a cool head, Harold.* He reached for his phone and called his lawyer.

He looked around his living room once again at the mess left behind by the detectives. He had to clean things up before Houdini came home – and fix his broken door. His lawyer promised to take care of everything and have Houdini home by nightfall. Now to call a handyman for the door.

***

"Cross," called a voice. Sam looked up from his desk. It was almost time to head home.

"What's up?" said Sam to the detective who'd hailed him.

"Your favorite kind of person is here," the detective said.

Sam made a quizzical look.

"A lawyer here to see you," the detective said with a chuckle.

Blah. I hate lawyers, Sam thought. "You coming?" Sam asked Alisha.

"Can't," she said pointing at the box next to her desk with Professor Barnes' ferret in it. "I'm on babysitting duty."

"Convenient," said Sam as he made his way alone towards the lobby.

The lawyer was easy to spot in his crisp white shirt, red tie, and testy disposition. As soon as Sam entered the lobby, the lawyer walked briskly towards him.

"Where can we talk?" said the lawyer curtly.

"This way. I have just the place," Sam said, leading him to the interrogation room.

The lawyer shot him a hostile glare at the sight of the interrogation room. "Sorry," Sam said. "All other space is currently occupied. What can I do for you today?"

"You can stop harassing my client, Harold Barnes. You can release all seized items from his home. And you can return his beloved pet ferret," the lawyer said.

"I'm sorry if he feels harassed," Sam replied with a very not sorry tone. "Everything was in order with the search warrant, as I'm sure you've seen for yourself. Mr. Barnes was not home, so we made entry to execute the warrant."

The lawyer placed a stack of paperwork on the desk. "You will not talk to or approach my client again. If you have any questions for him or need to communicate anything to him, it will be done exclusively through my law office. I would also like to see the probable cause affidavit you presented to the judge to justify the search warrant."

"You're welcome to request that, but it was partially based upon a confidential informant, so there's a good chance the judge sealed it," Sam replied.

"We'll see," the lawyer said. "You took several personal items from my client's home. I would like to retrieve those today."

"You know that's not possible," Sam said. He'd played this lawyer strong-arm game before. "It will be released as it's been cleared through evidence – if it's cleared. You realize your client is suspected of a very serious set of crimes."

"And what might those crimes be?" the lawyer asked.

"We believe Mr. Barnes is the serial killer the media refers to as the Holiday Killer," Sam said.

The lawyer let out a laugh. "Harold? Not a chance. Ridiculous accusation. You're wasting your time. This is nothing more than police overreach – a fishing expedition." He tapped his finger aggressively on the paperwork he'd put on the table. "You had better leave my client alone. Understood."

"Anything else I can do for you? I'm sure you're a busy man," Sam said.

"I'll be picking up my client's pet if you'll show me the way," the lawyer said standing up. "Unless you think a ferret is a serial killer too."

Pranked

"I see what you mean," said Agent Verner, the lead FBI agent on the taskforce as he looked over the final report from the forensics team. "This dude is crazy careful."

The forensic team had completed their analysis of everything collected from the raid on Professor Barnes' house. Not one single shred of useable evidence had turned up. No fingerprints except the professor's. No foreign DNA – except the ferret's. The stationary they'd seized didn't match the letters. The knives didn't match the murder victims' wounds. And none of the rope they'd tested matched the burn victim.

"We're not all hick cops here in Oklahoma, you know," Sam said. "We're perfectly capable of doing good police work. It's just unreal how well the Holiday Killer has covered up his tracks."

"I've seen soap dirtier than that guy's house," Agent Verner said.

"Every crime scene was like that too. In a *Walmart* of all places the shelves were wiped clean," Sam said.

"So where does this leave us?" Captain Durant asked. Nobody responded. "Anyone? C'mon, we've got the best people in law enforcement here in this room and we're getting outsmarted by a glorified math teacher."

"And we're one hundred percent sure it's him?" asked one of the Marshals. "I'm just saying, we're taking the word of a college freshman and a hunch. We don't have one piece of physical evidence tying him to the killings."

"Ok, if we go that route," Alisha chimed in, "Whose house do you suggest we raid? The retired Army colonel in his fifties? The dentist? Good luck getting a warrant for either of those. We have even less pointing to them."

"Palmetto," began Captain Durant.

"Let me finish," she continued. "I said this like two months ago. Just because we haven't nailed this guy doesn't mean we're doing bad police work here. Past serial killers have often gone decades without being caught." Turning to the FBI agent, Alisha added, "Didn't it take you guys like forty-five years to catch Samuel Little during which time he killed sixty victims? Were you guys just terrible at your jobs or was it just that the bad guy was good at what he did and you had to wait to catch a break."

"Nobody is saying we screwed up," the Marshal said.

"Ok. Well, I'm just saying, we're busting our butts here and we might just have to wait until he makes a mistake," Alisha said. "We've got time to figure this out. Valentine's Day is still over a month away, so it's not like we have to solve the case today."

"Thank you for that, Detective. Let's get back on track though," Captain Durant said trying to steer the conversation back to a happy note. "Anyone got an idea?"

"I say we tail him. We're already monitoring his mail, so let's see if he slips up," the Marshal said. "We lay low and just watch. He's probably expecting us to make another move of some kind. Let's let him make the first move."

"It's not much, but it's something," Captain Durant said. "Alright, go to lunch."

***

Alisha's phone rang at 4:04 the next morning. She reached for it and knocked it on the floor. She grumbled a curse word and dropped to her hands and knees to retrieve it from where it'd bounced under the edge of the bed. "Mmhmm, hello?" she mumbled sleepily.

Only heavy breathing answered her. "Hello? Who's this?" she repeated as she sat on the edge of the bed. More heavy breathing.

"Sam? Is that you? Did you accidentally call me in your sleep?" she said.

This time the response was a soft, sinister-sounding chuckle, and then the line went dead.

"I'm going to kill him," Alisha said. She checked the caller ID. It was a blocked number. Alisha dialed Sam's phone.

"Yeah," he answered a couple rings later. "What is it? Did something happen?"

"Did you just call me?" Alisha asked.

"No, you're calling me," Sam responded.

"No, before this. Just like a minute ago," Alisha said.

"No. I was out like a lightbulb," Sam said.

"Sorry. Someone prank called me or something. Goodnight," she said and ended the call.

***

The next night, again at 4:04 a.m. Alisha was awakened by her phone. She fumbled for it, managing to pick it up without knocking it on the floor this time. "Yes, hello?" she said barely conscious.

Heavy breathing was the caller's reply. "You've got to be kidding me," Alisha said. "What are you, like twelve? I'm surprised you're not saying, 'go catch your refrigerator because it's running'," she said. "Stop calling me and get a life."

Alisha was about to end the call when once again the caller gave a low chuckle and hung up.

She dialed Sam again. "What? Yes. Hello?" was Sam's sleepy reply.

"That jerk called again," she said.

"You woke me up at four in the morning to tell me your secret admirer called you again?" Sam said.

"Very funny. Never mind. I'll see you at work," she said and hung up. She checked her call log. Blocked number again.

***

"You look rough," Sam said as Alisha walked in.

"Thanks, that's what every girl wants to hear," she retorted.

"Who's your lover-boy? Can't get enough of you so he has to call you at four in the morning?" Sam continued to joke.

"You know, I couldn't fall asleep again for like an hour after that," Alisha said.

"Really? I fell right back asleep," Sam said.

"I hate you. That middle school jokester better not call back again tonight," she said.

***

For the third night in a row, Alisha's phone rang at 4:04 a.m. She picked it up and looked at the caller ID. Blocked number. She groaned and hit the ignore button and slammed it back down.

Fifteen seconds later it rang again. "Unbelievable," she moaned as she answered it.

Heavy breathing.

"Hey, you little punk," Alisha threatened. "I bet you didn't know that I'm a cop. I swear I will trace this call and show up on your doorstep. And I'll take your phone out of your pudgy little fingers and march you to your parents."

More heavy breathing. "Alright. I'm not kidding. If you ever call this number again, you'll be sorry. And don't give me that fake creepy chuckle. Bye."

She hung up the phone and almost immediately it rang again. She answered, but before she could speak the same familiar sinister chuckle emanated from her phone speaker. Then the call ended.

This is harassment, Alisha thought angrily as flopped back on her pillow. *I'm going to get you, you little twerp.*

***

"Did your secret admirer call you again," Sam joked.

"Shut up. Yes, at 4:04 in the morning for the third night in a row. I swear to God I'm tracing his number," Alisha said as she sat in her desk chair. "If he thinks blocking his number will keep me from finding him..."

"Maye it's the cute guy from forensics you're always flirting with," Sam laughed.

"You're not funny. At all. Probably some bored junior higher," Alisha said.

"You should've recorded the call," Sam said.

"Well, you know, at 4:00 a.m., I'm not exactly thinking that straight," she replied.

"Wait, did you say it was at four or 4:04?" Sam asked.

Alisha scrolled back through her calls. "Weird. Yeah, all three calls came in at exactly four past four."

"That's oddly specific," Sam said. "Makes me wonder if it's not a recorded thing – like some kind of spam bot."

"No, because last night – well this morning technically, I hung up before he could do his weird chuckle thing, and he immediately called me back just to chuckle and then hung up. It's a person," Alisha said.

"Definitely weird. Let me know what you come up with that trace," Sam said.

"Almost there," Alisha said. "Gotcha!" Her triumph was however quickly dashed. "Ugh, it's a burner phone. No registration. Probably bought at a gas station or something for cash."

"Well, I think we can probably rule out a kid," Sam said. "Burner phones are bit sophisticated for middle schoolers."

"That's even worse. My 'secret admirer' just turned into a pervert stalker," Alisha said.

"You can try recording him like I suggested. Set your alarm for 4:00 so you're ready by 4:04," Sam said.

Alisha rolled her eyes. "I do not have time for this garbage. I'm supposed to be trying to catch a serial killer and instead I'm trying to catch a prankster."

"Hold up. What if…" Sam began.

"No. Don't say it. That creepy professor better not be calling me," Alisha said as she looked at her phone in disgust. "4:04 doesn't even fit the pattern. The next major holiday Valentine's Day is on February fourteenth, so if it was 2:14 a.m. then I'd agree with you."

"Just a sec," Sam said as he dug through his desk drawer for the list he'd made. "Look, he said pointing to the second entry on the list. "Easter is on April fourth – four and four."

Alisha shook her head in disbelief.

"What does he say? Anything identifying?" Sam asked.

"He says *nothing*," Alisha said. "He just breathes in the phone all heavy and then does this lame attempt at a creepy chuckle before hanging up."

"So, are we going to take it as fact that it's the Holiday Killer?" Sam asked. "And should we tell the taskforce?"

"We don't *know* that it's him. Let me record him tonight and you can hear it tomorrow," Alisha said. "But if it's him, then why's he skipping Valentine's Day?"

"Maybe he's not. Maybe he's just getting a head start on Easter." Sam said. "But yeah, it won't change anything to hold off one day. Record him and let's see."

***

Alisha's alarm went off at 3:59 a.m. That gave her five minutes to wake up and prepare. She'd tested the record function on her phone with Sam before leaving work. Everything was ready to go. At 4:03, she hit the record button and waited.

Exactly on schedule, her phone rang at 4:04 a.m. Alisha answered. "Hey, good of you to call again. Love a guy who's dependable," she said.

Heavy breathing answered her. She waited. More heavy breathing. "Is there anything you'd like to say – something you want me to know? Do you want something?" she asked.

More heavy breathing. "You know, this is getting old. How am I supposed to pursue your advances if you won't tell me who you are?"

The voice responded with the sinister chuckle and then the line went dead. Alisha left the recording running in case he called back, but after another minute, she ended and saved the recording. She resisted the urge to listen to it again immediately, but instead went back to sleep. It would wait for the office.

***

Later that morning, Alisha marched in the squad room and placed her phone on Sam's desk. "I got it."

"Nice. Let's hear this lover-boy of yours," Sam said.

Alisha smacked him on the arm. "Just play it – but not too loud. The rest of the squad room doesn't need to hear it."

Sam listened to it twice. "Not exactly an Oscars winning performance, but decent for 4:04 a.m.," Sam joked. "Yeah I'd definitely say that's a grown man not a kid or teen. What do you want to do? Take it to the taskforce or see if he gets bored of you."

Alisha massaged her face and sighed. "Tell the taskforce I guess. If we weren't chasing a serial killer and if it wasn't for the oddly specific timing of the calls, I'd just change my number."

"I think you can still block a caller even if the caller ID is blocked," Sam said. He turned to his computer and typed a quick Google search. "Yeah. It's super simple."

Alisha hesitated, biting her lip as she thought. "Just pass it to the taskforce. If it's him, I'd be mad at myself for passing on a potential clue. Maybe forensics can isolate a background noise from the call that will produce something helpful."

Alisha emailed the audio recording to Sam who threw it on a thumb drive and shared it with the taskforce. They agreed, while not much to go on, the timing of it seemed coincidental. The team would look into it further.

"I guess I'm going to have to start going to bed earlier from now on since my stalker plans on getting me up at four every morning from now on," Alisha said as they walked out of the briefing room.

"You should keep recording them each night. Maybe he'll finally say something or a new background noise will turn up," Sam said. Alisha nodded.

The calls continued night after night with Alisha recording and bringing the audio to the taskforce. If this was him, he was executing his usual caution. Forensics failed each day to pull anything useful from the recordings. Days ticked by, ever closer to his next kill – but no closer to catching the Holiday Killer.

Bait

Tiffany's heart pounded and her eyes darted anxiously from side to side as she walked into Economics 102. Despite her initial refusal, after an anguished internal debate, she'd decided to take the second semester of Professor Barnes' class. Sam had been right – her professor had no reason to suspect her of anything. She was just another student in his class. And all she had to do was take the class and record the lectures. Nothing to worry about.

She found a seat towards the back of the class and did her best to be as invisible as possible. She was fifteen minutes early – nervousness had caused her to rush out of her dorm room long before she normally would. Now she felt like a cornered animal alone in his classroom.

Professor Barnes walked in. He glanced her way as he set his lecture notebook on the podium. "Hey, always love a student who's excited to learn," he said to her.

Tiffany laughed uneasily and mumbled that she'd read the clock wrong. She stared at the black screen of her phone pretending to be busy.

Professor Barnes walked towards her. He stopped about a desk-length in front of her. "I appreciate your input in the class last semester, Miss Gunn. Most freshmen students are either too shy to speak up or say too much as if they know more than their professor."

Tiffany nodded. Her voice cracked as she muttered "Thanks."

"What are you majoring in, Miss Gunn?" Professor ,Barnes asked. "You strike me as having the makings of a lawyer or a reporter."

"Maybe," was all Tiffany said.

Professor Barnes continued to pry. "So, you haven't settled on a major yet?"

"Not yet. I was thinking about some kind of police work – maybe in the forensics lab or something," Tiffany replied. She hadn't meant to say that much, but his ominous presence made it hard to think clearly.

The voices of two girls talking as they entered the class rescued her as Professor Barnes turned to greet them. Tiffany exhaled her pent up breath and fought back the sudden urge to cry. This was going to be a long semester. Tiffany agreed with Jennifer: Sam needed to hurry up and put this guy away.

My Valentine

For the rest of January and the first week leading up to Valentine's Day, the taskforce made virtually no advancements. Alisha continued to record her early morning "conversations" with her prank caller, yet nothing revealed his identity. Though he had switched burner phones at the beginning of February. The FBI intercepted every piece of outgoing and incoming mail from Professor Barnes' home plus his mailbox at the university, but it was all normal stuff – bills and junk mail. The Marshals tracked the professor's every move, but it was boringly routine: to the college, the store, the pet store – what you'd expect from an ordinary citizen.

Frustrations were running higher than ever. The feds were under pressure from their headquarters to break the case due to the mounting cost of their deployment to the city. Their daily meetings in the conference room with Captain Durant grew increasingly tense as he demanded new ideas and strategies to catch the Holiday Killer. Valentine's Day was only five days away. If they were right about the pattern, then the next murder would be on Saturday.

The amount of time that had passed without a murder had at least put Sam's wife more at ease. She'd also expressed that she felt much safer, now that Sam and Alisha had a taskforce working with them. They even had their first date in months planned for Friday night. It wasn't technically Valentine's Day, but the idea was to get their celebration in before the Holiday Killer struck again and Sam's schedule became once more unpredictable.

Valentine's Day was particularly special to the Crosses because it was the day that Sam had proposed to Jennifer. Things were still strained by Jennifer's continued stay at her folks' house along with their boys, but they were working through it – and they knew it was only temporary.

The week flew by and Friday arrived. At three that afternoon, Sam said goodbye to Alisha to get home and cleaned up for his date at six.

"Hope you have a great time. Maybe my lover-boy will call me early," she joked.

On his way home, Sam stopped at the grocery store to pick out a bouquet for his wife. He selected her favorite: red roses with baby's breath. Since it was Valentine's Day, Sam forked over the extra twenty dollars to have the florist arrange it in an upgraded frosted vase.

Their dinner reservation was at their favorite restaurant, a fancy Italian place in Bricktown. And Sam had an extra surprise up his sleeve – he'd rented a red Corvette. He glanced at his watch: 3:50. He had to hurry home. The Corvette would arrive at 4:30.

Sam had barely walked through his front door when the doorbell rang. It was the car rental company. "Mr. Cross?"

"Yes, that's me," Sam said stepping outside. The car in the driveway was not a Corvette – it was a red Ferrari.

"Our sincerest apologies," the rental agent said. "The last customer who rented the Corvette you reserved had a minor collision last night and we weren't able to get the repairs completed in time, so we've upgraded you to one of our exotic cars: a Ferrari 458."

Sam laughed. "That's quite the upgrade. I don't think my wife will complain at all."

"Great to hear. We just need you to sign the paperwork and do the walk-around with us and you'll be on your way," the rental agent said cheerfully.

Sam chuckled. *Jennifer's going to get a kick out of this*, he thought. Memories of his first case that now seemed so long ago came flooding back. It of course would be *that* red car. After wrapping things up with the rental agent, Sam took a hurried shower, splashed on some cologne, and then returned to the Ferrari. He chuckled as he sunk into the leather seats. He couldn't wait to see the look on Jennifer's face.

As much as Sam wanted to, he resisted the urge to floor the gas pedal and feel what two hundred and two miles per hour felt like. He did speed – slightly, because how can you drive a Ferrari and not speed a little. A few minutes later he pulled along the curb outside his in-laws' house. For some reason Sam felt jittery like it was a decade prior and he was picking up Jennifer for their first date.

Inside the house, his boys were bouncing around hyper, yelling and cheering "Daddy's here! Daddy's here!" And then when Jennifer came out – "Wow!" Sam exclaimed. She must've gone shopping. He really had married a goddess.

"Stop ogling me and let's go," Jennifer said, embarrassed by Sam's reaction.

Back outside, it was Jennifer's turn to be in awe. "What is *that*, Sam?" she asked, her hand covering her mouth as she stared at the Ferrari.

"Oh, just our new car," Sam said with a wink.

"Funny. Not unless you're one of those dirty cops working with the mob or something," she said. "Where'd you get it? And really Sam, a red Ferrari?" she added as she recalled the events of Sam's first case.

"Just gotta treat my girl right," Sam said. "It was actually supposed to be a Corvette, but there was a mix-up and this was what they brought. I was just as surprised as you are. Now come on, let's go. We've got to be in Bricktown by six."

Parking was a nightmare, but since it was a special occasion, Sam splurged for valet. As Jennifer walked ahead, Sam whispered to the driver to bring the flowers he'd stashed in the trunk back inside and give them to the hostess. Soon they were seated and ordering drinks and an appetizer to share. A moment later the hostess caught Sam's attention and motioned for him.

Sam walked over. "Yes?"

"Which bouquet did you want brought to the table first – the one you brought with you just now or the one you had delivered earlier this afternoon?" she asked.

Sam's forehead wrinkled in confusion. "I don't know what you're talking about. I didn't send any flowers – just the ones I brought with me a few minutes ago."

Now it was the waiter's turn to be confused. "Just a moment," she said. The hostess reappeared with two vases: the one he'd brought in the Ferrari and then a second one he'd never seen.

"That one's ours," Sam said pointing at the one he'd purchased at the store earlier that afternoon. "That other one's not mine."

"Sorry for the confusion then. This other one was delivered around 1:00 p.m. and the delivery guy said it was for a Jennifer Cross from a Sam Cross. That's you, right?" the hostess asked.

"I'm Sam Cross but I didn't send those, so I don't know why the delivery guy would say that," he said. "Can I see the receipt or the order slip?"

"The delivery guy didn't leave one, but there is a greeting card attached," the hostess said.

Just then Jennifer walked up. She'd apparently gotten tired of the mystique. "Awww, Sam! Those are so beautiful," she exclaimed at the sight of the two bouquets. "You didn't have to – and two of them!"

Sam smiled awkwardly. The surprise had kind of been ruined. And he still didn't know why there were *two* of them. "It's fine, we'll just take them both," Sam whispered to the hostess.

Sam carried one and the hostess the other back to their table. Sam tried to arrange them on the table so that his bouquet was near her and the imposter one was nearest him. It worked for about thirty seconds before Jennifer said, "Oh look, this one's got a card."

Sam had no idea what the card would say, but he prayed it was something generic like "I love you, happy Valentine's Day" since he still didn't know where the extra bouquet had come from. Sam watched as her smile changed to a look of horror.

"What is it?" Sam asked, reaching for the card.

She opened her mouth to speak but nothing came out. Finally, she exclaimed, "Is this your idea of a sick joke? After everything?"

"What is it? No," Sam sputtered. "What does it say? Give me the card."

She threw the card at him, hitting him in the face with it. He picked up the card from the floor under the table where it'd fallen and read it.

"Hey. It's me. I don't have a Valentine this year. Will you be mine? XOXO your secret admirer. HK"

Jennifer stared at him indignantly, waiting for an answer.

"Babe, this isn't from me," Sam began but she cut him off.

"That's worse, Sam," she said in a disgusted tone.

"I can explain – sort of. I'm just as confused as you are. I brought this bouquet," he said pointing at the one he'd purchased, "with me tonight in the trunk of the Ferrari. And I had the valet driver give it to the hostess while we were being seated. I have no clue where this other bouquet came from or that it even existed until she brought it out."

"The envelope has my name," his wife said.

"The hostess said that it arrived from some delivery company about one this afternoon. Apparently the delivery driver said it was from me," Sam tried to explain. "So that's why I was up there at the counter. She was asking which bouquet I wanted brought to the table first, and I was trying to tell her that I'd never seen this other one before. And that's when you walked up. If you would've just stayed seated, I would've handled it and avoided all of this."

"So, this is my fault now?" Jennifer said, raising her eyebrows accusingly.

"Babe, no," Sam said exasperated. "I'm just saying, I was trying to handle it without you knowing – *I* didn't even know. I'm sorry you're upset. I'm trying not to ruin our night."

"I want them off the table," she demanded.

Sam sighed. "They're evidence now. I can't just toss them. Or the card. Give me a sec. I'll call Alisha and see if she doesn't mind running over here and pick them up."

Their waiter returned with their appetizer, fried calamari. "Oh, those are beautiful," he said, pointing at the flowers. "And two. You're a lucky lady." Sam smiled weakly and asked the waiter to come back later to take their food order.

He was able to get ahold of his partner and she agreed to swing by and pick up the card and the flowers and get whatever information she could from the restaurant about the delivery company so they could track it down later.

Sam and Jennifer sat in silence, neither looking at each other, their untouched calamari growing cold. Sam reached across the table and took his wife's hand. "Let's not let this ruin our night. He doesn't deserve that victory. Let's enjoy ourselves. We've got an *awesome* car, a hotel reservation. You love this restaurant. Let's make it a good night. We need this."

Jennifer sighed and somewhat relaxed her stiffened posture and took a bite of the appetizer. "It's decent calamari," she said. "And I'm sorry too. I know none of this was your fault. Thank you. But I'll feel a lot better once it's only your flowers sitting here."

"I know. Thank you. I'm hungry. Let's order," Sam said.

Alisha arrived a few minutes later and was gone with the imposter flowers by the time Sam and Jennifer's meal arrived. The food was fantastic. Sam ordered lasagna and Jennifer got a pizza, and they split a slice of cheesecake for dessert along with coffee.

Jennifer said that it seemed a shame to waste such a nice car so they went for a drive. "Oklahoma may not be Paris, but it sure is pretty once you get out in the country," she said. Sam spotted a park and pulled in, and moments later they were making out in the car like newlyweds. Just after eleven, they arrived at their hotel, a five star historic spot in downtown.

***

It was nearly noon when Sam arrived at the office. "About time," Alisha said. "Must've been a really good night."

"It was. Thanks to you saving it," Sam said. "You really did rescue my evening. I owe you one. But yeah – I had to check out of the hotel, drop my wife off, and then return the rental car."

"I think you already owed me one, but ok. And I'm glad you had a good evening. Anyway, I did some digging already into those flowers," Alisha said.

"Nice. What'd you find?" Sam asked.

"Well, as per our usual luck – or lack thereof, I didn't uncover much. But at least I have what I think the whole story is," Alisha said. "The order was placed online – which of course normally would be a good thing because then there's an electronic trail we can trace."

"I feel like there's a 'but' coming," Sam said.

"*But*," continued Alisha, "the purchase was made with a gift card instead of a credit card. And the gift card purchase, as best as I can tell was not purchased through any online retailer, but probably bought in person at a store – and I'm guessing with cash."

Sam tossed his pen on the desk. "He thinks of everything doesn't he?"

"How'd he know you were going to be eating down at Bricktown?" Alisha asked.

Sam hadn't thought of that. He'd been too focused on his date with Jennifer to really analyze

281

the situation last night. All Sam could come up with was, "I don't know."

"I think your wife's right to be scared. He knows where you live. He apparently knows where you eat. You need to be careful," Alisha said.

"He knows your phone number," Sam said. "You need to be careful too."

***

Saturday came and went, but the Holiday Killer did not kill. The early morning phone calls to Alisha also stopped. Instead, in a stack of mail she found a Valentine's Day card that read:

"Hello, beautiful. Happy Valentine's Day. I hope you enjoyed our nightly calls. I sure did. Now enjoy the Holiday off – this one's on me. See you soon. XOXO HK."

Next to the Holiday Killer's initials was an Easter egg sticker and a cross – an indication of when, and perhaps where, he planned to strike next.

Easter

The case had been at a virtual standstill now for over a month, and though Easter was less than a week away, the taskforce began to dwindle. Without new evidence to analyze, the lab techs from State all left, and both the FBI and the Marshals thinned their teams down to just one agent each. Captain Durant had also suspended the daily conference room gatherings – there was nothing to discuss.

"Knowing who the perp is and not being able to march him in cuffs to a jail cell is literally the most frustrating thing ever," Alisha complained. "It's got to be torture for Tiffany, staring every day into the face of a serial killer."

"She's safe though," Sam said. "Oh, hey, what if Tiffany could get him to laugh in class and record it? Then we could compare it to the recordings."

"One, I don't think that was his real laugh in the phone calls – he was trying to make it sound sinister; and two, I don't know if 'laugh analysis' is a thing," Alisha said.

"Work with me here," Sam said. "I'm just trying to come up with ideas. Easter is this Sunday and I'm pretty sure we can expect him to strike again this Saturday."

"I still can't figure out why he skipped Valentine's Day," Alisha said.

"Only thing I can come up with is either he doesn't hate the holiday or he wanted to lay low since our raid created a lot of heat," Sam said.

"Yeah, I don't know," Alisha said. "People spend a lot of money on Valentine's Day – something he seems to hate."

"Maybe he doesn't have a problem with people spending money. Tiffany said in his lectures he calls himself a capitalist," Sam said.

"So, you're saying he felt like the spending on Valentine's Day is justified – buying chocolate, cards, and flowers is ok, but buying Christmas Gifts isn't? I'm not sure I'm buying it," Alisha said.

"Except that buying chocolate, cards, and flowers for someone you love is literally the point of Valentine's Day," Sam countered. "It's hard to argue that buying a new TV is the point of Christmas."

"Ok, but if you go that route, then why do the first murder on Halloween? Aren't costumes, carved pumpkins, and spooky decorations the point of Halloween?" Alisha asked.

"You know, I'm just spit-balling here," Sam said rolling his eyes. "It's called a theory."

"We could both be right after all," Alisha said. "I mean, we're up against a psychopath here – can't expect it to all make sense."

"Any theories for his next crime scene? An Easter egg hunt?" Sam asked.

"I mean, we're just speculating at this point," Alisha said. "But who's to say he doesn't just hit a store again? The first two were in stores. The third one was at a mall – even if it was an abandoned one. The fireworks stand, though it was outside, was still a store of sorts. He seems to target retail locations."

Sam breathed an exasperated sigh. "I keep having this pipe dream that we're going to figure out his next move and stop him first, but literally everywhere sells Easter candy, so it's just impossible to guess."

"And it doesn't help that the taskforce all but disbanded right before he's going to kill again," Alisha said. "Honestly, why did they even come if they're not going to see it through?"

"Government red tape and dollars – and egos," Sam said. "They thought they were going to swoop in here three months ago and solve the case for us 'hick cops.' But now that it's gone on longer than they thought, they've moved on to – whatever else it is that the government does."

"I just feel bad for whoever's going to die this week," Alisha said dejectedly.

"I try not to think about it – but yeah, me too," Sam said.

***

At 4:04 that morning the calls returned. Alisha groaned. "Not again."

Instead of the heavy breathing over the phone like before, this time she heard the scratchy static sound of an old record player being turned on. Alisha winced as a moment later music blared through her phone. It was an upbeat vintage country song about Easter that she had heard before as a child but couldn't recall the name of. For the next minute, the old country singer crooned about the Easter bunny and candy for kids before abruptly stopping in the middle of the song after a lyric about Easter being on its way. Then the line went dead.

Alisha tapped Sam's name in her phone and waited for him to pick up.

After a couple rings Sam's groggy voice finally answered. "Yeah, what is it."

"He called again," Alisha said.

"Ok, just bring the recording to the office. Bye," Sam said.

"Don't dismiss me," Alisha said. "And I don't have a recording because I wasn't expecting him to call. It was different this time though."

"Different how?" Sam said.

"He played some old Easter bunny song and then hung up," Alisha said.

"At least it wasn't creepy breathing and sinister laughing," Sam said. "Did he call at 4:04 again?"

"Yup. I guess there goes my chances of sleep this week," Alisha said.

"I'm very sorry about that. But at least one of us should get some sleep," Sam said.

"That doesn't sound very sympathetic?" Alisha said annoyed.

"Sorry, that's the best I can muster at four a.m. Wanna meet me for breakfast at seven before heading in?" Sam offered.

"Sure. I'll text you a place. Bye." Alisha hung up. She attempted to fall back asleep, but that cursed song was stuck in her head. After a half hour of tossing and turning, she stumbled to the shower.

***

The phone calls continued every day through Friday with Alisha recording each one. They were all the same: the Easter song that Sam also now hated with a passion, but nothing more. Tomorrow the Holiday Killer would kill again.

Or at least he was supposed to. The remaining Marshal had called to report that the professor had boarded a plane to Dallas that morning. And his return ticket wasn't until Sunday night.

"What's his move here?" Alisha asked. "Is he skipping Easter after all, despite ruining my sleep for the entire week?"

"It doesn't make any sense. How is he supposed to kill again if he's not here? You think something personal came up and he had to go out of town at the last minute?" Sam suggested.

"Are we sure he even boarded the flight?" Alisha asked.

"The airlines confirmed he did," Sam said. "He's definitely not in town."

"I hate this guy with every fiber of my being," Alisha said. "For all we know, this trip was planned all along and the phone calls were just a red herring and a mind game to torment me. Is it too much to ask for him to – I dunno – get hit by a semi while crossing the street?"

Sam laughed. "That would definitely solve the problem. I may or may not have laid awake a few nights myself wishing for his untimely demise."

"You know, this is how characters like Batman get created," Alisha said. "Honest police work can't bring the criminals down so some vigilante's gotta do it."

"What're the chances he's going to kill in Dallas instead?" Sam said. "You think we should notify police there?"

After a moment's pause Alisha said, "I don't think so. It would be a dead giveaway that it's him if he flew there and then a Holiday Killer crime scene showed up."

"True, true. Seems like we're back to the ol' 'wait and see,' I suppose," Sam said.

***

Alisha's phone rang early the next morning. The caller ID, instead of reading "caller unknown" as she expected, displayed her partner's name.

"Seriously, Sam. You're as bad as *he* is. Can't I sleep in just one day?" Alisha asked.

"It's almost nine. I'd call that sleeping in. Still, sorry to wake you, but he's killed again," Sam said.

"In Dallas?" Alisha asked as she sat up in bed.

"No back here," Sam said.

Alisha cursed. "How? Where?" she asked as she grabbed her clothes.

"The northwest side again. You know that huge church near NW 50th street – Triumph Community Church?" Sam asked.

"Yeah, I know the area. See you there as soon as I grab coffee," she said.

***

Professor Barnes pulled back into his hotel just after 8:00 a.m. He hated road trips, but the around-the-clock surveillance of his house made it necessary.

"No worthy cause is without sacrifices and costs," he said to Houdini, whom he'd brought with him in a small travel carrier designed for a cat. The plane ticket, plus hotel and rental car, in addition to the supplies for his "decoration" made this his most expensive murder to date.

It had also created a logistical headache – almost tempting the professor to call it off. But Easter was too important to skip. In addition to the six hour roundtrip drive, being out of town also meant he had to do everything last minute, including acquiring his victim. But, in the end, he was able to pull it off.

"We'll be home soon, Houdini. And then just one more decoration, and we can return to normal life," he said. He took a photo out of his wallet. It was badly wrinkled and faded with age. He ran his index finger over the woman's face. "I think she'd be proud of the way we've honored her memory."

***

Sam arrived at the crime scene before his partner. The church lawn was marked off with police tape, and several officers stood as guards to keep any sightseers, reporters, or distraught church members from disturbing the scene. Speaking of church members, if Sam had to guess, the upset bearded gentleman on his cell phone standing near the church doors was probably the pastor.

Alisha pulled up and Sam exited his car and joined her. "Looks to be over there on the church lawn," Sam said.

"Are those the kinds of great deductions that made you get promoted to detective?" Alisha asked sarcastically.

Sam snorted. "Funny. Good morning to you too."

Alisha continued her ribbing. "If only there was some yellow crime scene tape to give it away so we knew which way to go. Odd he would do it at a church though. I'm not religious, but even I know that Easter is literally a church holiday."

Before he could answer, they reached the crime scene. In the middle of the church lawn was a gazebo decorated in pastel streamers. A big sign dangled from the gazebo roof that read "Easter Egg Hunt and Airplane Flyover."

Sam changed directions and instead walked towards the gentlemen he'd seen earlier on the phone. "Excuse me, sir. Do you work here?"

"Yes, I'm the Lead Pastor, Tom Crist," the pastor replied.

"Can you tell me about the Easter event you had planned for tomorrow?" Sam asked.

"*Have* planned. Not had," the pastor replied.

"You're still going through with it?" Alicia asked.

The pastor nodded. "I'm not going to let the Devil keep us from going forward as planned for the most important Christian day of the year."

"Were you expecting a pretty big turnout?" Alisha asked.

"Yes. We run several thousand on a regular Sunday and we are planning for as many as ten thousand, including guests, for tomorrow's service," the pastor said.

"And I suppose that having a huge Easter egg hunt plus an airplane flying over dropping candy helps bring them in?" Alisha asked.

"Jesus brings them in," the pastor retorted. "We consider some candy and a little harmless Easter fun just tools God uses."

"Were y'all planning on having an Easter bunny for photos or anything like that tomorrow," Sam asked.

"Yes, we were. One of our volunteer workers, Gill Vance, will be wearing it," the pastor said. "He's great with kids and heads up our children's ministry."

"Alright. Thanks. That should be sufficient for now," Sam said, handing the pastor his card.

Sam started to walk away and then turned back around. "Do you know about how old Gill is?"

"Not his exact age. Mid-forties. Why?" the pastor asked.

"Just a question. Thanks," Sam said and rejoined Alisha.

As they ducked back under the crime-scene tape and approached the gazebo, Sam said, "Call it a hunch, but I have a feeling that we're going to find Gill Vance inside that Easter bunny costume."

The Easter bunny costume, clearly with a body inside of it, lay on the deck, its hands cuffed behind its back. Around the body was scattered several different colors of plastic eggs that had been crushed. There were also several large caliber handgun bullets strewn around the body as if they'd hatched from the smashed eggs. Sam picked one up with a gloved hand. Forty-four caliber.

Alisha nudged Sam's shoulder and pointed at something under the Easter Bunny's head. On closer inspection, he saw that it was an old record. "It's the Easter Bunny song that the Holiday Killer has been playing to me over the phone every morning at 4:04," she said.

"So that confirms this as his work rather than some kind of anti-church hate crime," Sam said. "Plus, these .44 caliber rounds. Four, four – that's tomorrow's date for Easter."

"You're right," Alisha agreed.

"I guess let's take the Easter Bunny's head off," Sam said.

"That sounds so wrong when you say it like that," Alisha replied.

"You know what I mean – to see who's inside," Sam said.

Sam joined Alisha in sliding the bunny costume's head off. Their noses were greeted by a sickening mixture of warm death and sugar.

"That's just disgusting," Alisha said.

Their victim was a male. Sam was no coroner, but it was pretty obvious that the man had died of asphyxiation – a look of panic frozen on his face. In his mouth had been stuffed, several of what Sam was pretty sure were yellow marshmallows – the Easter candy kind made in the shape of chicks. There were so many stuffed in the man's mouth that they bulged beyond his blotchy lips. Dried yellow drool stained his cheek.

"At least I didn't really like those marshmallow candies anyway," Sam said. "But any thoughts of ever having one again are ruined from this moment forward."

Just then the coroner walked up. After a moment of inspection, the coroner asked, "Did you ever play that game 'Chubby Bunny' as a kid? Not a game I recommend. It's kind of dangerous."

"Yeah, I played it as a teen," Alisha said, nodding. "I don't know who decided that seeing who could stuff the most marshmallows into your mouth was fun."

"Well, the premise of that game is the cause of this man's death. Someone forced so many of these little yellow marshmallow chicks into the victim's mouth that it obstructed his airway. And with his hands cuffed behind him, the poor fellow suffocated," the coroner said.

"Sheesh. What a way to go," Alisha said.

"How many of them were used," Sam asked the coroner.

"Well, I haven't counted yet, but let me see…two, four, six. Nine, eleven, fourteen, sixteen. Yes, I'd say sixteen," the coroner concluded.

"Sixteen. That's…" Sam began.

Alisha interrupted and finished his thought. "Four times four. Four and four again."

"I was just going to say that," Sam said.

"Well, I said it first," Alisha said smugly.

The coroner motioned towards the man's wrists. "If you'll remove his cuffs, I can finish removing this bunny suit and see what else there is to find."

A couple minutes later the suit was off and the coroner handed Sam the victim's wallet. Sam was just sliding out the man's ID when the coroner said, "You'll want to see this, Detective."

The coroner held up a red envelope. It was another greeting card. Sam opened it and gently lifted the greeting card out of the envelope. It was a Hallmark Mother's Day card – but not one of the cheap $2.99 ones. A fancier one. In fact, Sam had no clue they even sold Hallmark cards this intricate. The back of the card said it cost $8.99.

Inside, the Holiday Killer had left them a message that read:

Detective Cross,

We now count down to our final event. It's been a wild ride, am I right? Which one was your favorite? I suppose it's not fair to ask that since you haven't seen what lies ahead. I promise you it'll be a blast!

I know you want to catch me, but I have a proposition: I promise you that after one final decoration, my work will be done and I'll quietly slip away. I know you don't approve of my methods, but surely you see the necessity of my cause. I love this city and if I can save it from the addictive and poisonous drug of Holiday spending, then my mission and sacrifices will have been a success. And sometimes losing someone you love drives you to desperation.

So, what of it? How about you and your pretty partner stay away for my grand finale and then just let me go into retirement? I give you my word: Mother's Day is the last you'll see of me. And then I'll disappear like a paycheck at Christmas.

It's been fun, but time is almost up.
–The Holiday Killer

"I don't know whether to be flattered or creeped out that he thinks I'm pretty," Alisha said, reading over Sam's shoulder. "What does he mean by 'losing someone you love?' Not to alarm you, but is he making some kind of threat against your family?"

"That's not how I read it. It sounds like he's saying that he lost someone," Sam replied.

"Yeah, I see what you mean. But who? His parents are both in that nursing home, and our search showed he'd never been married or had any kids."

'I don't know. Barnes is one enigma after another," Sam said.

"Oh, and your hunch was right. Our victim is Gill Vance. Wanna guess his age?"

"Forty-four, huh?" Sam asked.

"Bingo. I guess I'll go notify the pastor," Alisha said.

Sam nodded and in the meantime finished snapping crime scene photos before joining Alisha with the distraught pastor.

Mother's Day was five weeks away. Thirty-five days to catch the Holiday Killer or risk losing him forever. Sam shuddered to think what the final murder would be like. The Holiday Killer had promised to go out with a bang.

Close to Home

"Cross, give me an update!" Captain Durant barked. "And I want to hear something other than 'We're doing the best we can.' I will not accept losing that murderous professor!" Captain Durant had not responded well to the Holiday Killer's latest communication.

Sam searched his thoughts for something clever to say. The truth was, they didn't have anything new. Neither the coroner nor the lab had uncovered anything useful to nail Professor Barnes. And that morning, the last remaining Marshal had left, recalled to chase down an escaped convict. With Mother's Day now less than two weeks away, the trail was cold as a cadaver.

Sam's silence was answer enough. Captain Durant glowered as he turned and stormed back down the hallway. A moment later Sam – and everyone else in the squad room – heard the office door slam.

Sam resisted the urge to bang his head the on desk. Though he was better at controlling his anger than Captain Durant, Sam felt the same way. The thought of Professor Barnes slipping away, or even worse: returning to normal life right under their noses was not an outcome Sam was willing to settle for.

"Let's go over it again," Alisha said.
"To what end?" he asked bitterly.

"To put away a psychopath. To get your wife and kids back home. To do our jobs and not let the bad guys win," Alisha said.

"Ok fine, Miss Positivity," Sam said. "How do we do that?"

Alisha held up the stack of case files and smiled. Sam groaned. That evening – and the rest of the week – dragged by without any new revelations.

It was Friday. With Mother's Day in only two days, Alisha convinced Sam to work late. Sam texted Jennifer to tell her not to wait up for his bedtime call.

***

Professor Harold Barnes watched from his car as two young boys played in the front yard. As it grew dark, an attractive, brown-haired woman opened the screen door and poked her head out. "Boys! Dinner!"

The boys ignored her and continued playing. "Jason, Drew! It's getting dark. Come inside for dinner. Don't make me say it again! Hey, and make sure you wash up."

As she was about to close the screen door, Professor Barnes reached up to the left of the steering wheel and flashed his lights. She noticed him and lingered. *Good*, he thought. She stepped out on the porch and made her way tentatively down the steps and across the lawn to where he was parked by the mailbox. She raised her hand to her face to shield her eyes from his headlights.

Professor Barnes, still wearing his dress clothes from his afternoon lecture at the college, opened the door. "Howdy ma'am," he said as he stepped out.

"Can I help you?" the woman said from where she'd stopped a few feet from his car.

"Mrs. Cross – Jennifer, correct?" Professor Barnes said.

"Yes, that's right. And who are you?" Jennifer said.

"A friend of your husband's. With the Holiday Killer on the loose, he asked me to keep an eye on you this weekend," he said.

"Oh, well, nice to meet you. He told me he was working late tonight," Jennifer said.

"Right," began Professor Barnes as he nonchalantly closed the distance between them.

"Look," interrupted Jennifer, "I really do appreciate you swinging by, but honestly it's not necessary. I'm with my folks here. My dad's got a shotgun. We'll be just fine. Thank you anyway."

"Just doing my job, ma'am, and doing a favor for an old friend," Professor Barnes said. He was now within arm's reach.

"What did you say your name was?" Jennifer asked.

"I suppose I didn't. It's Harold Barnes." As the name left his lips, he attacked. Jennifer was still facing into the headlights and so she didn't see his left hand fly up and strike her across the side of the head with a wrench he'd pulled from his waistband. She crumbled to the lawn, groaning painfully.

Quickly he moved half on top of her from behind and looped a section of rope around her neck. She fought briefly, but her body went limp a few seconds later, unconscious. Professor Barnes dragged her to the rear of his car, and deftly tied her hands with the rope he'd used on her neck. He then pulled a second length of rope from his coat pocket and tied her feet before lifting her into his trunk.

Professor Barnes walked back to where she'd fallen and picked up her phone. He then returned to Jennifer and used her thumb print to unlock it. He closed the trunk lid just as she began to stir.

As he drove away, Professor Barnes texted Jennifer's parents: "Going out for the evening. Sam surprised me by picking me up just now. Kiss my boys for me. Bye."

A faint thumping from the rear of his car informed him that Mrs. Cross had awakened. "Patience," Professor Barnes said aloud. "We'll get you more comfortable soon enough."

***

It was nearly nine the next morning when Sam arrived at the office. He was not surprised to find his partner already there, Holiday Killer files once again spread out on their desks.

"Good morning. Sorry I'm late," Sam said, extending a coffee cup as a peace offering. "I couldn't sleep last night – couldn't get my mind off of how we're about to lose him forever. I don't think I fell asleep until sometime after three."

"Don't sweat it," Alisha said, "You didn't miss anything. I've just been making my eyes cross staring at all of this for the umpteenth time."

Sam pulled out his phone. Still nothing from his wife. He'd tried to call her for their usual good morning chat, but she hadn't answered or replied to his texts. *Hopefully, she isn't mad at me for not calling her last night*, Sam thought.

"I'm sorry," Sam said as he put his phone away. "What did you say again?"

"I said, my eyes are going to fall out of my head if I stare at these files any longer," Alisha groaned.

"Yeah, I don't know if it'll make any difference at this point," Sam conceded.

"So, I was thinking – Mother's Day," Alisha said. "I don't really talk to my mom since she walked out on us when I was fourteen. What are people giving their moms for Mother's Day nowadays?"

"It's honestly not a whole lot different than Valentine's Day: a card, chocolate, and flowers," Sam said.

"I've been wondering all morning if a florist shop might be his next target," Alisha said.

"A florist shop is a good call actually," Sam said. "There's got to be dozens of them around the city though – and even more if you count the ones inside grocery stores.

"How about the florist shop where he bought the flowers for your wife on Valentine's Day?" Alisha asked. "Sorry, to bring up that awkward moment."

Sam laughed. "No, it's all good. Uh, yeah, that's a good call too. Dang, you're full of good ideas today."

"That's what happens when you, I dunno —
show up early at the office and actually work,"
Alisha jabbed.

"Yeah, yeah. I brought you a coffee though,
didn't I?" Sam replied. He poked through their files
until he found the name of the florist: Hamilton
Brothers. It was a shot in the dark, but at least it was
a potential lead.

"I guess you're thinking stakeout tonight?"
Sam asked.

"Maybe. Or maybe it's my turn to sleep in,"
Alisha said.

Sam shook his head. "No one's sleeping in.
He strikes at 5:09 a.m."

"Yeah, I know. Though, kinda seems like
we're putting all our eggs in one basket with the
flower shop being nothing more than a hunch,"
Alisha said.

"Well, it's better than the zero ideas we had
just a minute ago," Sam said.

"True, and it's better than sitting around
waiting for him to kill and then disappear for good,"
Alisha said.

Sam's phone vibrated. He pulled it out and
looked at the screen. It was a text from his mother-
in-law. Sam unlocked his phone and tapped on the
message. "Hey, are you bringing our daughter back
any time soon? Your boys need a mother."

Sam stared at his phone not sure what to
make of the message. His mother-in-law had a dry
sense of humor, so Sam was sure there was a joke
in there somewhere — he just wasn't sure how to
respond. He hovered his thumbs over the keyboard

on his phone for a second and then typed back, "Funny. I haven't seen her, but can I borrow her when you find her?"

Sam was about to put his phone back in his pocket when it rang. It was his mother-in-law. "Hey, Mother," Sam answered.

"Very funny, Sam," his mother-in-law replied. "I'm glad y'all are having a good time. No rush. I just wanted to remind you that the boys have their dentist appointment this afternoon."

"Mother, I honestly don't know what you're talking about. Jennifer is not and has not been with me. I worked late last night, and I'm at work right now," Sam said.

There was a long pause, and then his mother-in-law said, "Sam. She texted me last night saying she was leaving with you."

"Everything, ok?" asked Alisha, but Sam waved at her to shush.

"Mother, read me the text, exactly as she sent it," Sam said anxiously.

"Ok, um…It says, 'Going out for the evening. Sam surprised me by picking me up just now. Kiss my boys for me. Bye.' That's all she said," his mother-in-law relayed.

"And what time was that text," Sam asked, furiously writing on a notepad.

"It was…7:43 p.m.," she said. "Sam, you're scaring me."

Sam took a deep breath to steady his voice. "Mother, you and Tom need to get the boys and stay inside. I'm sending a detective there as soon as I hang up. I did not pick up Jennifer. And I've not talked to her since yesterday morning. Stay inside until officers arrive."

Sam hung up the phone. Alisha was now standing next to him. "Sam, she'll be ok."

"He's got her. That monster's got her," Sam said choking back tears of rage.

The next hour was a whirlwind. Officers were dispatched to Sam's in-laws house and a quick strike force was assembled to assault Harold Barnes' house. Forty-five minutes later Sam, Alisha, and Captain Durant watched as SWAT smashed in Professor Barnes' new front door.

Sam waited outside the home for several intense minutes as the SWAT team cleared the house. The raid, however, turned up nothing. There was no trace of Jennifer, the professor, or his pet ferret inside the house.

Sam could hold back tears no longer. He jogged to his car where he could at least let them flow somewhat privately. They were no closer to catching the professor than before and unless something miraculous happened in the next eighteen hours, it looked like his wife would be the Holiday Killer's next and final victim.

He pulled his notebook from his pocket and found where he'd written down the phone numbers for Walt's contacts. Sam lifted his phone and punched in Professor Barnes' number. Two rings later, to Sam's surprise, the professor answered. "Hello, Harold here."

"Hi, this is Detective Sam Cross – but I think you already knew that," Sam replied.

"Oh, hi. No, your name didn't come up on my caller ID," Professor Barnes said.

"Look, let's just cut the charade. Please…" Sam cleared his throat as tears tried to return. "Please tell me where my wife is."

"Your wife? Has something happened to her?" Barnes asked.

Anger replaced his grief. "You know exactly what happened to her! You took her from my in-laws' home. Don't play stupid. Where is she?"

"Detective, I am terribly sorry if your wife is missing," the professor said, "but I had nothing to do with it – just as I had nothing to do with any of those other awful murders. I sincerely hope you find her alive and well, but you have no evidence to blame me for it."

"Where are you? I'm at your home and you're not here and neither is your smelly weasel," Sam said.

"Ferret," Professor Barnes corrected. "And I don't see how it's any of your business where I am. You're very upset – understandably, but I don't think it's in my best interest to answer any more of your questions or accusations. You have my lawyer's card. Leave me alone and call him instead."

"Harold. Please!" Sam said, but the call ended. Sam held his phone for a moment and then threw it towards the passenger door where it hit and bounced somewhere under the seat. Alisha must've seen his outburst because she jogged over and knocked on his passenger seat window. Sam hit the unlock button and Alisha sat down.

"What is it, Sam? Something else at your in-laws?" she asked.

"No, it was him," Sam said.

"Barnes called you?" she asked, her eyebrows raising in surprise.

"No, I called him," Sam said.

Alisha's eyes widened. "You what? What did he say? What did *you* say?"

"I don't even know. He denied knowing anything. I yelled. I pleaded. I insulted his ferret," Sam said with a grim chuckle. "He lawyered up in the end."

Alisha rummaged under her seat, retrieved Sam's phone, and handed it to him. "You might need this in case he calls you back – or your wife calls you. Forensics should be here soon and they'll search the house high and low. They'll find something."

"You know they won't. He never leaves a trace. But thanks," Sam said.

Alisha placed a hand on his arm. "Hey, Mr. Negativity. None of that talk. We'll find her in time."

Hallmark

For all his gruffness, Captain Durant could show up spectacularly when the situation called for it. The amount of resources he'd coordinated over the last hour, both state and federal, was nothing short of impressive.

"Sam, I just hung up with – well, I don't think I'm supposed to say who that was," Captain Durant said. "But the minute he turns his phone back on, or your wife's phone turns on, there's an aircraft standing by to take off and triangulate their position. And they're supposed to be really, really good at what they do."

Sam nodded. He'd been trying to concentrate and come up with anything helpful, but he couldn't get the image of his injured wife out of his mind. The detectives at his in-laws' house had found traces of blood on the lawn near the mailbox. The lab was still running it, but Sam knew what the test would say.

***

Professor Barnes walked into the dingy hotel room where he'd left Jennifer, along with the rest of the things he needed for his final decoration. It was one of those pay-by-the-week places with no housekeeping so he didn't have to worry about being discovered or having his work interrupted. He'd also requested that the room be on the backside away from the street "to cut down on road noise," he'd explained.

She was right where he'd left her, bound and gagged in the bathtub. He opened the bag of snacks he'd picked up at the corner convenience store and pulled out a sandwich and a package of white powdered donuts. "Ok, Mrs. Cross. Which would you rather have – ham and cheese, or donuts? Oh, that's right. You can't talk because of the gag. I suppose I'll have to remove it for you to eat too. But you strike me as the screamer type. Can't have nosy neighbors calling the cops. I bet you're hungry though. Sorry you missed dinner last night and then breakfast. It's been a busy day."

Professor Barnes continued to ramble on, more to himself than to Jennifer. "You know, I talked to your husband a bit ago. He misses you terribly. He even begged me to tell him where you were. It was actually touching. Of course, by the time he finds you, you'll be dead. I promise you, it's not personal though – well, ok maybe a little. Your husband took away my best friend from me, so now I have to take his away from him too. But it's rather fitting – that a mother should die on Mother's Day. Sends quite the message, am I right?"

At this, Jennifer turned her head towards the wall to hide her tears. "Come now. I'll make sure you don't feel a thing. And I'm sure there will be a very nice funeral. I might even attend."

"It's all for a good cause though," he continued. "American consumerism has gone off the rails and needs to be reined in. They have 355 other days of the year to sell products to customers that they actually need and want, without desecrating our Holidays. Honestly, I could've kept going. There's Father's Day and Grandparent's Day – wait, I skipped Memorial Day. But you get the idea. Consumerism has ruined Holidays turning them into one giant spend-fest. It's far more damaging and disturbing than anything I've done here. But no. Mother's Day is where it all began and it's where the Holiday Killer ends as well. We'll leave our final message tomorrow."

"Oh, sorry, sorry," Professor Barnes said focusing once again on Jennifer. "I forgot about the food while I was sermonizing. Now, if I uncover your mouth, are you going to be quiet? I'd hate to have to use my wrench again. I'm sure it gave you a nasty headache last time."

"Good," said the professor in response to Jennifer's nod. He gently pulled back the duct tape over the lower half of her face, untied the bandana between her teeth, and lastly pulled the balled up sock out of her mouth. "Water?" he asked, extending a plastic hotel cup towards her.

She nodded and then tilted her head back slightly so he could pour some into her mouth. "Alright now, sandwich or donuts," he asked.

"Sandwich," Jennifer croaked.

It took nearly ten minutes for Professor Barnes to handfeed the sandwich to her with sips of water between bites. "Good, good," he said when she finished.

"Why even bother?" Jennifer asked. "You're just going to kill me tomorrow."

"I'm not a sadist," Professor Barnes replied, as if wounded by her question. "I don't take any pleasure in the act of killing. It is an unfortunate side effect of broadcasting my message. You can't tell me I'd be receiving the same kind of coverage if I only graffitied some slogan on businesses during the holidays. No, death sends the strongest message."

"It also destroys an innocent life," Jennifer began, but the professor cut her off.

"And so do the holidays!" he said bitterly. "Want to hear a story?" Without waiting for her reply, he continued. "I had someone special once. We were even going to be married. Her name was Kim. She was a good woman too – a nurse. One morning, the day after Thanksgiving – that consumerist abomination called Black Friday – she got up to go to work. She never made it. A motorist, racing to the next Black Friday sale, cut her off and clipped her front end while travelling in excess of ninety miles per hour. Both cars flipped, scattering the other motorist's purchases across the highway."

Barnes paused to collect his emotions. "Kim was killed. Mercifully, they said her death was almost instantaneous. And you know, I don't count that driver as my wife's murderer. She died too. No, I blame those who created the frenzy by their aggressive and manipulative marketing that has desecrated our holidays."

"I'm sorry about Kim," Jennifer said, "but what have I done to you to deserve being taken away from my husband and my two boys – on Mother's Day no less?"

"Like I said, it's not personal. Somebody has to die. A mother – and the wife of a cop at that

– sends a poignant message," Professor Barnes said. "But enough chitchat. There's work to be done. Which means time to put the sock back in. Gotta keep you quiet until the morning. Open up."

"Sam will find me. He's going to catch you and save me," Jennifer said before the professor stuffed the sock back into her mouth.

Professor Barnes laughed as he affixed fresh duct tape to her face. "His track record so far isn't very good. The odds are in my favor. Try to get some sleep. You've got a big night ahead."

He switched off the bathroom light and shut the door.

***

"Sam. Sam!" Alisha's voice broke through his mental fog. "Come on. We got this. We've got to be overlooking something here," she said tapping her fingertips on the case files. "There's a clue here somewhere. We're going to find it. Something has to be staring us in the face."

Sam stood up without saying a word and walked to the bathroom. He splashed cold water on his face and willed himself to think clearly. A minute later he returned to his desk, face still glistening with the cool water.

He stared a moment at the case files and then began shutting the ones from past cases. "It's not in these. They don't matter right now. We're not trying to pin the entire Holiday Killer case on him. All we need to do is figure out either where he's at right now with Jennifer or where he's going to stage his crime scene tonight – and hope he doesn't kill her first. We catch him for this last one and we pin all of them on him."

"Ok. So, what clues do we have that point to the next attack?" Alisha asked.

Before Sam could answer, Detective Arnold called his name. "Cross, we found your wife's cell phone. After the text he sent your mother-in-law, it looks like he powered it off and tossed it out the window. It landed in a grassy area, so it survived. It's not much to go on, but it does tell us that he drove back towards the city rather than keeping her somewhere rural."

"Thanks, and that does help," Sam said.

"Prayers up, brother," she said as she headed out.

Sam was about to turn back to Alisha when his phone dinged with a text message. It was Tiffany. Sam had forgotten he'd texted her earlier to tell her about Jennifer and to ask her if Barnes had said anything in class that might hint to where he was going. Sam scanned the text. "I'm so sorry, Sam. I can't think of anything helpful. He just said he'd see us Monday. I can go be with the boys if you'd like me to. I'm so sorry. "

Sam sighed and texted back, "Thanks, and no need. They're with their grandparents. I'll update you when we find her."

"Alright," Sam said, turning his attention back to Alisha. "Show me clues."

Alisha held up the Mother's Day card the Holiday Killer had left at the Easter crime scene. "This is all we've got that spoke of tomorrow morning."

They read again the message the Holiday Killer had written inside the card. "I'm not seeing anything," Sam said.

"The only weird line maybe is where he said, 'I promise you it'll be a blast,' but maybe I'm just reading too much into it," Alisha agreed.

"And even if 'blast' means a bombing, it still doesn't tell us where," Sam said.

Sam flipped the card over and looked at the back. "You know, this is a really fancy greeting card," he said. "I wonder if they're stocked everywhere or only in select locations – like maybe just in Hallmark stores."

"Do they still have Hallmark stores? Or is it just a cable channel now?" Alisha asked.

Sam did a Google search. "Yup, it's still a thing. There are three of them in the metro area."

Sam dialed the first store on the list. "Yes ma'am, this is Detective Sam Cross, Oklahoma City Police Department. I've got an urgent question for you. If I show you a particular Hallmark card, can you tell me where it was purchased? Great, I'll take a maybe. We'll be there soon." Sam hung up.

"What'd she say? Can she trace it?" Alisha asked.

"Not exactly," Sam said, "but she can tell us whether it's carried in all retail locations, like in grocery stores, or if it's only available in Hallmark stores – and then whether she stocks it."

Sam drove lights flashing the few miles to the Hallmark store. They were greeted inside by a librarian-looking clerk. "Hi, are you the detectives I spoke to on the phone?

"Yes, Detectives Cross and Palmetto. Here," Sam said as he extended the greeting card.

"Ooo, that's a pretty one for sure. I have not seen it," the clerk said.

"What does that mean?" Sam asked.

"Well, it could be good news for you," the clerk said. "I'm going to look it up, but I can almost guarantee you it's a special order. Now, it could've been purchased online, not in-store, but we'll know soon enough."

A few clicks later in her computer and she confirmed her initial assessment: the card was not widely available, only by special order – though it could be purchased to carry in individual stores if the shopkeeper chose to. "We haven't sold one at this location," the clerk confirmed.

"That's a huge help. We'll check with the other locations in the city." Sam thanked her again as they left.

"It's fifteen miles to the next store," Alisha said. "Can we grab lunch? I'm starving."

"I'm not hungry," Sam said, "but sure we can grab you something."

On the way to the next Hallmark store, they swung through a drive-thru and grabbed Alisha a burger. Twenty minutes later, they parked out front of the second store.

A burly, but jovial shopkeeper greeted them. "Need a last minute Mother's Day card?" he asked as he walked towards them.

"Actually, we have one. We're detectives here in the city and need your help hopefully to track down this greeting card," Sam said as he handed the Holiday Killer's card to the clerk.

"That's a beauty. And you think it might've been purchased here?" he asked.

"We're hopeful. Did you stock this card this year? Or did you put in any special orders?" Alisha asked.

"Lemme see," the man said as he navigated his way through the displays back to his computer. A moment later he said, "Why, yes we did. Looks like our other clerk, Carla, put in the order back on – wow, way back on the twenty-ninth of March. The buyer must've wanted this particular card really bad to order it that early."

"Yeah, I bet he did," Sam replied.

"I'm sorry, what was that?" the clerk asked.

"Oh nothing. What's the name of the person who ordered it?" Sam asked.

The clerk hesitated. "I don't know if I should be sharing personal order information."

Sam took the card back from the clerk, lifted it out of the evidence bag and opened it before handing it back to the clerk to read. The clerk's eyes grew wide. "The Holiday Killer purchased it?" he exclaimed.

"That's right, and so you see why it's imperative that we get that name," Sam said.

"Of course, of course. You know business has been down since that maniac started killing," the shopkeeper said.

"The name please," Alisha urged.

"Right – one Sam Cross made the order," he said.

Sam shook his head ruefully as he looked at Alisha.

"Does that help? Did I catch the killer?" the clerk asked.

"Not quite," Sam said, showing his ID to the clerk. "He used my name. But it does tell us where he bought it, which is a huge help." Sam pointed at the security camera in the corner. "We're going to need to see that tape."

"Sure thing, Detective," the shopkeeper replied. "Oh wait. I won't have it still. It's on a thirty-day loop. You missed it by ten days or so. It's been recorded over. I'm sorry."

"It's fine. How about getting your other clerk, Carla, on the phone. Maybe she can provide us a description," Sam said.

A few minutes later they hung up with Carla. Her description of the purchaser was unhelpfully generic – white male, dressed nice. She did mention that he kind of reminded her of a college professor.

They thanked the shopkeeper and returned to Sam's car. He checked what time the store closed. Not until six – four hours away.

"What's our play?" Alisha asked.

"I have a feeling about this store. I think this is the place," Sam said. "We're going to set a trap and wait. And then catch him when he arrives."

Mother's Day

It was fifteen after six when the shopkeeper locked up the Hallmark store and drove off. By half past eight it was dark outside. The shopping center parking lot cleared out except for an abandoned car with a flat tire.

Over the preceding six hours, a carefully coordinated net of officers in unmarked vehicles dubbed "the outfield" had fanned out across every possible route leading to the store. Sam had suggested the tactic from something he'd observed during his first case as a detective. Assuming the professor was still driving his sedan, there was no way he could get to the Hallmark shop without being spotted.

Several other undercover officers, including SWAT snipers – designated as "the infield," were staged within sight of the store. And then finally both Sam and Alisha, "home plate," were hunkered down inside the shop. The remainder of the SWAT team was assembled in the back storage room. They'd convinced the clerk to give them a key before he left for the evening.

Though he felt fairly confident that they were in the right place, on the right night, and would finally catch the Holiday Killer in the act, he still whispered a prayer he was right. Sam was slightly less confident about his wife being alive. It would all come down to the kind of staged scene the killer intended. Unfortunately, most of the Holiday Killer's victims had been killed elsewhere and their bodies brought to and then staged at the crime scenes. However, the two most recent victims on New Year's and Easter had been killed on site. Sam hoped that would be the Holiday Killer's intent with Jennifer.

Nervous, Sam whispered his fourth radio check of the night. The point of contention had been around when to apprehend – or potentially take out the Holiday Killer. The US Marshals had recommended an early arrest – as soon as his car was spotted. Sam had nixed that idea, worried it could turn into a dangerous high-speed chase and the cornered killer harming his wife.

The SWAT team had lobbied for their snipers to shoot on sight, arguing that Jennifer's life was in danger simply by being in the Holiday Killer's custody. The Legal office had pushed back against this route, but it was officially "Plan B." If any aggression was shown against Jennifer or if the Holiday Killer produced a weapon, he would be immediately taken out.

After much deliberation, the plan Sam had agreed to was to initially watch and observe – let the Holiday Killer come all the way inside the store, become distracted with part of his setup for the night, and then rush him and take him into custody. As much as Sam wanted the killer dead, he knew that apprehending him was the right move – as long as he didn't threaten Jennifer. If that happened, Sam would not hesitate to shoot Barnes himself. Sam also had to fight for his position on the inside of the shop. Captain Durant had initially said no: "You're too close to this; too emotional."

Sam had argued back, "Exactly, and nobody cares about my wife's life more than I do. I'm going to be there." Sam didn't want a gung-ho tactical team putting his wife's life in unnecessary jeopardy. He wiped the sweat from his palms on his pants and gripped his gun tightly. Ten minutes after nine. There was no way to know when the killer would arrive. It likely depended on the complexity of the killer's plan. All Sam could do was wait – and say another prayer.

Sam was jarred out of his meditation by his phone ringing. The caller ID said, "Unknown Number." Sam's first instinct was to ignore it, but his partner nudged him and mouthed *"Answer it!"*

He did and turned speakerphone on. "Hello, this is Sam."

Heavy breathing answered him. Alisha jabbed him in the arm and nodded. It was the same heavy breathing from the calls she'd received months ago from the Holiday Killer.

"Who is this?" Sam demanded.

The heavy breathing stopped but a moment later it was replaced with the muffled but distinct sound of a woman screaming.

"Hello? Jennifer is that you?" Sam practically shouted.

He couldn't be sure – maybe his mind was playing tricks on him, but it sounded like the woman's screaming changed as if she was trying to say his name. Then the line went dead.

Sam let out an anguished cry of rage mixed with sorrow. He pounded his fist repeatedly on the store counter he was crouched behind. "I swear…" he muttered under his breath.

"Sam. Sam. It'll be ok," Alisha said. "Think of it this way: that was proof of life. She's alive, Sam. And we're going to save her. You're going to save her. You hear me?"

Sam nodded and composed himself. Alisha was right. He checked the time. The call had come in at 10:18 p.m. Perhaps it was a sign that the killer was on the move.

More waiting. Seconds crept by as if mired in eternity.

Four hours later, just after two the next morning, a Marshal in an unmarked "outfield" police car radioed that they'd spotted the professor's vehicle. The Holiday Killer was coming. He was driving cautiously, taking unnecessary turns, doubling back instead of driving a straight shot to the store.

"Is he alone?" Sam radioed.

"Seems to be," the Marshal responded. "No sign of anyone else with him."

"She's probably in the backseat lying down or in the trunk," Alisha said.

Sam nodded. The sweatiness in his palms returned.

A few minutes later, "the infield" reported that the professor's car had entered the shopping center parking lot, keeping to the outskirts and then circling around back. "Target in sight," confirmed one of the snipers.

"What's he doing around back?" Alisha asked.

They'd scouted the rear as a possible entry point for the Holiday Killer, but the back door was solid and bolted. He had to come through the front.

"He's stopped," radioed an officer. "He's exiting his vehicle. Still alone. He's now doing something near what appears to an electrical or telecommunications box on the back of the store."

Sam looked up at the security camera. Its red light flickered off. "He disabled the security camera," Sam said.

"He's doing the same now to the neighboring store," the officer radioed again. "Now he's walking back to his car. He's on the move again."

Sam peeked out from around the counter to watch through the front door. The professor's sedan, headlights off, pulled alongside the curb in front of the store. Sam informed the "infield" team that they were going radio silent. He sent one final communication: "Kill him if he touches my wife."

Sam ducked back behind the counter. They'd set up a tiny camera to observe the front doors that could be watched on a monitor that Alisha held in her lap.

Sam felt Alisha startle next to him when the Holiday Killer's silhouette appeared at the glass shop door. He was dressed in disposable operating room scrubs like they'd found in his house during the first raid. A dark mask was over his face. Gloved hands fiddle with the lock for a couple minutes followed by a faint click as the door unlatched and slowly opened.

The Holiday Killer returned to his car and retrieved a medium-sized black duffle from his backseat. He placed it just inside to prop the door open and then returned to his car a second time. The trunk popped open and he struggled a moment to lift something out. Sam squinted at the screen and finally realized it was a hand cart with a second, but much larger and longer black duffle strapped to it.

The Holiday Killer left the hand cart next to the curb, closed the trunk, and then parked it in the nearest spot. A moment later he returned and began wheeling the cart towards the store. It bounced heavily as it went over the curb. Once inside, he turned the tumbler, locking himself inside with them. Sam could hear the killer's heavy breathing only a few feet away.

Sam rose silently to a crouched position. The Holiday Killer was now just on the other side of the counter, gathering Mother's Day cards from the displays, no doubt to use in the staging of his "decoration."

The killer returned to his duffels and removed a large knife from the smaller one and turned towards the large duffle strapped to the hand cart. That's when Sam saw movement towards the bottom of the bag. His wife was in there and she was alive!

Sam charged the Holiday Killer ramming his entire frame, linebacker style, into the killer's side, sending them both tumbling and Hallmark cards scattering about them. The knife clattered out of reach. They scuffled as Sam tried in vain to subdue the killer.

"Gun!" shouted Alisha.

The Holiday Killer had pulled a handgun from his waistband. Sam grabbed the killer's wrist, trying to wrench the gun away. The Holiday Killer managed to break free, but instead of pointing the gun at Sam, he pointed at his own head.

"Don't do it!" Alisha ordered.

For several tense seconds, the Holiday Killer held his gun against his temple. Finally, he dropped his gun and put his hands behind his head. Sam rushed forward and pinned him face down on the ground. SWAT swarmed around them and someone flipped the store lights on, causing Sam to wince from the sudden brightness. Once he'd cuffed the killer, Sam turned to the large black duffle, fumbling for the zipper.

"Wait, it could be a bomb!" ordered one of the SWAT members.

From inside the bag, a muffled scream answered them.

"Does that sound like a bomb to you?" Sam asked. He didn't wait for an answer and practically tore open the bag. The zipper only retracted a few inches before the straps around the cart impeded its movement. But it was enough for Sam to see matted brown hair and his wife's terrified – but then relieved eyes.

Sam frantically patted his pockets looking for his pocketknife. Alisha held up the one belonging to the Holiday Killer. Sam cut the straps, careful not to allow the duffle to topple to the floor.

Moments later his wife was free and cradled in his arms.

"It's him," Alisha said.

Sam turned to look at the unmasked killer. Professor Harold Barnes stared back defiantly. No words were exchanged between the two as an officer hauled the cuffed killer upright.

They were just about to lead the Holiday Killer away when Sam's wife spoke up. "I told you he'd come for me – that he'd catch you and that he'd save me. I told you. I know my husband."

Sam squeezed her tightly as he helped her to her feet and led her towards the waiting paramedics out front. He kissed her on the forehead and said, "Happy Mother's Day."

***

Three Weeks Later

"Are you absolutely, positively sure that's what you want to do?" Captain Durant asked as he held up the paper Sam had just given him.

"Yes sir, I am. I'll miss the field. And I'll probably hate the Academy. But it'll make my wife super happy," Sam said.

"Alright then. I'll put it in. You're twice the hero now, so I'm sure you could get any assignment you wanted – so you're sure?" Captain Durant asked one last time.

"One hundred percent," Sam replied.

"Ok. You know, you can always come back. Like you said – you're gonna miss field work," Captain Durant said.

"Thanks. I'll see how this goes for now. Inspiring new recruits might not be half bad," Sam said.

Sam hurried to his car. He had a busy day ahead. There was an awards ceremony for him and Alisha at eleven and then at five that evening Tiffany was getting married. Sam still wasn't sure about the groom, but maybe the cop and dad in him never would be.

The disgraced professor, Harold Barnes, had been charged with six counts of murder, one count of attempted murder, plus a litany of other charges ranging from kidnapping to arson, and making terroristic threats. He'd never see the light of day again. He'd be lucky to avoid the needle.

"Thank you, Sam," Jennifer said later at home when he told her the news of his reassignment.

"You know, the Academy can be dangerous too – green, wannabe cops wielding a firearm for the first time. I could get shot," he said with a wink.

She laughed. "I'll just have to bubble wrap you each morning before I send you off to work."

"That would be cute," Sam said.

"I swear though – it's someone else's turn to be in danger. The Cross family has had enough," Jennifer said.

"I'll make sure the criminals get the memo," Sam said.

"Alright, handsome. Time to get you dressed up. Can't be late for your own awards ceremony," Jennifer said pushing him playfully towards their room.

Sam laughed. "What are they going to do? Give the award to somebody else?"

***

The awards ceremony was exactly the kind of thing Sam hated: three hours of him in the spotlight, posing for photos, dodging reporters and eating questionable hors d'oeuvres. Why didn't they ever serve decent food at one of these events? Maybe the food at Tiffany's wedding would be better.

It was much better. Tiffany had insisted on preparing the food herself – steak, shrimp, and veggie kabobs. And she was a gorgeous, very happy bride. She'd asked Sam to walk her down the aisle, on account of her father's death the year before. Sam even shed a tear as he gave her away.

As the sun set and they watched the newlyweds drive away, Sam put his arm around Jennifer and smiled. The Holiday Killer had failed. Monday was Memorial Day, and Sam looked forward to doing his part to contribute to the Holiday sales. After all, Jennifer needed a new dishwasher, and they were on discount.

THE END

About the Author

Stephen Zimmerman was born in a small town in west Texas. From Texas, to Oklahoma, Missouri and Africa, simplicity and modest living shaped Stephen's childhood. In 2006, Stephen joined the United States Air Force. During this time, he served two tours in the Middle East and was awarded a Commendation Medal, seven Air Medals, and the rank of Staff Sergeant. That same year Stephen also met his wife Leanna, and they were married in Spring 2007. Together they have four children, two dogs, and six fish tanks. In 2012, Stephen graduated with a Bachelor of Arts in Biblical Studies and began his pastoring career in Arizona in 2015.

When not with work or family, Stephen enjoys devouring True Crime, psychology, and anything mysterious. This passion has blended those elements into a love for writing stories of his own.

Books by this Author

The MISSING

The Holiday Killer

www.SwordandSuspense.com